What read
STARS or

by Mariana Williams

Reading Mariana Williams' *Stars or Stripes 4th of July* is like going on the best vacation you've ever had. It's funny, thrilling, suspenseful, romantic, and always highly entertaining. Veronica is a delightful companion in this fast-paced romp. As with any great vacation, you will miss her when it's over—and hope that you'll see her again in another adventure. The sooner the better!

Raymond Obstfeld
New York Times bestselling author of *On the Shoulders of Giants* and *Anatomy Lesson*

Veronica opens up and lets you in—to her life, her bedroom and the backstage of show business. Mariana Williams is a storyteller who knows how to write and keep it real. I enjoyed it from cover to cover.

Alan Kalter
Announcer for *The Late Show with David Letterman*

I would say it's a page-turner except I was laughing so much that I had trouble sometimes turning the page. Sometimes you are lucky enough to read a book that not only keeps you in suspense but lets you giggle along the way. *Stars or Stripes 4th of July* is a real treat.

Andrea Abbate
Comic, TV Writer

Wacky con men and witty hijinks dominate this guilty pleasure of a novel. A female version of Carl Hiaasen, Williams substitutes Hilton Head for Florida, as main character Veronica Bennett heedlessly meanders into one sticky situation after another. Effortless enjoyment—you'll be reaching for another Veronica Bennett novel when finished.

Penny Bernal
Juror for Elle Letters, Elle Magazine

I could not put down Mariana William's novel, *Stars or Stripes 4th of July*. Okay, I lied. I put it down a lot—so I could rest from laughing! I was truly captivated, entertained, and even titillated. I needed a cigarette after reading, and I quit smoking 10 years ago. Like a carnival ride... I want to go again!

Craig Shoemaker, Comic,
"The Love Master"

Mariana Williams prose is bubbly and her dialogue crackles with humor and truth. She is a good storyteller to boot. *Stars or Stripes 4th of July* is not only a fun read but will leave you wanting a sequel.

Tracey Jackson
Author, screenwriter and blogger

STARS or STRIPES 4th of JULY

A Veronica Bennett novel

Mariana Williams

INFINITY PUBLISHING

Copyright © 2010 by Mariana Williams

ISBN 0-7414-6135-8

Printed in the United States of America

This is a work of fiction. Names, characters, places, and incidents either are the product of the author's imagination or are used fictitiously. Any resemblance to actual events or locales or persons, living or dead, is entirely coincidental.

Published October 2010

INFINITY PUBLISHING
1094 New DeHaven Street, Suite 100
West Conshohocken, PA 19428-2713
Toll-free (877) BUY BOOK
Local Phone (610) 941-9999
Fax (610) 941-9959
Info@buybooksontheweb.com
www.buybooksontheweb.com

Also by Mariana Williams

Wince-Worthy Tales

Happy New Year, Darling!
(by Veronica Bennett)

A special thanks to my critique group, Writer's Roundtable, as well as Barbara Stokes, Carol Hastings and Patricia Owen. Also, for Paul's encouragement. He leaves me fraught with joy.

CHAPTER 1

"And so I've decided—we'll make love every *other* night," I cleared my throat, adding, "Instead of every night."

Jack's eyes smiled over the top of his coffee cup. Sitting with his back against the bed's ornate headboard, wearing the hotel's plush robe with the collar circling his chiseled jaw, he looked positively regal. His dark hair was slept into peaks and valleys and he needed a shave but a sly grin betrayed a boyish charm.

"Oh...*kay*." He tilted his head with an expression one would use when standing in front of a Jackson Pollack painting.

I let go of the door handle and my purse slid off my shoulder and down my arm, weighing heavy on my wrist. I squared my shoulders and spouted my memorized speech. "Since I've been in Sydney we've hardly worked on the book. You know I'm grateful to be here—the Park Hyatt is gorgeous." I waved toward the expansive window overlooking the glistening harbor. "But I've flown fourteen hours and we need to finish your biography, Jack. Not just shag in the suite."

"I'm not sure 'shag' is the Australian word. You may be quoting Austin Powers, a Brit."

I slid my purse up to my shoulder and straightened up. "I've got five days left. How about we get together every day

1

for three hours? We can meet in the back of the restaurant at ten, each night. That gives me at least fifteen hours of interviews to work with." With that I walked into the hall and closed the door softly behind me.

My room was a few doors down and in minutes I'd changed into my pink and gray Bebe running suit and tennis shoes. I took the elevator down to the lobby. Outside, "The Rocks" district of Sydney Harbor was waking as the sky gently lightened from charcoal gray to lavender. Floor-to-ceiling windows stood between the water's edge and the lobby of the city's finest hotel. I walked outside onto a wooden porch, stepped down five steps and turned left onto the boardwalk. Then I recalled last night's dinner with Jack, balancing on those planks trying to keep up with his quick gait. A stiletto heel stuck between the strips of wood would have toppled me. My head had bobbed up and down as I tried to concentrate. "Lovely view"—heel in center of board—"Yes, that is quite a yacht"— heel in center of board. It wasn't easy being a fascinating *and* limber companion.

Companion? Is that what I am? Something less than a date, but more than a fan. As Jack's biographer, I knew the publishers wanted me to present an intimate look at his life. I got that all right. I sighed, remembering my bare legs in the air a few hours earlier, toes pointing like a freakin' ballerina. No, I didn't come to Australia to be a mistress. Not even Jack Swanson's. Yet, it was so hard to distance myself from the actor who played Chet the racecar driver in my favorite movie in college. That doesn't make me a groupie, does it?

I jogged past fishermen who ignored my mumbles of discontent. *What a morning*, I wheezed in the damp air. Pfft, movie-of-the-week action star—Jack Swanson, puhleeze. The expressionless fishermen gripped their poles and focused on the water.

North of the harbor a walking path led to an angular condo village of glass and chrome. Known as "quays," the little bays along the boardwalk were calm inlets. The sky was gray and the water looked like mercury as it rippled, making gentle lapping sounds against the wooden pilings. The screeching gulls looked formally dressed. Their black tail feathers were polka-dotted with white, like a skirt. In the distance a church bell rang out six chimes, heralding in the morning.

I slowed my jog to a trot, as cockatoo's squawked at me, taunting as they circled in the air. An ibis with legs about a foot tall stood as still as a wooden lawn flamingo as I passed. Its body was white with a jet-black head and large curved scythe-like beak. Even *he* looked elegantly judgmental. *You can't even stand still—like me. You're too A-D-D to finish anything you start.* His round eye was white and the size of a fifty-cent piece. In the center there was a small black dot, a pupil. *Squawk, return the publisher's advance —give up.*

I wondered if he saw me cry.

******

Seated on the back row of the crowded auditorium, I leafed through the program reading the bios of the guest speakers for the tenth time. Naturally, Jack's photo looked like it was taken a few years ago. Hmmm, after this what next? The big question: How would I stand around the sea of glombers when they darted from their seats to pounce on the actor "from Ah-mer-ee-ka." Among them, but trying hard not to *be* what I call the fan-geese, I'd do what I usually did. Paste an expression on my face of contented distraction as I shuffled papers, and waited for his cue.

I was jolted back to the present with the sound of laughter by three or four hundred film students. A new question followed. "What's it like working with some of the famed musical composers who have scored your films? Anything come to mind?"

Jack's steel gray eyes perused the ceiling as he stroked his chin. "Quick story about Andrew Lloyd Weber." He paused.

"We were sitting at a dinner party at Michael Bennett's home. You have to understand, Andy is somewhat of a social misfit. What I mean by that is, he's uncomfortable with himself and it shows. He turns to my friend, the esteemed lyricist, Allen Lowe…"

The moderator cut in, "Of the Lerner and Lowe songwriting team, of course. Go on, please."

"Yeah, Andy turns to Lowe and says, 'I don't know why people take such an instant dislike to me.' And Lowe replies, 'Oh Andrew, it saves so much time.'" More laughter from the crowd.

"Oh, that's cruel!" The moderator cackled as he rocked back in his seat. "Economy of words spoken by a truly brilliant lyricist."

"He certainly had a knack for words," Jack agreed. As they chatted, I cringed, recalling my daring proposal to Jack this morning.

"Okay," was all he said. *Okay?* I wondered how he really felt about my feeble stab at restraint. At least I could count on fifteen hours of interview to finish his autobiography. That was my purpose here, wasn't it?

"We have time for one last question," the moderator said. Hands shot up and the mic was passed to a pretty redhead wearing a leopard headband. "Are you involved in a relationship at the moment, Mr. Swanson? You're hot!"

A wave of giggles rippled through the auditorium and I stopped breathing. It was like being sucked backwards down a wind tunnel with Starbucks cups, hotel suites, and calendar pages all flying past me. NO! I didn't want to know, but to plug my ears and sing "la-la-la-la" wasn't an option. So, I slunk down in my seat as the collective female audience leaned forward in theirs.

"Is this a film student, or someone from the tabloids;" Jack looked from side to side.

"Purely academic, I promise," she answered and dropped to her seat amidst a flurry of high-pitched laughter.

Jack looked skeptical but then gestured as if to say, so what. "Since this won't go any further than this room, I am passionately involved..."

I squeezed my eyes shut.

"With a script I may direct, as well as working on my autobiography that will be available in the U.S. by the end of the year. Thank you for the question."

Muffy Potter, the student who organized the symposium, ushered Jack off the stage. They were engaged in an animated discussion near the exit by the time I walked up a few minutes later.

Jack swung his straight arm in my direction, as if presenting a car for sale on a lot. "Say hello to Veronica Bennett, Muffy. She's a writer from California who made time in her busy schedule to come down under for a few days. We're working on my life story."

Down under? The covers, maybe.

Muffy jumped into the air. "*Oh, stop it!* You're writing a book!" Her eyes widened, and she patted Jack's forearm. She withdrew it quickly and turned to me with a respectful nod and smile.

"Much of it's been said before," Jack said, "but there are still some juicy stories about old Hollywood, you know, back lot gossip."

"That's fan-*TAST*-ic," she swooned. "Bravo, good on you, dah—leng!" Then, turning to me, "How thrilling for you to hear it all and to decide what goes in."

"Yes, surprising all that *has* gone in. Right, Jack?"

He sputtered. "Excuse me for coughing. This good weather has brought out my hay fever."

"Veronica," Muffy chirped, "we have a table at a great place. You must join us for deen ah. How long have you been a writer, dah—leng?"

I took a deep breath. "Not too long. I've been musician and singer for the last ten years. Jack and I met through a friend and I offered to give him a few piano lessons."

Jack shook his head. "I'm furious my mother never made me practice, as a kid."

I picked up the story, "I wrote a novel last year and once my publisher heard I knew Jack Swanson, well, he put my book on the back burner and suggested this biography. Jack was gracious enough to let me tell his story."

Jack gave me a warm smile. "Veronica is a wonderful singer, too. I was plunking along with a piano primer for little kids, but now I can accompany myself using cool chords. Although, I'll never play like she does."

Her interest in me evaporated like a drop of water on a hot griddle, once she heard Jack had yet *another* talent. There was no getting back to me, although God bless him, he tried. I accepted her invitation to join them for dinner and we walked behind the building where the limo waited.

Muffy wore tight jeans, black calf-high boots and a long sweater to her hips. A cute knit hat, a scarf rakishly wrapped around her neck and various chain necklaces of different lengths and sizes completed her ensemble. Young girls in Sydney seemed to be walking out the door like hat trees dangling a gazillion accessories. Either that, or her apartment was on fire this morning and she grabbed everything she owned on her way out.

Their profiles were illuminated by the parking lot lights as they strolled in front of me. Muffy had an adorable nose that scooped up like a pixie's. Her lips glistened in the dark with a dewy gloss. Young girls don't wear lip color either, I noticed. Without lipstick, I have cat lips—nothing but a line, I thought as we climbed in the back of the limo.

Muffy sat in front with the driver, and turned to face us. "We've reserved a table at a restaurant famous for seafood. It's in Rose Bay. Have you been to 'Pier'?"

"No, I only arrived two days ago," I explained. "I've stayed mostly in the hotel." I looked out the window as I spoke. "It sounds lovely, thank you for including me."

The Pier was a long narrow restaurant like a pier. Walls of windows looked out on the calm blue water of one of Sydney's numerous harbors. We were led to our table where four other Aussies from the film school were ordering drinks. They greeted us with enthusiasm.

"Skinny flat white," Muffy said as the waiter pulled the chair out for her.

I must have blanched, because Jack smirked and leaned in to me, saying, "She ordered coffee, skim milk."

"I thought she was introducing herself," I murmured back, taking my seat on the other side of him.

Introductions were followed by a recap of the symposium with great attention focused on how well it was organized and how much Jack Swanson's presence added.

When the compliments ran their course, I spoke up. "So Muffy, is that your given name?"

"It's Margaret. Muffy is a nickname that stuck. Have you heard it in America? What kind of girl would have that name?"

Jack and I looked at each other and shrugged.

"Seems Preppy." I ventured. "A nice college girl."

"A perpetually youthful name," Jack said, agreeably.

Muffy beamed. "I'm not sure Muffy was professional enough for an aspiring film producer. I sometimes feel on the back foot. Recently a distinguished gentleman asked me, 'What kind of name is Muffy?' I told him it was Egyptian, short for Mufumi." She batted the air. "You know he couldn't say anything—it would appear racist."

We all laughed. It seems PC is alive and well on both continents. Actually, Muffy was adorable and what she said was secondary to her charismatic presence and charming accent. Knowing Jack as I did, he was probably relieved to have the attention off himself after speaking all afternoon. I was just a fly on the wall looking to fill pages of the actor's life for the biography I began months ago.

"Anyway, I asked the universe to give me a sign. Do I stick with Muffy or do I become Margaret? A week later I went to the re-launch of my school, a big black-tie event filled with the 'crème' of Australian film industry. I desperately wanted the producer/director George Miller to be a guest on a show called Master Class."

Jack turned to me tapping a finger in mid air. "He directed *Happy Feet* and *Babe*."

I nodded. "Great films."

"He was *very* nice and said he'd love to be on the show if it would help. I gave him my card and he looked up and said, 'Muffy? What a great name.' I told him, how funny you should say that, George, because I was wondering if I should keep it. George Miller grabbed me by the shoulders, looked me in the eye and said, 'Muffy Potter, you cannot change this name!' So, I got my sign from the universe! I've been Muffy Potter ever since. I own it."

We saluted her with a toast. As our glasses clinked, I felt happy for her auspicious start in the art world, then slid into doubt about mine.

Our delicious seafood dinners were eventually delivered and devoured. Our table fell silent. I felt clumsy switching the fork back and forth between my left and right hand. Like the English, the Australians eat with a downward pointed fork, while the knife in the right hand slices feverishly like a sushi chef. I wanted to sword-fight with my fork on the plate too, but it felt too risky.

We were zoomed back to our hotel and Jack invited Muffy and me to join him in the bar for a cognac. Our little fresh-faced hostess was thirty-one years old and therefore it wasn't unseemly to reciprocate the fancy dinner with this gesture. As the three of us made our way to the bar, I suddenly remembered this was the "other" night of the pre-dawn agreement I'd made.

I bade them goodnight with a flurry of double-cheeked air kisses at the bar's entrance.

******

Spring in America coincides with Australia's Indian summer. The sun shines all day, occasionally interrupted by a burst of gentle rain. I've decided the Botanical Gardens that rim the harbor are the Garden of Eden. From a distance, the icon of modern Sydney, the Opera House, looks like a pile of helmets backstage at a giant's production of *Don Quixote.*

The sprawling garden paths are alive with well-dressed birds in fancy feathers, three-D spider webs the size of a small trampoline, and trees heavy with flying foxes hanging upside down. They are fruit bats and thanks to a taxidermy display, I saw up close they have cute Pekinese dog faces and reddish brown fur. They hug themselves with leathery large wings and hang high like big avocados from treetops. My cheeks ached from the prolonged smiles long before my legs tired of walking the fragrant path. It was nature's symphony, with the chatter of ducks, screeches of birds, and underscored with the constant hum of insects.

Signs encouraged us to walk on the grass, smell the flowers and touch the leaves. Mums chatted while pushing prams, seniors strolled while holding hands, and joggers in Lycra jetted by as cameras clicked from every direction. I'm sure I'm not alone in thinking my pictures, taken with a disposable camera, were ready for the cover of National Geographic.

The most common tree in the gardens is the Morton Bay Fig tree. Since its roots grow above ground, the tree's mahogany-colored tangle of thick wood ropes makes up the base, the limbs eventually branching out beneath the heavy boughs of an emerald shade.

This setting would have been a perfect place to interview Jack, but his day was spent with Peter Garrett, Australia's Minister of Culture, and former member of the 80's rock band,

"Midnight Oil." Since meeting, the two were inseparable. Peter was smart and articulate; rock-n-roll royalty who was a force for positive change. How could I compete with that?

Still blissed-out from the Eden experience, I got back to the hotel and rang his room. "Remember me? The writer who's on the brink of fictionalizing your biography for lack of data?"

He laughed into the phone. "Go ahead. Make up something, I've probably done it anyway."

"Indulge me a little. Come see this authentic puppet- maker shop. The husband and wife are French and he makes the dolls and his wife makes the wigs and it's like Gepetto's work-shop..."

I heard him speaking through a yawn. "On George Street. The narrow cobblestone alley is a nice touch too. It's another world going on downstairs in the little cave-like rooms."

"Yes, exactly! Oh, so you know it?"

"Been there, done that, bought the marionette. See I told you, whatever you come up with I've already done."

I slumped into my chair. "Which one?"

"Which what? Oh, puppet. Let's see. Last trip here I bought a very elegant Puss in Boots that's dangling in my office. He's dressed in a purple and green silky waist coat, very dapper. I should have one made for myself."

"Wow, I can see you both wearing matching outfits, with you pulling the strings and the puppet dancing," I laughed. "Let me call my agent in L.A. and see if he can book the act. There has to be interest in a puppet-animal-fetish duo."

"Veronica, back to the shop, did you find something magical, dear?"

"I bought two boxing kangaroos. You push a lever with your thumb up under its skirt and he jabs the air. I've got two." Then, in a sultry voice, "Wanna fight?"

"Maybe later, I'm on my way out."

A silence stretched out and I refused to pick up the slack. I pictured his elegant cat in its silk waistcoat then disloyally scowled at my boxing joeys, still in the plastic, with the "Two for $18" tag.

Jack finally broke the tension. "How about hot chocolate in the restaurant tonight. Was it ten you said? I should be back from dinner by then. I'd include you, but I was invited by…"

"Ten is good, Jack. I'll be there. Bye for now." We hung up.

It was disarming how his husky voice thrills me. Spending time with Jack was like gliding on ice skates on a frozen pond in the moonlight, not knowing that while coming out of your graceful spin, the ice will be too thin and you'll drop into a freezing hole. Slumped into my chair, I kicked my feet into the air. My low-heeled sandals flipped off and hit the ground. I'd been spinning on thin ice trying to write *Jack's Back,* for almost a year.

CHAPTER 2

This was *the* night for sex in my every *other* night program. My nerves had nerves. After anxiously downing two bitter espressos, I checked my mirror again. My eyes bulged like a Chihuahua and I was just as jumpy. Prepared to speed write for three hours to fill gaping holes in his story, I couldn't risk dulling my wits with a glass of Chablis. At 9:55 Jack strolled to the last table where I was poised with a pen boring a hole into the first page of a legal pad. Dressed in black jeans, a buff-colored leather jacket and salmon silk cami top, I felt I'd struck the perfect chord of professional writer and good kisser. The sheerness of the top just hinted at the salmon lacy plunging bra.

"Table for one, just coffee," he sang as he approached. "A song I wrote. Would you like to hear it?" Without waiting for an answer he leaned over and kissed my cheek. *"Not meeting someone, not coming undone...just coffee. Then, out of the rain an angel came..."*

I wrote the words as he sang, like a court reporter getting every word. Songwriting? Another facet of the shining diamond before me. We picked his life up where we had left it in Los Angeles. His memory was prompted by old calendars he brought, and we traveled back through the years.

About one I checked my watch. We stood up and gathered our things. He pulled my chair out for me and waited as I stood up. We were inches apart and his dreamy eyes said the writing session was over.

"Precious girl—forgive me," he said softly.

"For?"

"I've thought about your words the other morning and I'm afraid in my eagerness to see you I wasn't a gentleman." He eased back and looked me over while holding my hand. "Your little frame, well...fits so well with mine. It's hard to let you go. What are you? Five two? Three? Your hazel eyes draw me in, Veronica. *Hmmm.*"

He tilted my chin up, then ran two fingers along my jaw line then down my neck. His fingertip gently traced the outline of cleavage along the lace trimming of my bra. Through the silk I felt the heat of his touch drawing down my breast. Aware of the sounds of workers cleaning at a distant table, I stood perfectly still—not wanting to disturb our connection of intimacy.

He whispered, "I've been unfairly using our writing time together. You're right. I haven't been as available as much as I thought I would be. Please accept—"

"No apology is necess—"

"Accept this gift." He withdrew a small felt box from his pocket. "I passed by the window of the jewelry shop on the way to the lobby enough times to grow fond of it." He put it in my hand.

I struggled with the tight fitting top, then it sprung open. A shimmering opal pendant on a platinum chain was inside. "Jack? Why, it's so beautiful! How sweet, and what a surprise."

"You've been so patient with me. I can't thank you enough for coming all this way to finish my story."

I looked at the opal, then at him. "I want to try it on right now, but why don't we go upstairs?"

"Jack!" Peter's voice called out.

I turned to see Muffy and Peter shuffling toward us. Their boisterous words were garbled because of their accents and echo in the empty restaurant. "There you are!" Muffy pointed. "You weren't in the bar, and it closed at one-fifteen."

Peter slapped Jack's back, then turned to me. He raised his eyebrows and flashed a warm smile.

"Hello, dah—lings!" Muffy embraced me first with a whisky-soaked hug.

I clamped the jewelry box shut and dropped my arm to the side.

"Are you coming to Brisbane too, dah—ling?" Muffy blinked several times then hiccupped once and giggled.

"Hello, Veronica." Peter saluted me for some reason. "We're trying to coax my mate, Jack here, into coming for the weekend to a film festival in Brisbane. They'll be thrilled to have him." Slapping Jack on the back, he continued with, "*Imagine* the excitement, Chet the racecar driver arriving without announcement. You have some real fans there, mate."

Muffy gave the thumbs up. "They can probably quote *Moon over Miami* chapter and verse."

It seemed that Jack and I had stepped outside of the eye of the hurricane with their arrival.

Peter forged on. "I have a plane, a Cessna 310 all fueled up...it's only about ninety minutes away."

As Peter and Muffy rambled, I just stood there, fighting my way to the surface after being submerged in the romantic moment. Their intrusion jolted me from romance-land and I landed with a thud. Jack's eyes scanned the ceiling. Peter's words trailed off. "I hope we aren't interrupting anything, mate. I just thought you'd be meeting us for a pint around one, then the bar closed."

Muffy giggled. "Then the bar closed and they saw us to the door."

I stepped back from our circle. "That film festival sounds great, you guys. I was about to tell Jack that I won't be staying till Friday after all. You see, I...I have another job starting soon in, in..."

"America?" Muffy jumped in.

"Yes. In America. I moved my flight up. Don't miss seeing Brisbane on my account, Jack. I'm sure we can finish up via email." Clutching my legal pad to my chest with the jewelry box tight in my fist, I extended my right hand and shook everyone's hand goodbye while backing toward the door. Their voices started up immediately and I heard Jack call my name as I disappeared around the corner. The business center was open all night and I suddenly had some emails to get out. Using my room key I let myself in and sat down at the computer desk. I felt my face flush with heat as I frantically typed.

TO: Virgin Airlines

FROM: Veronica Bennett

SUBJECT LINE: Emerg.flt needed due to death. Next tx from Syd to Lax Please!

TO: Creative Entertainment Agency

FROM: Veronica Bennett

SUBJECT LINE: Need a piano/voice gig. Available immediately. ANY WHERE

*****

Gamely, I boarded the plane in Sydney, and stopped at home for a twelve-hour layover to grab mail, clothes, and music. The agent had arranged two other flights from there: Charlotte, North Carolina, and apparently an hour and fifteen minute puddle jumper to Hilton Head Island. I would be in a humid tropical paradise three days after leaving Jack in Sydney.

A gig at a resort in a place I never heard of. I assumed Hilton Head was the headquarters for the world-wide hotel chain; I pictured a training facility for housekeepers and chefs,

surrounded by a running track with valet parkers and room
service waiters sprinting. Like in most hotels, the top floor
would be a lounge. Maitre d's would be perfecting fake accents
and lounge singers faking song requests. The "special of the
day" would be memorized by headwaiters and described in
mouth-watering detail. "The monk fish was caught off a reef in
Peru, and flown here first class, at 8 a.m. this morning." But, I
suppose skyscrapers aren't built in locations that have a season
named after hurricanes. Hilton Head Island is actually
surrounded by water—as in *island*, and was a golf resort
destination off South Carolina.

My pride kept me from staying in Sydney. I hated leaving
Jack, but the fear of slipping another wrung of his priority
ladder made me run and hide. My ability to compartmentalize is
either a blessed gift or a ticking time bomb of resentments.
However, by compartmentalizing I'm able to function. (A skill
which, if refined, could be taught at the Learning Annex.)

I literally had two Jack envelopes. The first one was simply
labeled J. Inside was the only picture I had of us together, and
some bad poetry—whining missives about our time spent at the
piano bench and other surfaces. Song requests he'd sent up to
my piano were inside too; three rippled cocktail napkins with
smeared ink were my treasures. Now the tiny jewelry box was
safely tucked inside.

The second jumbo-sized envelope was labeled BIO.
Jammed inside were notes scribbled on binder paper, the backs
of envelopes, old clippings with notes in the margins as well as
calendar pages. Most disturbing was the contract from our
publisher clarifying the expectation of a 90,000-word
manuscript. IF I didn't come up with *Jack's Back*—the money
they had advanced me—the money that I'd long ago spent on
living —would need to be returned. Yikes.

With my clothes in two huge suitcases, and music books
and shoes in a carry-on, I was flying to the East Coast to sing at
a resort for the season. I remember a commercial where Carly

Simon sang a lilting song to support an aspirin ad: *"Haven't got time for the pain."* I must begin again. *Again*-again.

*****

The airport in Charlotte is awesome. There's a long row of potted ficus trees planted every few feet in front of a window and in between are dozens of lovely white wooden rocking chairs. A musician plays a jazzy grand piano near an open bar where people sit on tall stools with their backs to those rocking.

As I made my way to the gate for my connector flight, I looked longingly at those lucky commuters flopped over massage chairs getting rubbed down by masseuses. They were sharing a spa-like area beside contented girls leafing through magazines during pedicures.

Unlike LAX with its unflattering overhead lights and annoying babble of flight announcements, I had flown into a Southern comfort zip code.

The fifty-five minute flight to Hilton Head Island was more excitement than I wanted. It was a buzz kill boarding the tiny plane with ten rows of two seats on one side and a solo seat on the other.

More troubling was the male flight attendant who looked like a contestant on the first week of "The Biggest Loser." The ridiculous scale of the plane versus the size of the flight attendant made me suspect I was in a sketch for "America's Funniest Videos." As our well-meaning sumo wrestler informed us of the safety features, I briefly considered a mutiny. Leaving him on the tarmac while the rest of us took our chances buckling our seatbelts without instruction, suited me just fine. But no one made eye-contact with me and I couldn't overtake him myself. So I sat in blink-less terror—and gave him my complete attention.

The psychic energy I normally use to keep the plane in the air now had to be diverted to mentally "vibe" the giant to stay in the center, fearing if he moved in either direction the plane would tilt over. With grim foreboding I knew even Neil Armstrong in the cockpit couldn't steer us out of the spin once our US Airways giant sat in the jump seat.

Somehow the little puddle jumper managed to lift off the ground. Our portly flight attendant stayed in the center aisle, wedged between the aisle seats as his long arm reached up and down the rows, never moving his cart. He served an alarming amount of booze to the very, very, almost *reverently* quiet passengers.

*****

After checking into the Crowne Plaza Hotel, I trudged to my room for some sleep. I didn't want the word to get around that their new singer was a sunken-eyed, wrinkled dullard. They'd have to find that out for themselves. Frizzy hair was a major problem in the high humidity. Catching my reflection in the brass walled elevator, I looked like the love child of Albert Einstein and Diana Ross.

It was seven-thirty p.m. by the time I got up to my room on the fifth floor, conveniently located next to the ice machine. How delightful. The rumblings of metal would be the sound of home for the next three months. There was a note on the table with a small basket of fruit, from the food and beverage manager, David Lindsey. I was invited for coffee at 2:00 p.m. the following afternoon at Brellas Café, the hotel coffee shop. Sleep came easily once I pulled the curtains shut and clipped the heavy drapes with my traveling clothespins—the fix-all travel accessory for closing snack bags and darkening a room.

The east side of the hotel faced the Atlantic Ocean and my room faced north. I could wait to see the ocean tomorrow. Now it was pillow time.

CHAPTER 3

David Lindsey, the Food and Beverage Manager, was a fortyish, curly-headed brunette, with a slight build. Within minutes of our meeting, it came out he was a musician who had recently married the General Manager's daughter. That explains how a friendly, creative, slightly zany musician crossed over to the dark side, i.e., management. (In all of my ten years accompanying myself on piano, I had never met a suit with a clipboard that was fun, till now.) By our second cup of coffee, I suspected that happy-go-lucky David was better suited to the piano bar and was now experiencing the down side of nepotism. Instead of guzzling free drinks and chatting between songs for hours, his days were ten-hour shifts scheduling bus boys, revising menus, and meeting with pushy liquor salesmen.

With pride and a tad of melancholy, he escorted me to the bar next door, called Starz. We made our way to the corner stage and he pulled out the bench from the white baby grand piano. He lifted the lid carefully, and then launched into playing *Great Balls of Fire*; he was a monster on those ivories, pounding out like Jerry Lee Lewis.

"I hope you don't expect me to follow that!" I gasped.

"I just show off sometimes. Don't worry, Veronica. You're a wonderful singer. Your agent over-nighted your CD."

"I'm sure the crowd loved your playing here, David. And, by the way, what is the crowd like?"

"Mostly upscale families on weekends. Golfing tournaments bring in people, and of course we've got honeymooners." He swatted the air. "Not many young singles. Are you married?" David looked at the floor, and then shrugged. "I might as well get the question out of the way. You know the other employees are going to ask. We can't ask marital status before someone is hired."

I nodded. "Single but not looking."

"Sorry for asking. Here, let me move to a chair and you can try out our Yamaha. We have it tuned every six weeks, due to the humidity."

The action on the keyboard was perfect and with the carpeted floor, the sound didn't boink around the room, as is the case in glass and hardwood-floor clubs. I played a medley starting with "On Broadway" then, "New York State of Mind" and ended with a brief "New York, New York." Besides the obvious theme, it offered a pop tune, a blues and a show tune. David Lindsey applauded like a hyperactive kid. "I love it, I love it!" His reaction was over-the-top enthusiastic and gushy. I wondered if he was on something—and if so, where could I get some?

"Veronica," he bounced in his seat. "I'm dying to tell you my idea about how to build the business and put this place on the map!" He crossed his legs and leaned forward with a toothy grin. It seemed he wanted me to drag it out of him. I was mute, but he continued anyway. "It has to do with you!"

"Something *I'm* supposed to do?" I asked, "beyond just singing from eight to eleven-thirty?" I squeaked, "Six nights a week?"

"Listen," he urged. "We get just a few locals coming to the lounge—oh, remind me to get someone to drive you around to see all the plantations."

"Plantations? Wow, I guess we really are in the South. Yes, I would love to see—"

"Later. So here's my idea. You and I—mainly you, organize a talent contest and we will hold it here." He paused dramatically and swept his arms open wide, "We'll call it…American *Island* Idol!"

I felt myself twitch. "I thought you said there were only a handful of locals, that it's mostly retirees and honeymooners. Do you think there's enough talent here?" I looked around the vacant lounge with concern. "In Hilton Head?"

"Since you're new in town," he said breathlessly, "I can't think of a better way for you to get acquainted with the people here."

I slumped. Still sitting on the piano bench it was impossible to hold up my spine. "Gee, David. I've never done anything like that before. When you hired me, I assumed you had enough business to validate bringing in someone for three months. Now, you need to build *it up?* I thought this was the vacation season coming up?" He looked crestfallen, but I forged on. "I mainly keep to myself. I'm quiet."

He looked at the floor.

I peddled backwards, "Well—aside from the gig, when I am, uh, an extroverted, heh, heh, charmer."

David sighed deeply and looked to his folded hands. His index fingers tapped like miniature applause. I pressed on anyway.

"If you hired me to come all the way from L.A., there must not be many people around here who can sing and play."

"I've heard the local entertainers," he said softly. "We like to bring in talent from L.A. or New York. New Yorkers are too sophisticated. California is just right, ya know?"

I had to drop my head lower to try and meet his eyes. "I know you did this gig for, what was it, four years?"

"Five years," he sulked. "Since I've been in management I keep brainstorming on how to bring some real excitement to this place. So, I thought this would get the community involved and turn into a big celebration. I spoke to a few of the purveyors and they've agreed to donate cash prizes." He was cracking his knuckles now. "I was really hoping you would emcee the contest and we could have some fun."

Now it was my turn to sulk.

"American Island Idol," he said softly. "Well, just sit on it." David got up and shook my hand. The sudden shift in his demeanor hinted at the shame that he felt by telling me his idea too soon. It seemed his second personality kicked in, replacing Mister Giddy with Mister Sad Clip Board. As we walked past the white rattan furniture and small glass-top tables, the ceiling fans swirled lazily. The walls were tinted mirrors making the lounge seem larger than it was. Even though it's meant to be quiet in the morning, an empty bar is a lonely sight.

What I didn't tell him was that I'd barely watched the TV show. *American Island Idol*, geeze, what does that bring to mind? A tiki with torches? Painted red, white, and blue? There's an island idol for ya. Poor David. What a blithe spirit he was, now trapped trying to make sense of numbers. He was so anxious to meet a fellow musician that he had dreamt up this stupid plan to show his new wife and in-laws that he could be more creative than just coming up with a new tequila drink. But the idea was full of flaws.

"Okay, I guess I can, uh, help you with the talent search," I heard myself say. "Can we just call it, *Island* Talent Search?"

I almost fell backwards with the surprise bear hug. "Yes! Yes, thank you! This will be so awesome! Thank you again! Now let me call valet parking and get you set up with one of our rental cars. To use while you're here."

"Oh, good. Thank you so much."

"Instead of suburbs, we have plantations. We are in the Shipyard Plantation now."

As he pulled his walkie-talkie from his belt he said to me, "The concierge could get you a map. The island is only 26 miles around, but I'm afraid you might get lost."

"I'm sure I would," I said, feeling as lost as I've ever been.

CHAPTER 4

It was 8 p.m., Monday—the first night of the gig; four people in a lounge that seats eighty. Flickering candlelight reflected off the glass tabletops of the white rattan furniture. Maybe the decorators figured if the lounge looked like a patio, the guests wouldn't know they came inside.

I tested the mic and warmed up my fingers with a little five chord blues. Then I played some instrumental songs by Antonio Carlos Jobim, assuming the tropical vibe of this beautiful island setting.

The pink little spotlight cast a gentle beam of light on me and my white, lacquered grand piano situated in the corner of the Starz lounge. Over the bar a TV screen was tuned to a soccer game with the sound off. This was something I had to get used to long ago; a moving ball, any shape, is a necessary evil in most bars. The season was ten weeks and then I'd be back in California, hopefully with my book completed. It always amazed me that my fingers had music memory, leaving my brain to wander.

David Lindsey flew through the door and with long strides, crossed the room to stand at my elbow. "Meditation? I love that song. Sorry it's empty on your first night. Mondays are slow."

"It's okay, I'm just easing into the gig," I whispered. "How does the P.A. sound?"

"You sound great." He pulled a chair loose from a table setting and plunked himself down. "I've got good news! I found our first contestant for the American Island Idol talent search."

"I thought we changed it to just, Island search, David?"

"Oh, yes, of course. Got it." He waved his arms as if conducting the Philharmonic. "Island Talent Search."

"You found someone?" I swung the boom stand holding the mic to one side.

"Her name is Lucinda. She is the dental hygienist for my dentist. She is always singing along with the Muzak and I thought, what the heck? I told her about the talent contest and she's ready to sign up."

"Were you wearing a bib and spitting into a cone during the negotiations?"

He erupted into a donkey bray of a laugh. "Anyway, here's an info sheet. It tells the dates of the event and the amount of the prize money. There should be a signup fee, just to hold people to coming, so I made it $20. How does that sound?"

"Sounds fine with me, but I am new to this. Are you sure you even need me to do it? You know people and have an idea how it…"

"Veronica, I have to meet with the Seagram salesman at eight in the morning. Before that the fish monger is coming and I've got to figure out how many catfish we'll be selling by Wednesday. Believe me, I need you to run this. I just got the first sign-up. Aren't you excited? Gotta get home now. No drinking on your shift," he smiled apologetically, "and after your shift, if you want to drink, it has to be at a different bar in the hotel."

"I know. I read the contract. Thanks for dropping by. I love the feel of this piano."

"I do too," he said with his head down, then scurried off.

The rest of the night was uneventful except for finding a cell phone at an abandoned table. I thought of turning it in to Lost and Found but then decided to call the owner myself. I didn't know anyone on the island and maybe the person who lost it would be interesting.

On my first break, I dialed the most recent outgoing call. A woman named Mrs. Cunningham had met the phone's owner for lunch at the Crowne Plaza that afternoon.

"Gertrude will be so happy to get her phone back, dear. I don't know if there will be a reward, however."

"Oh, to be honest, I'm not looking for a reward. I just want to return it. If it goes into the Lost and Found, it would probably just sit there."

The woman on the line laughed. "It is kind of ironic Gertrude doesn't know where it is—she is the leading psychic in the South. But, like all of us, she can be forgetful when she isn't in a trance."

"I can relate to being forgetful—so, she really goes into a trance? Did she do that—here in the lounge at the hotel?"

"Oh, gracious no! My birthday was this week and she took me to the hotel. We love sitting on the patio and the shrimp club sandwiches are to die for. Gertrude Anderson is a third generation oracle and regarded as royalty. Let me look up her home number for you, dear. Call her there. She'll be so grateful."

*****

To: Jack

From: Veronica

Re: Biography

Hey Jack, Sorry I've taken this long to get back to you. I listened to your messages on voice mail. I agree my departure was too sudden, but I needed to take this job right away. I'm guessing you enjoyed the film festival in Brisbane. It sounded like a good opportunity and I didn't want to hold you up in Sydney talking about your past when you could be experiencing an interesting "present." Or, perhaps when I left you took to your bed with severe melancholia and you've spent the last week sprawled about your unmade bed in a dark room amidst a sea of empty whiskey bottles.

Seriously, as for the remaining one hundred pages of our biography, I'll make it easy. We're covering the last fifteen years. I'll do the chronology of your contribution to cinema and pop culture and just email you questions and ask for quotes. We should be able to knock it out. I'm sorry if I sound so clinical. I just don't know how else to do this. I adore the sparkling pastel opal necklace, and Sydney was terrific. But once I crossed the "line" of professional biographer I was doing the limbo *under* the line. Maybe I should have just stayed on and worked at the hotel while you were in Brisbane. See how schizoid I've become?

Hilton Head is a safe tropical island resort town with tons of civil war history. I adore the hotel and the piano. The Food & Beverage Mgr., David, is like a St. Bernard puppy that runs up to greet you and jumps on your blouse with wet paws. Friendly, extroverted and manic, means well but needs to tone it down.

I agreed to co-produce a talent search. I can't believe I took it on. Since he is a frustrated musician, I related to him and felt like a self-centered heel saying it was a *stooo-ped* idea. The last thing I need is a distraction from the writing; I tried to slither out, but caved in...*Grrr*...okay. Maybe it won't take up much time.

Anyway, I started singing last Monday night and I walk the hard white sands of the shore in the afternoons. To swim, I just dive into the warm water and go for what seems like miles, but when I put my feet down, I discover I'm only in waist-high water.

Tall grasses grow all the way to the white sand on the beach. There are countless ponds surrounding the area. Alligators lurk about the golf courses, and I've seen baby turtles swimming freely inches from the drowsy alligators' long snouts; surprisingly, they both co-exist nicely. I was warned that I was too close as I crouched near the edge of a pond. Supposedly, the gators eat small dogs and a customer told me when they have opened up dead gators they find numerous dog collars inside their stomachs. Funny, I never thought to ask *why* anyone would slice open a gator's stomach to discover such a treasure trove in the first place. Anyway, I believe it. Do you? So far, my only friends are Flora and Fauna. Today is my night off and I'm going to get a manicure and pedicure at the local day spa.

G'night,

Veronica

P.S. I found a cell phone and it belonged to the local psychic. They call her Gertrude the Oracle. Anyway, I left it at the registration desk in an envelope. She thanked me with a card for a free reading. I promise not to snoop into your future.

CHAPTER 5

"What time do you close?" I asked the manicurist who was briskly brushing my heels.

"Sorry, I usually just work mornings." She called out to the back, "What are the hours tonight, Patrice?"

A slender and stylish woman appeared around the corner. "Tonight we close at 7 p.m. You're the last appointment." She lingered a moment. "Hi, I'm Patrice, the owner. Is this your first time to FACES Day Spa?"

"Nice to meet you," I held out my hand. "I'm Veronica. Yep, first visit. I just moved to the island a week ago. But I'll be putting your number on speed dial. I love the scented candles and great service." I nodded to the gal meticulously painting Plum Crazy on my toenails. "Maria has brought me back to life with this glorious foot massage."

Patrice smiled then walked to the window and pulled the curtain back. She peered down the palm tree-lined strip mall. "Did you see all the cars in the parking lot?"

"I didn't notice."

"There's some promotion next door at The Jazz Corner. They're celebrating their five-year anniversary. I should probably stick my nose in to see what's going on."

"Are you a jazz fan?" I stood up carefully as Maria guided my painted toes into my sandals.

The owner drifted about turning off lights. "Oh, it's not just jazz. They have all kinds of music on different nights. Classic Rock is tonight. You're finished? Nice color. Look, give me a moment to close up. Since you're new in town, Veronica, you might as well see Hilton Head's local music scene. One drink, on me."

I agreed and thanked her for the invitation. A half hour later we were toasting margaritas and shouting over a loud band.

*****

"Are you going to tell me your name, or do I have to guess?"

I swiveled my bar stool to the left. A smoky-eyed guy with a good build and dark shoulder-length hair was smiling at me. "Oh, go ahead and guess," I said, then turned back to my drink.

"You look like a, *Gina*."

"That would be me," I said as I lifted my drink in salute. We bantered about like that for a short while and then headed for the dance floor. A few minutes later the band took a break and the dance floor started to clear. Patrice was in an animated conversation with the guitarist. As we approached the bar ready to reclaim our stools, the musician waved in our direction.

"Cuz! Over here! Say hello to Patrice."

My dance partner nodded to her with a grin. "Hey, Patrice."

As I hopped up to the barstool next to her and slid my drink in front of me, he said, "This is Gina, everybody," and patted my shoulder.

Patrice cocked her head to one side, and looked at me quizzically. "Gina, huh? Well, Gina, say hello to JT. As you heard, a killer guitarist. But I like him because he's one of my clients."

I nodded at JT. Then looking back at my dance partner. "I didn't catch your name."

JT stepped closer, slapped him on the back and with pride in his voice announced, "This is my cousin, Hippy Bob, a good ole Southern gentleman."

"I do drink Southern Comfort, if that qualifies," he replied. "Nice to meet both you ladies. How about a drink?" Before we answered he caught the bartender's eye and twirled his index finger in the air.

Patrice leaned into me, saying, "Gina? I thought you said—"

I looked at Hippy Bob and confessed, "Now that we're drinking together, and we have no secrets—my name is Veronica."

"The main thing is, we have no secrets," Hippy Bob said gamely. "Veronica…hmm, I like that." Then, he lifted his glass to salute JT, and added, "That was a good set. It's no secret you set that guitar on fire, with 'Smoke on the Water,' cuz."

Patrice and I agreed the band sounded great and for the next few minutes we talked about songs and the nostalgic appeal of classic rock. Our drinks came and after a few sips it was time for JT to return to the stage.

I caught his sleeve as he got up. "Say, JT, I play piano at the Crowne Plaza and this may sound weird because I just met you, but I've been told to put together a night of local talent. I'll try my best to not make it hokey." I swallowed. "But there is $5,000 in prize money for the first place winner. They don't have enough stage for bands to compete, so to keep it simple we're… they're… looking for the best solo acts. If you would agree to do a song, I would so, uh, appreciate it. You play fantastic." I didn't add, 'and look hotter than the hinges on hell's gates.'

"I'll think about it." He smiled and set his drink on the bar. Then he kissed Patrice on the cheek with a "See ya, girl," and disappeared into the crowd as he made his way toward the stage.

It was so hard to blurt out that lame speech to this darling guy and have him brush me off. I got the sense that everything came easy to JT. He was about six feet tall, had fair skin, a smattering of well-placed freckles, and strawberry blond thick hair. His teeth were perfect porcelain soldiers lined up and ready to do some lady-killing. Especially in his line of work—musician. JT's singing voice was a gritty growl in, "Fooled Around and Fell in Love," and although hardly moving on stage, he had charisma to burn. Exactly the type I needed to steer clear of. Even in our brief encounter I analyzed his flawless features and got lost in his eyes, trying to figure out which shade of blue. As I watched him on stage, I suspected his life was a series of open doors and all he had to do was stroll through.

"I'll talk to him about it," Hippy Bob spoke in my ear, although I was so focused on JT, I didn't remember the subject.

"You know, the talent thing?" he prompted.

Patrice spoke up. "I'm surprised the Crowne Plaza came up with the five thousand dollars for prize money. They've never done anything like this before. That shows a lot of confidence in the idea, Veronica."

"Yeah, right," I mumbled. I didn't reveal I'd never pro-duced anything more complicated than an omelet, and that stuck to the pan. But, if there ever was an Island *Idol*, or a local Adonis, it had to be JT. "I guess some liquor company is sponsoring it. They want to award the prize money to one person, rather than splitting it between first, second and third. That's a better incentive, don't you think, Hippy Bob?"

"Probably for some people," he said. "JT doesn't care about money. He only plays here for fun once in a while. He has a standing invitation to sit in and since they do cover songs, he knows most of them. It's cool that you're a musician too. I'll have to come down to the Crowne Plaza and heckle you."

"Now, now." I swatted his shoulder. "You were introduced as a Southern gentleman, so…."

As Hippy Bob backtracked on his threat to heckle, I noticed he was a better than average hunk of man, too. He was as tall as his cousin although his brown curly hair was in need of a haircut. He had a lazy way of looking at you through partially closed eyelids. Was he stoned? Maybe that's where he got his name. A neatly trimmed goatee framed his thin lips and his smile was as white as the crisp shirt he wore. Not knowing any Southerners, I thought it was charming to see a good looking guy in a cowboy shirt with tan piping on the collar and silver snaps on the pocket.

"Which nights do you work?" Patrice asked me. "We'll meet over there this week, okay, Hippy Bob?"

"That sounds so formal," I said. "Do people ever just call you, Hippy?"

"Or Mr. Bob?" Patrice asked.

He laughed. "Call me anything but late for dinner. Crowne Plaza, huh? I've never been over there. But if your music is half as pretty as your smile, I'll make the trip."

Glancing over my shoulder toward the stage, I said, "Thank you, but what about JT entering the contest."

"JT just might come by one night and do the show."

"That's the rub," I said grimly. "There'll be two nights of it. The contestants need to qualify. We'll come up with fifteen or so acts to be semi-finalists, do a show, then the finals on Saturday, July 3ʳᵈ. He'll have to compete twice to," I drew quotations in the air, "win the Island Talent show."

I shrugged. We all burst into laughter.

"Bacardi is promoting new rum drinks at the same time," I explained. "They're hoping that after a few Cuba Libres the title won't sound so craptastic. Hippy Bob, where do your talents lie? Can I get you signed up at least?"

"No, not me," he drawled. "Unless you want me to open a horse's mouth and tell you how old he is, by lookin' at his teeth. I'm studying to become a vet."

"That is so noble," Patrice swooned. "This island needs a vet. I used to take my cat all the way to Beaufort to see a good doctor. Which plantation are you from?"

"Sea Pines." Just then the music got louder as "My Sharona" thumped its contagious bass beat. Someone Patrice knew grabbed her hand and pulled her off the stool and toward the dance floor.

"Let's go." Hippy Bob took my hand and I happily followed the sea of people to the edge of the stage.

At the next break Patrice and I met in the bathroom for a conference. She'd never seen Hippy Bob before, but apparently JT came in regularly to get acrylics on his right hand, to play guitar. We were a bit tipsy and it was exciting accidentally bumping into a social life. Maybe I would have friends here; Patrice sure seemed fun-loving and spontaneous. I caught her checking her watch and so I suggested we go.

We hugged Hippy Bob good-bye, waved to JT on the stage and then went next door to Faces to soak our feet in hot soapy water and have coffee before I drove home. It was a terrific perk partying with a spa owner.

"Does it seem odd that two very eligible bachelors live together and neither work?" I asked. "Hippy Bob said JT doesn't need money or care about it—something like that. A musician who doesn't need five grand? And, I bet he'd win."

"Hmm. Yet, they're not gay," Patrice murmured. "They live in Sea Pines, which is stylishly expensive too. We can wonder all day, but never really know what's going on."

I took another gulp of the coffee and swished my feet in the soapy water. "Bar relationships are so shallow—and fun. The guys live by the beach—alone. Maybe their cars have car seats and bumper stickers saying 'My kid is on the honor roll.'"

"No, I've seen JT's new Cadillac Escalade. No car seat. The bumper sticker says, 'Don't blame me, I never voted in my life!' He's single."

"Maybe we need to follow them home. Maybe they live in one of those little trailers off the highway behind a fruit stand."

"And they get those gorgeous tans from picking the fruit they sell?"

"The bar lets out any minute…they don't know my car," I said. We giggled a moment and the words hung in the air. We patted our feet dry then exchanged glances.

"Okay," Patrice grinned. "Grab your keys. I'll get the lights."

"You're on!"

CHAPTER 6

Patrice knew the roads so it made sense to have her slide behind the wheel of my Toyota Corolla. David came through with the loaner car for the duration of my stay. It was beige and nondescript and I was wishing I could mark it somehow to cut down on time searching for it in the hotel lot. Tonight, however, when trailing a couple of hotties a blah car was an asset. With the full moon it was easy to spot them leaving. JT was carrying a guitar case. We started our engine and followed the black Cadillac Escalade out of the parking lot exit. They turned right and peeled down the dark two-lane road.

"Which one of these guys do you like?" I asked Patrice, then cringed at my own childish banter. "I mean, you know."

"Oh, I'm not interested in men right now. I'm too busy at work. I barely know JT and just met Hippy Bob tonight." She threw me a sideways glance. "But, they are both tid-bits, especially since the island is full of retirees and tourists and those who serve them. Like me."

"And me," I said.

"How about you, Veronica? Do you have some studly main squeeze waiting back home?"

"Not exactly. I was getting main-squeezed, but it never really amounted to anything. This job came at a good time—I needed a break from guys." Somehow a pick-up truck got in between our car and the Escalade as we zoomed up the tree-lined winding highway. "Wow, it's dark out here. Can you still see their tail lights?"

"Yep, they're just in front of that truck. Has anyone taken you around to see the various plantations?"

"I got a short tour from the rent-a-car guy. These houses along here are nothing like those in California. These are so far apart."

In the moonlight I could see palm trees swaying and hear the sound of the wind blowing in the dark foliage. White picket fences and then stone fortresses dotted the country road. All the homes were set back with no sidewalks. A skunk scurried past our headlights. As it flashed its glassy eyes, Patrice tapped the brakes to miss it.

"We're crazy doing this, you know." I looked at my watch. "What if they live really far away? It's already one-fifteen."

"JT gets his nails done at my shop, he can't live too far. Wait a second. We're coming up on Sea Pines; this is the high rent district." She slowed down. "Okay, this'll be interesting. This here area is what you might call the Beverly Hills of the island. Look! JT is slowing down and turning—"

The Escalade pulled up to a stone-pillared, gated enclave. Two lion sculptures guarded each side of the driveway. They either punched in or said some security code, because a wide metal gate swung open. Their car jetted inside and the tail lights disappeared as the gate slammed shut with a loud clunk.

"Hot damn, will you look at that?" Patrice slowed the car down and flipped a U turn. We rolled along with our headlights out. She lowered the window and pointed at the large property surrounded by a metal-staked fence. Although no one could hear us inside the car she spoke in a whisper. "That is one of the oldest and finest mansions in all of Sea Pines."

"Mansion is right," I whispered too.

"It's dark," she said, "like no one's home."

"Either that or the house is so far from the road you can't see lights. Do you think they live here alone?"

"JT said it's just him and his cuz." She slapped the steering wheel. "Well, we trailed a couple tid-bits right up to their mansion gates."

"They even have stone lions on guard," I whispered. "Which one did you say you liked?"

We laughed in the way that makes you snort because we were trying to be quiet. As our car idled past, we peered through the semi-dark to where the tail-lights had disappeared. A few seconds later dim lights flickered back through the trees. I guessed they were home.

*****

The following Monday night I was scheduled for the last appointment at FACES Day Spa. Patrice greeted me at the counter when I arrived at six.

"Good to see you back, Veronica." We exchanged a brief embrace then Maria led me back to her station. After six days of wearing three-inch-high strappy sandals, my toes needed caressing. Patrice floated through the back salon area and disappeared inside a supply closet, then reappeared. "How's the new gig?"

"The first week went well. I love singing but—it's no fun shoving my toes down a narrow passage of leather straps for five hours at a time."

Her laugh sounded like the tinkle of glass chimes.

I sank my feet into the soapy bin. "I'm treating myself here every Monday so my feet don't look like a bag of French fries stuffed in a sandal."

"Whoa—wait a minute," Patrice dropped into the empty chair beside me. "I'm gonna need a minute to get that image out of my mind. Are you sure you aren't a writer?"

A thrill washed over me with her off-hand remark, but revealing that I'm actually writing Jack Swanson's biography was a secret for another time. "I did some writing, if you could call it that. I made a flyer for the contest at the hotel. I was hoping you'd be here and I could show it to you." I pulled it from my pocket and handed it to her.

"This flyer looks good. I'll write down some local spots to post them. Someone at the hotel can do that for you, right?"

"Don't worry," I winked, "I wasn't going to make you drive me around."

"Can you believe it's already Monday? Sorry I haven't dropped by the Crowne Plaza this week—where does the time go, Veronica?"

"No worries. I'm still getting used to the gig and would prefer friends come in next week anyway." Then I cringed having used the plural for friends. She was my one and only.

"Did Hippy Bob ever come by?"

"No. I guess he was busy too. What was it he does?"

Patrice leaned in close so Maria didn't hear. "Studying to be a vet online, remember? Aside from science classes, I can't imagine how you'd learn to treat animals tapping on a keyboard. That's a hands-on-fur business, but, oh well."

CHAPTER 7

My hotel room had two double beds, one for sleeping and the other for laying out clothes. I loved my horizontal closet, where I could display entire outfits, with accessories, and observe a thinner, version of myself.

My fifth-floor room looked over the air-conditioning units of the floor below me and then beyond to the parking lot. Oh, well, I didn't mind. After all, being from Seal Beach and having been blessed with an ocean view for the past year, I magnanimously allowed the hotel guests their turn at the coastline. Not that I had a choice. Clearly, the proximity to the clunking ice machine is why I got this room. I figure, if you've got lemons, make lemonade. If you've got a rumbling ice machine, buy a blender and make smoothies.

I also dined on Top Raman that I handily made in the room's coffee maker. The taste of shrimp, however, didn't go well with coffee. There was a guilt-inspiring desk where my bulging BIO Envelope of Jack notes waited along with colored Post-it pads, photo copies of news clippings and a thesaurus.

With whole days stretched out before me and no friends, I busied myself with tedious tasks. Daily maid service was divine but I still found cleaning was a way to procrastinate writing. So I washed my make-up brushes, hair brushes, contact lens cases, inside my purse, the *outside* of my purse, brushed the lint off my slacks, used a razor to clip tiny balls of yarn off my knits, and tightened buttons on anything that threatened to wobble.

While cleaning out a purse I found a thank you note left by Gertrude the Oracle. Without giving it a second thought—like saving the experience for a real cosmic crisis—I dialed her number.

An elderly man's voice answered and that threw me. Was a wizard living with an oracle?

"Oh? Hello, is this the home of Gertrude Anderson? "

"May I ask who is calling, please?"

"I'm Veronica Bennett. I found her cell phone last week. So she doesn't know me by name, sir. If she's busy, it's okay, I can—"

"She will be glad to speak with you, dear. I'll get her."

I leaned across my bed/closet, throwing things around, looking for my calendar, but gave up when I realized I had nothing going on but my gig.

"Hello," a normal woman's voice spoke into the phone. Maybe I expected an echo, or gentle harp music behind her. "Thank you so much for returning my cell phone, dear," she said. "Now, it's my turn to return the favor. Are you interested in a life-cycle reading?"

Life-cycle? Wasn't that exercise equipment they hawked on late-night TV?

"Sure," I replied. "I mean thanks. I would love a life...uh cycle...reading."

Gertrude's voice was warm and reassuring. She chuckled like a grandma. "It doesn't hurt. I would love to meet you, dear. Why don't you make an appointment and we'll see how it goes."

"You can conjure up the spirits at any certain given time?"

"My teachers are very good to me." Another chuckle, "They always show up."

"Is today okay then?"

"Let me see." I heard the sound of papers shuffling. "How about four?"

"Four sounds fine. I'm getting excited, actually now talking to you. Thank you. This will be my first time meeting a psychic, er, oracle."

She gave me her address before we hung up. Just like making a hair appointment, except that my sense of anticipation bordered on mania. I had to jump around and shake out my hands just to release the energy. How exhilarating to go from idly finding a piece of paper in my purse, to heart-thumping anticipation. The secrets of the universe, *my* universe, would be unveiled in a few days. I tried a cartwheel for the first time since Girl Scouts. Thud. My ankle clunked the TV. This would need some practice before I could take it outside. My once limber body had calcified. The day was far too exciting to confine myself to the writing desk, so I put my swim suit on, grabbed my beach bag and left the room.

******

On the way to The Oracle's, I called the spa and asked for Patrice. We agreed to have a quick drink Monday after my mani-pedi. Monday is open-mic night at the club, so naturally I wanted to scout out acts for my talent contest. Neither of us mentioned JT and Hippy Bob. But bumping into JT would be the only way to press him into performing at the talent contest. None of my new friends had come by my gig.

Gertrude lived in a very ordinary, smallish home. Possibly the most non-descript house on the street. I parked in front and grabbed my little spiral notebook. Barbie in a swimsuit on the cover was campy and cute at the time I bought it. Now I regretted not choosing the note pad with the Kahlil Gibran quote.

The man whom I assumed to be her husband (I'm going out on a limb here, but doubt oracles shack up) answered the door and led me into the dining room. He offered me some sweet tea and just as I pulled out a chair, the diminutive channeler appeared. She was sixty-ish and looked like a nun in street clothes—during the Eisenhower administration. Minus a hat. In this resort town where long shorts and sundresses were so common, this was a bit of a disconnect.

Gertrude thanked me once again for returning her cell phone and introduced her husband, Ted. We exchanged pleasantries as I acclimated to the time warp.

"Dear, come right this way. Bring your glass with you," she urged. "We'll be in the parlor. Do sit in that chair and I'll sit across from you in this one."

All the curtains were drawn and although the sun was shining at four in the afternoon, lamps on top of doilies lit the small dark room. Bookshelves lined the walls and pictures of various deities were framed and displayed like family members. All eyes were on me. Krishna smiled—looking slightly buzzed, Buddha smiled—looking contentedly full from a big meal, while Jesus looked wistful as he cradled a lamb; the Dali Lama looked studious in his glasses.

"I spent years in China when I was a girl," Gertrude said as she smiled serenely and for that instant I saw her as a ten-year-old staring back at me through pink plastic horn-rimmed glasses. "My parents were missionaries. I see you noticing all the spirits on the shelves."

My emotions bubbled to the surface. I felt safe with this kindly lady, but she couldn't help it if my future sucked, and she just might *tell me* that. Perhaps singing along to The Vandals' "Fear of Punk Planet" on the drive over hadn't prepared me for the cosmic shift in consciousness. I should have tried to meditate or chant or fast or at least done a head stand before I came over to this holy ground. Why didn't I prepare? I eyed a box of tissues on a nearby table and grabbed a few. There was a Holy Bible the size of a large phone book on a stand. It was open and the edges of the pages gleamed gold.

I surreptitiously folded Barbie's pinup picture back, and poised a pen on the lined page. "I brought along a little notebook."

Gertrude nodded solemnly and then suggested that I take notes after the reading. Next she rubbed her palms together and closed her eyes. "This is how we start." Softly, almost to herself, she started reciting The Lord's Prayer, "Our Father who art in heaven...." All the while she was swishing her palms together, her head bowed reverently.

After a moment of silence she looked up at me. "I channel souls from the other side. They are around us all the time and I just have a better time hearing them. Think of it as a frequency. When you dial the radio some things come in clearly, but you can lose the program if you drive out of range."

"So, you are dialed in...so to speak?" I asked.

"We all have the gift to channel energy, but mine is more astute. We'll begin with a life cycle reading and then you can ask questions."

I drew in a breath. "Go ahead, tell me anything. I can take it."

"Are you in law enforcement? I see you sitting in a police car."

I'm thinking, hunky detective might come into the bar. I must have grinned slightly because she held up her hand.

"Oh. I see you are I the backseat. Quite upset. Hmmm. The tears are justified judging from your aura." She arranged her horn-rimmed glasses on the bridge of her nose. After a pause, she said, "I see you as a counselor. Does that sound right?"

"No, that is not my occupation."

"Are you a social worker?"

"No, that is not my field either."

"That's funny, I see you advising people. Almost...interfering with people and their life paths."

"Oh, well, there *is* that." I agreed. "I spent last summer trying to turn my roommate into a fashion model and rehabilitate my handyman, but....never mind. Perhaps you could say that on occasion, I am *generous* with advice."

"How lovely," she purred. "You are a very old soul and feel much compassion for people. Because you've lived many lives you can put yourself in the mind-set of people easily. Maybe that's what I'm getting. At any rate, you have a heightened degree of empathy and, my goodness, you are creative as well. You would do well in any of the arts. You are a natural communicator. Music would be one expression, an excellent expression, of communication."

Sitting up straight, I blurted out, "I'm a professional musician."

She then went on to describe my gullible nature (sorry, she's way off), but all in all, her soothing voice coaxed me into such a comfortable mood that I hated to get up and leave.

Then all of a sudden she cocked her head to one side, almost as if she was straining to hear a voice. Gertrude looked me straight in the eye. "One thing, dear. I never give bad news, but my soul guides want to warn you. You need to be cautious not to lose something *very* important. You may not realize its value at the time."

"Is it Jack?"

"Oh, heavens no!" she scoffed.

"Is it, is it... losing my opportunity to becoming a writer? If I don't finish Jack's biography I'll blow my one chance." I squirmed in the chair. "Is it losing the money Kendal Street Publishers advanced me? 'Cause it's already lost—gone, is that it?"

"No," she said flatly. "Veronica dear, our time is up. The energy generated here today has been wonderfully astute. Let us embrace this wonderful energy we feel today and carry it forth into God's magnificent physical plane."

Reluctant to leave, I just sat still and took in a few deep breaths. Gertrude stood up, shook my hand and thanked me for coming. She wished me a pleasant stay in Hilton Head, then someone knocked at the front door. Her husband opened the door to greet the five o'clock appointment.

On the porch outside I scribbled into the Barbie notebook: Be careful not to lose something of great value.

CHAPTER 8

The original plan of having the talent applicants send me CDs of their music wasn't practical. I needed to meet the contestants. So we sent word out for open auditions.

The Banquet Room was buzzing with voices and instruments. Open guitar cases were strewn around the floor, dancers bouncing down in agonizing splits, and an accordion duo was facing off with a rousing version of "I Can't Get No Satisfaction."

I stepped over and around the happy mayhem as I made my way to the front of the room. "Thank you all for coming." I held a clipboard above my head. "If you haven't signed in yet, I'll leave the list here on this table. Right now, when I call your name, please describe your act. Tell me how long it is, and what you need by way of staging. I'm assuming you singers have a background track on the CD. If you're chosen today we'll need to keep your CD here. Not that we don't trust you to remember it next time, but this will make things run smoother."

Hands flew into the air and not risking questions I couldn't answer, I just blazed through. "Let's just start down the list of names. Oh, gee, I should introduce myself. I'm Veronica Bennett and I'll be emceeing, well, producing this wonderful event." My voice cracked. I smiled at their eager faces. "I play piano in the lounge six nights a week and I invite you all to stop by and say, hello." The dancers looked up from the floor. Some held their legs up in a skyward stretch. Other contestants held their heads close to their guitars, tuning up.

"When I call your name, please describe your talent so I can get a feel for how many categories we have." I wanted to sit down so badly but felt it would take away from my stature as producer. So I teetered on my heels.

"First name, let's see, Mary Ellen Delaney?"

A voice called out from the back. "Belly Dancer, I have my own CD. The Blue Hawaii song is about, I don't know, maybe ten minutes."

"That sounds really great, Mary Ellen. Do you think you could trim it to about two and a half minutes?"

A sturdy, six-foot red-headed gal, about forty, approached me. "The dance needs that amount of time to tell the story, ma'am."

"I see." I scribbled a note on the clipboard and flashed a smile. "Thanks. I see your phone number is here if we need to talk about it."

She pressed on, "Do we get our twenty bucks back if we aren't in the show? It doesn't seem right if—"

The question stunned the crowd into silent attention. I looked up from the clipboard and scanned a room full of suspicious eyes. "Uh, sure." I nodded vigorously. Where was David? The F&B Manager needed to answer the tough questions before it turned into an evil circus of disgruntled performers.

"By a show of hands, how many here are dancers? Looks like six, no, seven. Thank you. Singers? Are you in a group, or are you individual acts?" Trying to corral these aspiring artists into some kind of order was hard enough, then, three doves got loose. A violin's high pitch proved too much for the creatures and they blasted out of Merlinski the Magnificent's sleeve. Girls screamed and ducked as the flapping wings grazed their heads. The guys howled with laughter and jumped in the air trying to grab them mid-flight. Poor Merlinski ran about trying to coax them back into a tiny, wire dressing-room cage. As he ran through the room, the flapping cage door caught on a brunette's pony-tail, and now she was following in step with him. Her yelping added to the chaos.

By the time David galloped into the room, the accordion duo was belly-to-belly honking out a medley of hits by the Stones. I thrust a small stack of novelty-act resumes in his hand and excused myself for a restroom visit. When I returned thirty minutes later, the room was cleared out. Chairs were topsy-turvy and the floor was littered with pieces of cheap plastic Hawaiian leis, dove feathers, and empty water bottles. David was shuffling papers at a table. ·

"You did a great job, Veronica," he said, not looking up. "The flyers really brought them in. We have applicants from Bluffton to Savannah." He paused to squeal. "You remember I told you about our first contestant, my dental hygienist?"

"Uh, huh," I lied.

"I'm sorry she couldn't make it today. But I filled out her application and clipped it to the singers stack. Lucinda is really looking forward to being in our competition. Unfortunately she has another little part time job she does on weekends—well, once a month," David looked up with a weird smirk. "And it fell on today."

`"Okay, what is it?"

"It's in the health field, still." He put his hand over his mouth barring a snicker; then let loose a robust belly laugh.

"Come on? What's the dental hygienist's monthly job?"

"Out here in the country there are gas stations and roadside little bars that are miles apart. She has to collect the money and replenish the vending machines." Now his laughter almost knocked him off his chair.

I joined in. Like yawns, laughter is contagious.

"She's a condom route salesperson," he sputtered. "She tells me it's still in the medical field."

"Hygiene is very important. I can't wait to hear her sing."

"Don't let her know I told you," David said quickly.

"I'll just ask her, what do you do with 500 used condoms?"

"Huh?"

I leaned in close to him. "Roll 'em into a blimp and call it a *Goodyear*."

As the laughter died down, he smiled apologetically. "She's kind of a sex kitten."

"How nice for you." I winked, "Now that you mention it, your teeth look *really* clean, David."

"Bless her heart." David looked sheepish. He regained his management demeanor with a clearing of the throat. "With all these contestants there's a real sense of excitement. I can taste it—can you?"

I thought a minute. "Let's see. What would today's auditions taste like? Hmmm, Pop-Rocks? The candy that explodes when you eat it. Starts out sweet, then stuns you instead. Then you don't know if it was worth the shock and the weird sounds." I trailed off the fractured metaphor.

David ignored the comment, choosing to hum a happy tune as he arranged and re-arranged the stack of applicants. Contestants turned out, *yeah*—but wasn't talent the goal? People had to stay in their seats and be somewhat entertained. Didn't they?

He stood up with the applications in his left hand and thrust his right fist into the air. "Island Idol will be like nothing else that's ever happened here!"

******

TO: Jack@yahoo.com

FROM: Veronica@yahoo.com

SUBJECT: Questions for bio-years 1985-1995

Dear Jack,

I've attached your questions for the next decade of your history.

Things are going swell here at the gig, well, except for the talent show mayhem. It's amazing how, like termites, these hidden talents come of the woodwork and are now flying around. If only the contest was called The Island Circus Performer Contest. Then I think we'd have something. The funny thing? I love it. I love the energy of the performers. They're optimists, just like me, and maybe that is the soul of the artist—to whatever degree they *can* entertain, they want to put it out there. I'm reminded of first grade. Kids got to "share" every Friday. One kid brought a rock and told a good story, and another kid brought in an ant farm and you were bored—looking longingly through the window at the abandoned playground. I found a guy with real talent, a musician I heard last week, but he didn't show up. The acts are out there, though. I loved watching the ventriloquist *warm up* by talking to his hand puppet privately before they came out. I ended up talking to Casey the Duck, instead of Ken the human. Casey, are you guys ready to go out there? Ken has absolutely no expression, and the duck bobbles his head around with a long neck and raises his eyebrows and says things like, "See that man over there? I've seen more hair on a bar of soap."

Jack, on a more serious note, your biography. I bolted too soon. We both know we haven't committed the proper time to it, and now the deadline is looming over me, and not over you. If this talent competition goes well, maybe I can branch out and do more of them and even get paid next time. That way I could pay back the money Kendal St. Publishers advanced me. You know the old saying, "the expert is the guy from out of town?" Well, on this island of plantations, alligators, and white sandy beaches—*I* am the expert.

As for our unfinished book, I don't know if I can even do it. Maybe we can find a real writer to finish it. In the meantime, here are the questions I have for you, and I'll continue to plug away and hope I represent you well. It's so hard to be objective now, and not sound like a crazed fan. I probably can't even write. It's awful to let you down. I only wanted to bring joy into both of our lives and I know I got at least half of it right.

G'nite,

V

******

TO: Veronica@yahoo.com

FROM: Jack@yahoo.com

SUBJECT: Joy and circus tents

Vee,

You speak of joy? You brought more joy than these walls could hold. Still in the same suite, I look around and can't believe I let you slip away. Sydney's cloud has not lifted. I only blame myself.

As for your producing shows. You can do anything you set your heart and mind to. My strong feeling is—you were not born to be the Cecil B De Mille of the bayou. You're a writer and should trust your instincts to create something—new, not round up some wannabes that belong on the carnival circuit. Round up a collection of your *own* stories with your delightfully quirky view of everyday life. That's what you're meant to do. To shine the flashlight into corners of everyday rooms and show us what we overlooked.

Love, teetering on pining (*dammit*), J

Patrice greeted me with a glass of wine when I entered the salon. She looked adorable in her bright coral strapless sundress. Like in Hawaii, the islanders dress with more color than in Southern California. In Seal Beach I wore black and white year-round.

"Guess what?" She grinned, then pulled me aside to the cubbies where the salon stores the ladies purses; kind of like preschool, she shoved my bag into a green box on the wall. "You-know-who got his nails done here yesterday..."

"Tell all!"

She paused dramatically and whispered, "I asked him if he would be playing at Happy Hour tonight, and he said he would be. I said we'd see him there."

"Good work. All right!" Once I was settled in the nail chair, she excused herself. I checked my watch, vowing to myself that soon I'd get up my nerve and try to snag the local hotty for the contest. I needed something good to happen; my faith in the project was chipping away as surely as last week's nail polish. With new French on my hands and Berry Delicious on my toes, we set off to The Jazz Corner next door.

Like the one other time we were there, it was a pretty sizeable crowd, even at six-thirty. JT was on stage with the house band, playing, "Suzy Q." It was a sexy slow blues tune Credence Clearwater covered back in the day, and it gave the musicians on stage time to stretch out with solos. Some heavy-set dude was playing harmonica as we squished ourselves into a table alongside the wall. Next, JT took his turn. Cradling his Stratocaster electric guitar, he pressed the strings into a whining submission that soulfully pierced through the din of conversation. Straight out of that electrifying solo, he stepped up to the mic and sang, *I like the way you walk, I like the way you talk....* He stood with his legs together, kind of bent at the knees, as he closed his eyes and leaned into the mic—close enough to kiss it. His style was a sensual growl of blue-eyed soul. By the end of the song the audience was on their feet cheering.

Patrice waved the server over. Perhaps it was the down-home blues but we both felt like beers instead of fancy drinks. We bought three Coronas and sent one to the stage for JT. On the napkin I scribbled a few words to say we were seated by the dart board, buried by the people and loving his music. The candle on the table served as a nice anchor for the contest flyer.

"Do you think this is subtle enough, Patrice?" I pressed the flyer flat. "Can you see the print in this light?"

"Work it, sister," she said. "I don't see Hippy Bob around, do you?"

"No, but it's hard to say."

Patrice and I caught up on the news of our week. Before long, JT came walking up. He tilted his drink to me and mouthed a 'thank you.' When he got closer he kissed Patrice's cheek and gave me a one-armed embrace. He stood with his back to the wall since there wasn't a chair available. We had his attention and Patrice looked enchanted.

"Where's Hippy Bob tonight?" I asked.

"Oh, Bubba's back home. We don't usually go out to-gether, tell you the truth. Either he goes or I go. You know, when you live with your cousin 24/7...I see enough of his ugly face."

"I wouldn't exactly describe it *that* way," I shook my head. "But, I know what you mean about having a roommate around all the time."

Patrice was all atwitter, "Is it just you two?"

"And Becky." He looked from side to side and lowered his voice. "Becky is mine but he loves her too, so I imagine he's glad when I leave them alone for a while." He gleefully called out, "You should see your faces!"

"Whatever." Patrice arched her back and stretched.

JT lightly boxed Patrice's arm. "Becky is my German Shepherd. She's real special."

"Oh, I see," she said. I grinned to see the little flirtation dance playing out before me.

Patrice slapped his shoulder and shook her head. "I used to have a Shepherd. I love 'em. They need a lot of exercise. Do you take her for walks? They say a dog needs—"

"Becky?" Again, JT laughed, expressing his joyful side, which was a welcome change from his self-absorbed stage persona. "Becky has about everything a dog could want. Don't worry about her getting walks. She's straight-up spoiled. But, to answer your question, it's just the three of us. We live out in Sea Pines." He swigged his beer. "You two girls ought to come out sometime."

"We'd love to!" We sang out in stereo. Then, feeling sheepish after our rousing chorus, I changed the subject. I moved our drinks off the damp flyer and bent it toward him.

"So, JT, I think I mentioned there's a talent contest at the Crowne Plaza in three weeks? Anyway, I'm supposed to organize it, and, and—I need to know someone terrific is coming in. Can I sign you up?" With no reaction from him, I had to blither on. "I'll pay your entrance fee if you'd agree to play one song on Sunday, June fifteenth. Then, the finals will be on Saturday the third of July."

He chuckled to himself, then reached out and wrapped his arm around my shoulder for a little hug. "Veronica, I don't mind paying the entrance fee. My cousin was supposed to come by and see you play at the hotel—right? So, I owe you an apology for him. Us musicians gotta stick together, girl."

"It's no biggie." I squirmed.

JT gifted me with another dazzling smile.

"There is a $5,000 first prize, JT," Patrice piped in. "You aren't just helping out the new kid in town. I'd bet you'll be coming home with that five grand, my friend."

His lips formed an easy smile. "I don't play music for money; you should know that by now."

I wanted to ask what he *did* do for money, and why he *didn't* play music for money and how he got those hypnotic blue eyes, and thick blond hair and Adonis physique. "When do we get to meet Becky?" I blurted out instead.

"When do you want to meet Becky?"

"How about tomorrow?" Patrice sounded off the charts-eager.

"Sounds good to me," he said. "Happy hour tomorrow about five at our place."

"I start at seven," I said, "but I could come by for an hour."

"Wait a minute—" JT scratched his chin, then turned to Patrice. "How about the day after tomorrow?"

"Wednesday is good," we chorused, a little too loud.

We all giggled. Then he smiled. "Patrice, listen." He leaned in close to her ear. With his cheek against hers, I heard him whisper, "you should have my address. I know I get little post cards about facials and all that girly stuff in the mail." She nodded.

"So, ladies, see ya then. I'm gonna visit the bat room."

He disappeared into the crowd and we stuck around listening to music. Fortunately, the harmonica player also dropped by our table. JT had told him to come over and talk to me about a flyer. So, having secured at least one contestant, and possibly two, I was feeling okay. When the waitress came by later with the bill, Patrice tried to take it from my hand.

"Let me get this," I told her. "I'm supposed to be talent scouting here, so I'll turn it in as an expense." I knew I'd never have the guts to do that, but it felt good anyway.

Crossing the parking lot on the walk back to our cars, Patrice and I congratulated ourselves on landing an invitation to Tid-bit mansion. We talked about what to wear, what to bring and mostly wondered how many minutes would make up *that* happy hour.

In our inebriated haze we decided to put our "no-guys pledge" on hold for the summer and replace it with a new pledge: no more than two drinks at a sitting. Getting plastered could lead to accidental nudity and unlady-like puking.

I felt a queasy rush as the vulnerability door creaked open. That door was almost locked after the sting of Jack's snub in Sydney.

CHAPTER 9

"Are you okay to drive, Veronica?" Patrice watched me pull everything out of my purse as I looked for my keys. The hood of my car disappeared under make-up, hair brush, gum, pens, spiral pad, teeny flashlight and half a bag of sunflower seeds. I was down to the paper clips and gray Tic Tacs at the bottom.

"Have you checked your pockets?" she asked.

"Oh yeah, I remember now, I took the one key off and—" I pulled the single key out of the narrow pocket inside the hip of my jeans. "Here it is! I was going to leave my big purse in the car and just come in with money, lipstick and the car key. We got to talking and I never—"

Patrice cocked her head toward the spa. "Are you sure you couldn't use some coffee? It will only take a moment and we can soak our feet."

"Sounds good, thanks."

A few minutes later, we flopped into the huge reclining chairs with hands curled around mugs of coffee. Although the silence was a nice retreat from the cacophony of voices and music next door, I plunged into a moody valley. "Have you ever heard of a psychic named Gertrude Anderson?"

"I have. You forget this is a small island and women stay here for hours. We're like bartenders to men—we hear it all. I heard she's right-on, and not negative. Hmm, what else? Oh, she takes donations from her regular clients, but for the first time it's $125 for a reading. Are you thinking of going?"

"I already went."

"Get out—really?"

"She told me I may lose something really important through carelessness. I mentioned the first few things that came to mind, but she was adamant that it was something else. Now, I'm worried about what I have to lose—more than just car keys."

Patrice leaned in. "So now everything seems precious?"

I lifted my feet out of the bin of water, shook the bubbles off, and then laid them on the white terrycloth towel. "Patrice, I have a nineteen-year-old son who lives with his dad in Hawaii. Since we only see each other a couple times a year, I worry I may be losing him."

"Wow. How long has he lived with his dad?"

"A year. When he finished high school, my husband and I divorced. My son sided with him and they both moved away. At the time it actually was the best solution. There was an affair and forgiveness wasn't in the air."

"Oh, you poor thing. You can't imagine how much cheating we hear about in here. What a jerk to risk your long marriage like that." She reached over to pat my arm.

I took a big swallow of air. "Thanks for the compassion. But I was the cheater. It was probably stupid of me to fall in love while I was married. But Raymond and I got married so young...anyway, that's another story for another pitcher of margaritas."

She batted the air, then handed me a box of tissues. "Believe me, I'm not judging you."

"Right away my ex got a gig playing guitar in Kona. That's on the big island of Hawaii. He was sick of having a house in the burbs. He's an extraordinary classical and pop guitarist, so he can work anywhere there's a five star hotel. He picked the Royal Kona Hotel so he could surf and Devin liked the sound of that too. Since they both hated me and loved Hawaii—the moment my son graduated, they packed up and moved. The house wasn't even sold."

"What happened to the guy you were, uh—seeing?"

"Seriously, Patrice, he died. No doubt all the stress hit him hard. Also, he was older and had a heart condition. We never had a chance to be happy. It was one of those situations of the worst possible thing happening. You give up your family for the real thing and the real thing ticks-out. He died within a few weeks of...of...oh, it's all coming out." I sobbed into my hands. "Once this story comes out, it's hard to find a beginning and an end, which is why I never talk about having a son. See what happened? It opens up a silo of tears."

Patrice shook out a towel and placed it on the ground that bridged us, then carefully stepped out of her reclining chair. She dried her wet feet on the terrycloth and walked over to me. My head was down and she rubbed my shoulder. "What's his name?"

"Devin. He's a doll. He's funny and crazy and, well—I'll bring his picture next time."

"Better yet, why don't you invite Devin here for a week? It's summer. Is he in school?"

"He's got some weeks off before college summer school, I think." I blew my nose. "He acts like he doesn't even *care* if he sees me."

"There's no harm in asking him, honey, that way you would be 'careful not to lose something very important.'"

"Well, maybe with my being here, on this beautiful island, he would be curious enough to visit me. Do you think?"

"Even if it's not this relationship, at least you have heeded Gertrude's warning. Meanwhile, put your jewelry in the hotel safe."

It felt good to laugh. "My jewelry isn't even worthy of a hotel safe."

"I thought you might have treated yourself to some bling after the house sold. After all, *they* moved to Hawaii. Couldn't you at least get a trip to Tiffany's? Right?"

"I wish. Our house was mortgaged twice. We paid off bills after a quick sell at the bottom of the market. Then? I had an unproductive year of grieving. That was my vacation; seeing how crappy the world was, watching the bedroom ceiling. I couldn't get out of bed. Gawd, what am I doing?" I turned to face her. "I have a great new job, a new friend...a new opportunity to produce a talent contest and meet nice people..."

"Happy hour at the Tid-bit mansion Wednesday," she added with a smile. "Don't forget that."

"And a son." I picked each word cautiously. "Who will be... invited to...Hilton Head."

"Sure, do it!" Patrice slapped her knee. "We've been talking about painting the outside of the building. Would he be willing to help out with that?"

"Probably. Look how sweet you are." I brushed away a tear with the back of my hand, then sat up straighter. "Thanks for listening and helping me through this."

"Watch out, don't get me crying." She laughed and we embraced awkwardly, still in our recliner chairs.

CHAPTER 10

TO:Devin@yahoo.com

FROM:Veronica@yahoo.com

RE: Free vacation while you're on break

Hi Dev,

    I guess you got my last email about my new gig on the East Coast? I was hoping you might want to island hop to a different island. Kona is great and all, but Hilton Head is beautiful and lush and the ocean is so warm I end up swimming all the time. The ocean was too cold for me back home, but here I walk straight in without even a shiver. I don't have to enter the water in slow mo. Why not come here for a week, Dev? You'd like it, I think. The waves are small for surfing—like two feet, but there are crocodiles, bikes to ride on hard white sand along the shoreline, and a mom who misses you!!! The French fries are killer, too. What's it been, about seven months? How about if you come out here before summer school starts? I'll even get you your own hotel room. My friend needs someone to help paint, so you could pick up a few bucks too. Talk to your dad and if it's a go, book a roundtrip flight with the best price, put it on his credit card, and I'll reimburse him.

Love muchly,

Mom

P.S. Please pack the best clothes you have. XOXO

*****

TO: Veronica@yahoo.com

FROM:Devin@yahoo.com

RE: Free vacation while you're on break

K

*****

"Veronica?"

"Oh?" I was jolted from my concentration on piano keys to see a buxom brunette standing too close.

"Sorry if I startled you," she said, sliding into the stool rimming the piano. "You play so awesome. I love that song. Wasn't it in the original Superman movie?"

"Yes, 'If You Could Read My Mind,' by John Williams." Next I played a circle of five chords as we spoke. It was something pianists can do on auto-pilot when the brain engages in conversation. "I was looking down at the keys getting lost in the melody. I guess you did surprise me."

This woman didn't look like a regular tourist or local. Her blue eyes flicked, weighted down by heavy false eyelashes. As she dug inside her purse she spoke into it. "Where *is* my list? I just had it."

"You said my name. Do I know you?"

She looked up. "Oh, excuse me, I'm Lucinda. I'm the food and beverage manager's dental hygienist."

"David," I murmured, "mentioned something."

"He said he'd signed me up for the Island—ah*dol*—contest?" Her soft Southern lilt made the word idol sound legitimate. "Don't let me be a bother, honey. Just play, I l-o-v-e the music."

She pulled some papers from somewhere and pressed them onto the bar, ironing it with the palm of her hand. Then she ordered a glass of house wine from the waitress. As I played through the first set, I had a chance to watch the Betty Boopesque Lucinda.

Her turquoise blouse stretched tightly across her ample chest, threatening to pop the buttons off the fabric. She wore a wide belt that emphasized her tiny waistline and that was all I could see. Something told me she wasn't going to sing as well as she scraped teeth. You don't need a weather vane to know which way the floss is flossing. I could imagine her in a tight white uniform, leaning over to tenderly clip on the paper bib. Her smile so close you could smell cherry lip gloss. Oh yeah. Not to mention her other job. What did David say? Condom-route salesman? She probably had a trunk full of condoms in the parking lot.

A few songs later, I announced my break, then swung the mic and boom-stand to the side.

"Can I buy you a glass of why-in?" she asked.

"Why-in? Oh, wine. No thank you, Lucinda. I'll get some coffee and be right back to look at your list."

Lucinda's song list included two torchy ballads from the show *Dream Girls*, and an ambitious duet from *Phantom of the Opera*. She hadn't resolved who would sing the male's part but was open for ideas. I had ideas all right, but she was set on singing anyway.

"I always meant to sing professionally," she said rapturously, placing a dainty hand over her alabaster throat.

"Meant?" I asked cautiously. "Did you study voice?"

"Oh, goodness no!" Coquettishly she tilted her head to one side, looking up through the hedge of black eyelashes, "I'm just what you could call a *natural*."

All rise for Judge Mental. Without even hearing her, I knew she stunk out loud. My ex-husband used to say he could tell how good a guitar player was by the way he took his ax out of its case. He claimed he was never wrong and I believe him.

"As you know, the semi-finals are Sunday. Sorry you missed the first meeting, but David gave me your name, so, no worries. We're having a general meeting for the participants this Friday afternoon. We'll set the line-up for the program, and the acts will give me their introductions and leave their music with Audio-Al, our sound man. Since you're David's pal, don't worry about it if you can't make that meeting—you're in the show. Good luck! Just be sure to get here by six Saturday night."

"Which of these songs do you like best?" She handed me several sheets of paper, and leaned in close as I read down the list.

"These are some ambitious songs. Phantom of the Opera medley? How about 'Crazy' by Patsy Kline. Everyone likes that one and surprisingly, no one is doing it."

"You play and sing *so* amazing, Veronica, that—can I ask you something?" It's always silly that people need a prelude. Usually they are already talking, why not just say it.

I smiled modestly. "Is there a CD of me singing? I get the question a lot. Actually—"

"No," she interrupted. "Can you tutor me before the show? Is that too much to ask?" She flashed me her thousand-watt smile; her glistening lips stretching around neon-white teeth.

"Ummm—no, sorry, Lucinda. It would be a conflict of interest if I help just one of the contestants. I'm sure you'll be great. David said he's heard you hum along to the Muzak in the dentist's office."

"Aw, really?" She lifted her shoulders high to her ears. "That's so *sweeeet!*"

"Don't worry," I patted her arm, "let's just have fun."

CHAPTER 11

The valet parking guys were chatting me up as I waited in front of the Crowne Plaza. It was the lazy afternoon lull after lunch. The guys were so helpful, cute and wholesome. I tried to imagine my own son wearing the khaki uniform. The uniform hat would be backward on Devin's head. His pants would be hanging low on his hips. I shook off the image of his boxer shorts rimming the top of his butt-crack as he bent over to assist a snooty lady with her suitcase.

Checking my watch for the third time, adjusting my sunglasses, applying another coat of lip-gloss, I waited for Patrice's stealth Prius to roll up.

"Howdy," she called through the open window. She was striking in her straw cowboy hat. Stylishly swept up on the sides, it modeled the shape of a boat. One of the valet guys jumped to open my door. "Have a good afternoon, ma'am. See you later."

As we cruised out of the circular driveway, I said, "When did I become a ma'am?"

"As soon as you crossed the Mason-Dixon line," she laughed. "Very cute—I like that dress. Is that what you're wearing to work tonight?"

"You bet. It's casual sundresses like this during the week. On weekends I step it up a bit. Honestly, most all my clothes are black and it doesn't jive with you island people. Maybe I need to go to shopping."

"There're only a couple places in Wexford Village near my spa, but we could go into Savannah." She pulled out on highway 278 and turned south on Sea Pines Drive.

"Too cute, Patrice." I gestured toward her blue tank top and white shorts. She had layered a blue-and-white checked short-sleeve blouse on top. "I love the lace trim around the collar and pocket."

"It's pretty casual around here. Thanks. About today, we're only staying what? Hour and a half, right?"

I sighed. "Are you sure you don't want me to follow you over? Since the invitation was for five, we have to leave at six-thirty, for me to be playing at seven."

"You're playing it close, girl. Allowing only half an hour to get to work? It's about twenty-five minutes from here."

"That's how I roll," I said in a breathy, mock-mysterious voice. "Playing it close."

"We'll leave together," Patrice announced officiously. "I didn't want to come alone. JT is too cute for his own good. Or, for my own good."

Twenty-five minutes later we pulled up to the massive iron gate that stretched across the mansion's driveway.

"Look." Patrice pointed at a wooden sign about waist-high. Hanging by chains was an engraved board reading, Welcome to Pinewood.

"Pinewood, huh?" I said. "Do you think it would be wrong to repaint it to say, Welcome to Tid-bit mansion? Where did you get that expression anyway?"

Patrice giggled. "My girlfriend and I used to imitate this cat food commercial on TV. So, I don't know how it started but we would do a cute-guy alert with a meow, then say stupid stuff from the ad, like 'good cats deserves tid-bits.' It just evolved from there. Okay, we were in high school."

"Some things just stick, don't they?" I shook my head and laughed. "Like going to see a new guy for the first time at his apartment, and you get there and hang out with his six roommates all crammed around a TV watching sports. You sit and pretend to watch and curse the fact you're wearing a skirt. Aghhh! You have to excuse me, I'm just blithering 'cause I'm so nervous. This feels like high-school. I haven't been on a date *since* then. I got married the summer after high school. Well, I dated briefly when I was married..."

She glanced at me sideways. "Let's leave that part out of your biography, okay?"

"But I was married all my adult life—then, I told you what happened."

Outside the gate was a stone pillar with an intercom. She pushed a button on the panel and it responded with an electronic hum. I jumped at the sound and felt the tug of the seat belt. A distorted voice said, "Come on in," as the gates slowly creaked open.

Once inside, we found ourselves on a beautiful shady lane. Soft gold rays of summer filtered through the live oak trees. Green leaves rustled with the warm afternoon breeze. Beyond the Eucalyptus trees, a rolling manicured lawn stretched out edged by tall pampas grass, its alabaster feather plumes dancing in the breeze. Flowering tobacco with little pink stars bordered the grass, adding a striking contrast to the pale green hydrangeas. The ocean's briny scent grew stronger as we approached the huge house in the distance.

"Are these types of mansions actually called plantations?" I wondered aloud.

"No, plantations are neighborhoods."

"Is this anything like where you live?"

"Oh, goodness no. I live in a villa, in Palmetto Dunes."

"Villa? Wow."

"Think condo or townhouse. Not Europe," she clarified. "Palmetto Dunes is a nice area, don't get me wrong. There's a long tree-lined lane with a lagoon on the right. You'll have to come over to my place. Sea Pines was the first plantation, then Shipyard. In the '80s the developer went bankrupt, I heard." She motioned out the window and I followed her gesture.

"Oh, how darling—a little bridge over the creek." I lowered my window for a better look.

"It's a crick. It might even be jumpin' with gators." She laughed when I quickly rolled the window up.

In the half-mile driveway, on the right, was a boat house with open doors. From what I could see it looked like it housed kayaks, jets skis, and some trailers and hitches. On the other side of the lane, there was a clearing for parking and as Patrice guided the car into the wide area, I spotted JT sprinting toward us with a German Shepherd trotting at his side. He threw a tennis ball to the side and the dog dashed off after it as we stepped out of the car.

"Did you have any trouble finding the place?" He graced the top of Patrice's head with a peck and gave me the one-arm side hug.

"Drove right to it," she said.

"What a great day, huh?" I looked around. "What a lovely yard—uh, grounds you have here."

"Thanks for comin' out." The dog dropped the ball at JT's feet and he patted its head. "This here is Becky. She pretty much runs the place. Sit, Becky. Good girl." The dog sat at attention, her pointy snout sniffing the air, and then she politely lifted her paw. Patrice and I did a round of "ahs" as we shook hands.

"She looks like my old Shepherd," Patrice swooned as Becky sat in the soft dirt panting slightly. "Mine was a little bigger, but also had black and tan markings. How old is she?"

"She's about eight years old, but she'll be around for a long time." JT ruffled the top of her head, then straightened the red kerchief that was tied loosely at her neck.

"Hey," Hippy Bob called, drawing our attention to the long porch that rimmed the house. "Good afternoon, ladies, don't you look pretty?" As he sauntered toward us, his long hair reflected golden highlights from the sun. He wore long dark shorts and a red tee shirt and I felt completely over-dressed. This time I was the one that got the kiss on the cheek and Patrice the hug.

"Thanks for droppin' by." He made no apologies for looking me over. "This will definitely be a happy hour. What's all-ya'll drinkin'?"

Patrice nudged me. "All-ya'll is plural for ya-all, Veronica."

Bob waved us toward the porch. "I heard girls like Cosmos, so I looked up how to make 'em on the Internet." He made an adorable little dance step, like riding an invisible bike real fast. "Step this way to the Carolina Room. That's a fancy way a sayin' porch."

As we followed, I wished I'd dressed more Southern Bellish.

"We don't get much company," JT said. "So Cuz put away the local moonshine and six-pack of Olympia Beer we usually drink." He punched his cousin's arm and they exchanged a few jabs.

"You talking about me trying to impress?" Bob exclaimed. "How 'bout you at the club. You were on these girls like a hobo on a ham sandwich."

We migrated toward the house and stepped up three stairs to the wide porch. There was a cozy swing with green and white striped cushions. I paused to run my hand along the fringe hanging from its canopy. "That's a dream catcher, right there." Bob stroked the canvas with affection. "Best naps in South Carolina." He held open the screen door as we passed through.

We weaved through the various pieces of white wicker furniture making our way to a glass-top table. On a tray sat two pitchers, silver ice bucket and several tall glasses. "First, would you like some lemonade?" JT offered. "We've got a drink for thirst and a drink for libation."

Once we were seated, Hippy Bob disappeared around the corner and returned with another tray and set it on the table. "This is my famous Barb-B-Q shrimp. Here's more sauce in the little bowl if you want to add some, and these here are some hush puppies." He set the tray on the table.

We all exclaimed with delight at the aroma. A basket of corn muffins rounded out the buffet. "When we rang you in at the gate, I fired up the grill." Hippy Bob winked. "Perfect timing, huh?"

"Corn bread? Hush puppies?" I grinned. "Perfect. I need to carb-load, in case I run a marathon—next summer." They tittered politely and I realized it was Southern California humor. Back home for lunch, we girls split a salad and discussed exercise.

This was literally a taste of the South. I adored hearing the three of them speak in their soft Carolina accents as they discussed the flavor enhancing qualities of hickory wood on the barbecue. Everyone dug in and the only sounds were short groans of pleasure and laughter following.

"Thanks guys," Patrice said, wiping her hands on a cloth napkin. "Before I forget…" She reached for her purse and pulled out a package. Pink cellophane with a ribbon held together eight or so cookies in a tower. "These are for ya'll. I like molasses and sesame seed cookies for breakfast with coffee."

"Did you make them?" I asked, wishing she had warned me. I felt so empty handed. Should I pass around my half box of Tic Tacs?

"Baking is something I do to relax." She smiled. "I made 'em this morning. Here's some for you, honey." She pulled a smaller stack from her bag and handed it to me.

It was the guys' turn to fuss about getting homemade baked goods. Hippy Bob must have felt my pain, because he leaned over to say, "Patrice makes cookies, I make shrimp, but you and JT make music. That's the stuff that gets my attention. We've heard JT, now it's time we made it over to your gig. What time do you start tonight, darlin'?"

I loved how darlin' sounded. So natural coming from him. "I start at seven." As my I felt my face get hot, I reached for my glass. "This Cosmo is great."

Bob got that lazy-eyed smile I'd seen the first night we met. "How about we come down to the Crowne Plaza later, huh?" His voice had that sweet soft drawl that seemed to slow down time. "So, sweet stuff, how'd you get started singing?" Just then his cell phone rang out a brittle tune. He plucked it off his belt, read the incoming number, and for a moment looked like he was going to throw it. He stood up while it blasted yet another round of tinny music.

"Shut that dang thing off," JT said without looking over. He was focused on whatever Patrice was saying. Standing behind her chair, leaning close to her face, he pointed off in the distance. They appeared to have spun off into their own world.

Bob glared at the phone. It looked tiny in his large hand. When the beeps indicated a message had been recorded, he impatiently flicked it up to his ear. "Excuse me.." He seemed to wince as he listened. He clicked the phone shut and tossed it on the table where it skidded across the glass. "JT, Numb Nuts is coming in the morning, 'round ten."

JT whipped his head around. With a grimace he said, "Did you forget to fax that—that deal over we signed?"

Bob's voice rose with, "I sent it just like I *said* I would." He shook his head and shuddered as if shaking off a chill. "We'll talk about it later."

I looked at my watch. It was six-thirty already and the spell of the bucolic wonderland was broken. Our hunky hosts had drawn us in with their charm as easily as bees circling the honeycomb. Yet, after the call, it seemed both cousins lost a measure of composure.

JT stepped away from us then skipped off the porch. He walked a few feet, bent down and the next minute a horseshoe was flying through the air. It clanked with authority as it rounded the metal spike in the lawn. Patrice and I exchanged looks as I reached for my purse. I was agitated for a different reason, and it wasn't Numb Nuts. I was miffed that I hadn't got a promise from the island's hottest musician to do the talent show. Obviously I couldn't bring it up now.

Bob took my hand, turned. it over slowly and kissed my palm. "We'll be over a little later, Veronica."

"Sorry, ladies," JT said as he turned around to face us. "I owe you a tour, don't I?"

Patrice spoke up. "Veronica, do you mind taking my car? I'll just come over with the guys in a little bit. Okay, honey? I'll help Bob clear these few dishes and we'll see you later."

What could I say? As I drove away I couldn't help but notice that although their estate was pure Southern grace and old world class, the ornately furnished villa looked like it had been decorated by the original Daughters of the American Revolution, definitely not two hot guys in their thirties.

CHAPTER 12

At eight-thirty Bob walked into the lounge and sat at a bistro table just as I was getting up from the piano bench for my break. I saw that the other two weren't with him, and acknowledged him from across the room. Behind me was a dial on the wall, which I turned to adjust the canned music for break time. I then joined him at his table.

He pulled the chair out beside him. "I can't tell if my timing is good, that we get to have your break together, or terrible because I missed a terrific bunch of songs." His brown eyes were so friendly, and it felt wonderful to see a familiar face. He had changed into jeans and a fitted, crisp white shirt that showed off his slim physique. Around his neck was a small gold chain with a charm of some kind.

"There are more songs ahead, don't worry," I assured, sitting down. "Where's Patrice? Don't tell me she got lost on the tour...it *is* a sprawling—" Trying to avoid the word mansion, I muttered, "place."

A waitress appeared at Bob's elbow. He turned to her. "We'll have a Cosmo and a Jack and coffee, please, ma'am."

I loved how he took control and ordered for me, as if we were a couple, and I liked being his other half. "Oh, I'll just have the Jack-less coffee, Karen. No Cosmo, thank you." When

74

she was out of earshot I explained, "No drinking on the job. Orders from island headquarters."

"Jack-less is good too." He cocked his head. Bob was so focused on me it was like an artist holding a palette, intently taking it all in.

"Patrice and JT, I guess you could say, are still on the tour. They sent their apologies. He'll drop her off here to pick up her car later. She's got a spare key; they'll find it in the lot. Enough about them."

"Hmmm." I figured she could handle herself, given the two-drink-maximum pledge we 'd made to each other earlier in the week. Still, I was disappointed.

I checked my watch. "What would you like to hear?"

From then on it was a fabulous evening. We lounge singers have a saying: you can always dazzle if there's at least one cute guy in the room. Sometimes it's the bartender. Other nights I'd pretend the man seated alone in the far back was a studio head on his night off, maybe searching for a singer to do the title song for the next blockbuster movie. We have to play these games, as after reciting the same words nightly, no matter how lovely the lyrics, they lose their meaning. If tonight was an iPod playlist, it would be entitled, "Flirty Groove."

At twelve-thirty, I said good-night through the mic and returned to Bob's table. He applauded along with the fifteen or so tables of guests. He stood briefly as I sat down.

"Thank you, thank you. So, Bob, what's that charm on your neck?"

He looked down at the same moment his hand reached up to touch it. "Oh, this? It's a Sagittarius. You know, the archer with his feet on the ground—part goat, but he's a man looking up to the sky shooting an arrow into—into, what? Dark space, I suppose." He chortled at his remark. "It was a gift a long time ago. I suppose that's why they call me Hippy Bob, I was into astrology. Sagittarius aims high but can be accused of not moving off the side of the mountain."

"I would say learning to be a vet is pretty ambitious, Bob."

He looked abashed, then twitched his head slightly as if to shake free the shyness. "And, you are? Let me guess, Veronica. Maybe, I'd say, a Leo or Pisces?"

"I'm a Pisces. Wow, you're good—what gave it away?"

"When you two girls got out of the car this afternoon and you were wearing a dress...." He took a sip from his glass. "Pisces is a feminine energy. Have you ever been accused of being a girly-girl?"

At the moment, I had barrettes in my hair, wore hoop earrings, and a dainty sweater with vines embroidered on the front.

Bob continued. "I like to see a feminine side. It's something women can't buy, borrow or steal. You just have it or don't. You've got what I like. Hey, the music's great too. Have I forgotten to mention that?" His long hair dusted the top of his shirt and he smelled like soap from across the table. He looked down and then targeted me through those thick, dark eyelashes. I felt a whirl in my gut, like an elevator dip. I may've played some romantic songs earlier, but Hippy Bob's romantic vibe was in his eyes. Attempting to bring the needle down on the lust meter, I asked, "What sign is JT?"

"JT? JT is a typical Leo—places to go, leadership, ambitious."

"Really? I didn't get that from him. He didn't even want to enter the talent search, and that's offering a $5,000 prize. I'm guessing he could win too."

Hippy Bob stretched his long legs out and leaned back in his chair. "Let's see." He ran his hand through his hair and let out a sigh, then crossed his arms across his chest. "Just between you and me—the truth? JT has a buddy over in Malaga, Spain. This friend is fixing to open a nightclub that will cater to Americans. I guess there're tourists and students they're hoping to attract. Anyway, they see it as," he drew quotations in the air, "a Planet Hollywood type of hip crowd."

Aware that I may not see JT before the next weekend, I had to take a chance. "If you would just do me a big favor, Bob..." I scribbled a note on one of the flyers lying on our table. "Please give this to JT for me. Basically, it says I'm putting him in the show. He can go on last so he doesn't have to wait around. Just check in with me next Saturday night at nine." Letting out a long sigh, I was glad I'd finally said it.

"I'll make sure he comes out for it, darlin'." He folded the flyer and stuck it in his pocket, never taking his eyes off me. "Just ignore that he's not all jumpin' up and down to be in the contest. His head is in another place. JT's putting his ducks in a row to move to Europe. As soon as the place is ready, it's hasta la vista, Hilton Head."

"Is it almost built? Wouldn't he need the money to help him get started over there?"

In the silence that followed, I felt tacky speculating on his cousin's finances. Clearly these guys were living large.

"Our Aunt Lila left us Pinewood. Tell me, did you always want to be a singer?"

Clearly he wanted to change the subject. Okay, I could do that. "I tried a few things before I took music seriously."

"Let's see, you're gorgeous, but maybe too petite for a model, so?"

"As *if.* Thanks, Bob." I swatted the air. "Actually, my height may have been a factor in one of my stupid plans."

He leaned forward, and with a look that said, *I've got all the time in the world,* he took my hand. "Tell me everything about you."

I started to laugh at that line, but took the bait. "One day, a friend said he knew how to make $100 dollars a day—EASY. It took a small investment, it was legal, and I'd be providing a service. I was in my early twenties."

"Not so long ago, right?" Bob smirked.

"Electricity had been invented, let's just say. Anyway, I was an out-of-work singer, living on Top Raman, and ready to throw my whole self into this entrepreneurial venture *just* until I became the next Gwen Stephani. My friend said, to make a bunch of money quickly, I needed to become a PEEP HOLE installer! All it takes is a drill, extension cord, a peephole costs about 50 cents, you charge ten bucks to install it—you do ten a day...boom!

"I brought my best friend, Penny, into this money making BONANZA as my partner. She borrowed a drill and extension cord, I bought one hundred peepholes."

"That was optimism," Bob said.

"Knowing the business we'd be doing I didn't want to *constantly* be going back to the hardware store to get more." It was fun to make Bob laugh.

He took a swig from his glass and said, "All you do is drill a small hole on each side, one person holds half inside the hole and the other person is on the other side and you screw it in, right?"

"Easy for you to say, but the drill vibrates even more than a hair dryer—which freaked us out. We had to practice not screaming when it was plugged in. We had to try it, so, since we didn't want to ruin her apartment door, we installed on in her bedroom door. It took us three peepholes to get it on the *right* side of the door. Needless to say, she lost her security deposit on the apartment."

Bob chuckled, and added, "Not to mention looking like a pervert to anyone who came over."

"Come to think of it, she didn't have many dates after that," I murmured. "So, I bought a cute handyman outfit of white overall-shorts, cute top, put 100 peepholes in a purse...."

"Very professional," Bob nodded.

"Thanks, but we got no buyers. It was so discouraging."

Bob finished his glass and set it on the table. "I'd a been your partner. The whole thing makes sense to me. I can see you in those little overall shorts."

The lounge was emptying out. The lights were turning on bright for the cleaning crew. "I'm almost done with the story, let's go outside, okay?" I grabbed my gig bag and purse and we left the crisp air conditioned lounge, walking into warm, moist evening air. With Bob's arm draped over my shoulder, we strolled along the dimly lit path, and I picked up the story.

"So, after seven hours of knocking on doors, we decided to hit an apartment house and cover a bunch of houses at once."

"Good business plan," he said.

"We knocked on a door that was half open and there were about five people standing in the middle of the room speaking a foreign language. We offered them the peephole opportunity and they said, yes, to go ahead. I was spastic with joy, which is probably why I drilled too long and too big. Penny drilled her side of the door. Now for the big moment. I undid the package of the peephole, handed her half, I poked my half through my hole—while I stood outside. We tried to connect it, but the holes were too big and the peephole pieces sank down and clunked at the bottom of the cheap apartment door."

"Uh oh."

"It was a horrifying moment. The foreigners were very engaged in conversation and we played it off like we were still working. I pulled another one out of my purse, and the same thing happened. Then, again, and again. Now we had to leave but we were scared of the foreigners."

"Were they Russian spies?" He gasped with mock concern.

"It wasn't that, *anyone* would have beat us up. Penny and I looked at each other, then at the hole in their apartment door. It was definitely a gaping hole."

"So anyone passing by their door could see inside the entire room?"

"Yes, and forever, see inside the entire room. We tried again. This time we balanced it so carefully on the edge of the hole that it stuck. Well, I'm sure until someone *closed* the door. We gathered our stuff up and told the foreigners it was ten dollars and they wrote a check. O—kay, whatever. We took the check and crept down the hall, down the stairs and bolted to the car, speeding off like Bonnie and Clyde. Next morning, when the bank opened, I took the $10 check in to be cashed. The teller informed me that the check was written on a closed account."

Bob laughed. "I told you not to trust them! They were Russian spies!"

"They beat us for ten bucks—and we gave them a hole to remember. By the way, if you need a peephole...I have ninety-three left."

"Great story," he said, giving me a squeeze. "You better stick to singing. Now see that hammock right over there? Let's see if we both fit."

We did just that and our evening ended in a long, moonlight kiss in the parking lot. A sexy déjà vu of high school and frat parties. After that time in my life, I got married and took the action indoors. I had a strict policy to never kiss customers, and because I was married for eighteen of the last twenty years, it was easy to keep. But tonight I felt more like sixteen than thirty-eight. If this *were* college, we'd be excelling in chemistry class as he pressed me against the Cadillac Escalade.

CHAPTER 13

TO: Jack@yahoo.com

FROM: Veronica@yahoo.com

RE: Interview notes

Hi Jack,

Thanks for getting back to me with the names of those people in the pics. The pics with anecdotes associated with them, I'll leave in. I'll crop out the others. We'll definitely use the pic of you and Cher. How about the story about the bar fight at the Troubadour? I'm still trying to refine the timeline from 99-2009 we've got. There's enough material for three hundred pages—I just hope it's cohesive and a fun read. We can't really wait till everyone dies, you know. And the conflict is, how much spice gets in? Does the publishing company secure the photo releases or do I? Geeze.

You asked about the talent contest. It's going pretty well. I picked the best variety—and we'll call it the semi-finals. It's this Saturday. The finals will be a couple weeks later on July third.

The gig is going well. I've made three friends. Southern men open doors, call you ma'am and actually tip their hats…even baseball caps. Everyone speaks slowly, makes eye-contact, and they seem to have time for one another. It's been said Southerners readily offer food, where Yankees just offer drinks.

Oh, and they love to eat down here. There was a story on the news that Mississippi is the fattest state in the nation. I guess I should watch out for the cabbage cooked to oblivion with onions and bacon, and biscuits and gravy at breakfast and even boiled peanuts, if you can believe that!

I'll send you the pages as I go. I hope you enjoyed the Sydney Opera House production of Phantom, and give my regards to Muffy Potter. I assume she is still acting as your guide?

Hugs,

V

******

TO:Devin@yahoo.com

FROM: Veronica@yahoo.com

RE: Travel arrangements

Dev,

I'm so happy you're coming out in a couple weeks! Don't be worried by the little plane that takes you from Charleston, SC to here. Although, after riding big waves and skateboarding, this will be just more dips and glides. I'll have someone pick you up at baggage claim, since most likely you'll come in when I'm working. Let me know flight dates and times. I'll send one of the guys from valet to meet you. He should have a sign saying Devin Bennett. Hold on to the tickets, since I need to reimburse Dad. I can't wait to see you!

Love,

Mom

*****

It was a good Friday night. Patrice and JT had just strolled out after my last set. Bob sent his regards—whatever that meant, but I didn't care. It was fun seeing them from across the room, chatting away. They were so darling together that everywhere they sat it looked like a photo shoot for a brochure. Gratefully, I actually knew all their song requests: Fleetwood Mac medley for her and KD Lang for him.

Most often I resort to song counseling. It goes like this:

"Anybody has a request, just let me know."

"Do you know "All My Exes Live In Texas"?

"Ah—no."

"Okay, anything by Kenny Chessney?"

"Ah—no." I smile. "So it looks like you like songs by guys who play guitar and have been dumped." This comment usually illicits a grunt. I continue, "Maybe you'll like Kelly Clarkson's song, "Because of You." She came from Texas, and likes guitar music."

"She's from Texas?"

All further dialogue is drowned out by my hands pounding the keys.

I was singing the last song, "Never Can Say Goodbye," when David Lindsey burst into the room. He could never just enter a room. Although not large, he moved with such a lack of grace that all his body parts seemed to be in motion at the same time as he weaved between the tables like a drunken marionette. I finished the song quickly, clicked the mic off and closed the lid over the piano keys.

He slumped into the nearest seat. "Everything is in place, whew. The voting ballot card thingies are handed to the people once they buy their ticket. If they buy their ticket in advance they can show it and get a ballot at the door."

I walked around the piano and pulled out the chair beside him. He continued with, "I've hired a magician to entertain for fifteen minutes while we tally the popular vote."

With that, he consulted his clipboard. "Check. The three judges are: Sheriff Jimbo Clark, Prissy Wilson, the owner of Island Interior Designs, and, and the third—?" He shuffled his stack of papers. "The third is the owner of the dance school, Cynthia something."

"Bradley." I said. "Cynthia Bradley."

"That's right." David looked unusually glum. "I hope this goes well, the GM is very pumped about this promotion. I guess people have been talking about the flyers plastered around town."

"Do you always call your father-in-law 'GM'? Or, at home is it Larry or…?"

"When I'm with my wife's family I call him Mr. Pop." David scratched his neck and sputtered out a dry laugh. "It's respectful and family-like at the same time."

"It's also kind of dynamic," I said. "If things don't work out here, maybe you two could come up with a soft drink. Is your wife coming to the show?"

His face clouded over, "Oh, you betcha. She'll be sitting with the family at the GM's table. This is my chance to prove I've got ideas for the F & B Department. They'll be watching closely."

"Let's keep the drinks coming to that table, then."

"Right-on," he said. "I told my wife I have to be backstage to help get the acts on and off. I can't bear the thought of sitting with them all night." He looked from side to side and then, in a hushed voice, "Did you give Lucinda a good spot in the show? Have you heard her sing?"

"Yes, and no," I said, feeling uneasy. "She'll go on fourth so the crowd will be warmed up. I haven't heard anyone sing, though. I see the talent the same time everyone else does."

"Oh my gosh," he gasped. "Maybe it will be horrible? You didn't *screen* the acts?"

"David, you're the one who asked me to do this thing—I certainly didn't have time to watch all the acts. Most of them didn't have CDs of themselves singing. You want this by July fourth? I picked a variety of those who looked the most experienced. If they suck, they won't get votes. That's that. It's on to the next contestant."

"Lower your voice, please. No offense, but what do you do all day—you only play for four hours a night?"

"No offense," I shot back, "but I was *hired* to play four hours a night and not to run a talent contest I know nothing about." I felt my throat tighten. "Organizing this contest has eaten into my whole day and I do have *other* commitments." I stood, brushed off my skirt and reached for my purse.

David pulled on my arm. "I'm sorry. Veronica, please sit down. I just want to know what you do all day. Come on, we're friends."

"Pshh. I'm writing an authorized biography of someone—who has to remain nameless. I'm half way through and I have to turn it in at the end of the summer. Getting away to write was part of the reason I came all the way out here."

"Oh yeah? Who is it? "

"If I tell you, I'll have to kill you."

"Is he coming here?"

"Hardly. He's in Sydney, Australia."

David wiggled in his chair. "He *could* be one of our celebrities in the Nissan-Palmolive Golf Classic, Miss Bennett, so don't get uppity. Anyway, what if there's a line-up of sucky singers in a row and people just stampede out of the banquet room?"

"As much as they may want to, I'm sure they'll stick around to see their friend or family member's sucky act. So, it won't be a stampede. Most likely a trickle."

David made a gurgling sound and dropped his head into his hands. "Veronica, you don't know how important this is to me." He whimpered, "If people leave or, or—"

"Shout insults?" I offered.

"Yeah, shout insults about the Island Idol…I will…I will—"

"You will? What? You won't be on stage taking it, like me—what about me?" I cried. "I'm the one up there dodging tomatoes and hecklers. I have to emcee this…this—" my voice cracked, "show."

We looked at each other and froze. His eyes widened. I bit my bottom lip.

"You haven't seen *any* of the acts," he feverishly whispered, "perform?"

I shook my head. His elbows were already on the table and it was a quick drop sinking his head back into his palms. "Only JT, and he's great." I told him. "Oh yeah, I signed up a harmonica player who'll play along with a CD of blues music. I heard *him*." I didn't add he forgot to drop off his backup music so even that might evaporate.

"Each act only gets three minutes?" He peeked though his splayed fingers. "It's so brief."

"David, if you're bombing—three minutes is an eternity. That's why we have so many participants. A lot of participants means more audience. It's the kids' dance school auditorium theory of packing the house," I said.

David stood up and steadied himself on the back of the chair. "Maybe you're right. We have 264 tickets sold. People will vote for their friends and hopefully stay."

I patted his arm. "I don't know how to do it any other way. There's nothing we can do now—"

He hugged me in a desperate, rib-crushing embrace. Then, just as abruptly, he spun on his heels and bolted from the room.

CHAPTER 14

The Crowne Plaza banquet room looked great. I originally suggested they set up long tables coming from the stage, Vegas style, but the hotel only had large round eight-tops, so we opted for rows of chairs fanning out from the stage and put the tables in the very back of the room. Volunteer moms from the dance school greeted each guest with a program, voting sheet, golf pencil and drink ticket.

I bowed stiffly from the waist to acknowledge the applause. "Ladies and gentleman, thank you for coming to the first annual Island Idol contest." The ballroom looked fairly full with all sorts of people, from antsy toddlers to old folks. Since audience participation might focus the group, I scheduled our magician to go first.

"We will begin with the magic of Merlinski the Magnificent. Let's welcome him to the stage with applause." The poor guy who lost his doves at the rehearsal, stuck his long neck out from the wings and I waved him to the stage. "Let's have everyone's eyes forward. They say the hand is quicker than the eye, so let's find out!"

Merlinski's tape was cued to an accordion polka and as he strutted out to center stage the room quieted down. Perhaps they were stunned into silence by the cheese ball music. He showed us his palms, tugged at his sleeves and then pulled a rope from his pocket. Alas, the familiar rope restoration trick looked like it needed a bit more practice because after snipping the middle, we saw him try to slide the knots down. He abandoned the whole idea and tossed the full length of rope behind him. The audience laughed as he wiped his brow. Merlinski looked embarrassed as he walked to the edge of the stage. The polka droned on as he fumbled fanning cards and his own silence made the act seem even more dated. Bowing humbly in front of a woman seated in the front row, he gestured an apology. Somehow he was able to coax the volunteer to come up. I checked my watch. One minute into the act and I was desperate for something else.

Merlinski extended his gloved hand to the woman. She stood up from her front row seat. The audience applauded encouragement as she climbed the few stairs leading up to the stage. She joined him in the center of the floor just as the music switched to a dramatic tango. Merlinski skillfully swung the woman around to his side as the guitar music rhythmically accompanied the couple. As the music became more dramatic he sinuously pressed himself to her back as she arched her back in the passionate embrace. Her shapely leg was exposed by the hip-to-hem slit in her skirt as he dipped her low. Wait a minute, why was she wearing that? As the music got louder their four legs moved as one across the floor. This skillful dance team spun and dipped around the floor in a sexy tango, taking everyone by surprise with the thrilling opening to the show. The crowd cheered as the shill made a flamboyant curtsy, and extended a graceful arm to her dance partner, Merlinski. He smiled a crafty smile and bowed deeply.

The second act was the ventriloquist Ken and his impudent wooden duck, KC. Not surprisingly, this ventriloquist was a crowd pleaser with the kids as well as adults. The next act was a tap number by Bradley's Dance School Sweethearts. A dozen or so girls and one boy tapped away to the song, "You Are My

Sunshine." I felt it best to get the kids over with at the beginning. They were pretty squirmy, so David stayed backstage and helped calm the nerves of the stage mothers. Surprisingly, the kids were more confident than their parents. Of course, the parents had seen the act—the kids only the tops of their own shoes and the floor. When the adorable kidlets took a bow, David gave me a huge smile and thumbs up from the wings. Then he scooted down the hall to the little utility room where John, the CPA, hung out. We called it the "counting room."

As it turned out, Lucinda inherited a room full of positive people fully primed for a singer.

Reading off the card she provided, I announced, "Ladies and gentlemen, some of you may know our next performer from Dr. McWalter's office. Along with being a terrific dental hygienist, Lucinda Starlight has long aspired to entertain you with her singing." I paused for the hoots and whistles to die down. So far, things were going very well and I was loving every nerve-wracking minute. Patrice caught my eye from the front row and gave me an encouraging smile. She pointed at the empty seat next to her on the aisle. I nodded back.

"She chose to sing, let's see—" I checked the three-by-five card. "Lucinda will be singing a Whitney Houston song from the movie *The Body Guard*, written by Dolly Parton, 'I Will Always Love You.'"

Lucinda minced on to center stage amid whistles of approval that nearly drowned out her intro music. She wore an emerald green, skin-tight sheath-style dress and matching four-inch strappy heels. The familiar intro was met with anticipation I suppose, since people clapped even before she began.

I skipped down the three steps at stage right and took my seat next to Patrice. Softly I leaned in to say, "Do you suppose 'Starlight' is her stage name?"

She patted my knee and smiled. "You're doing a great job. This is so much fun!" Glancing over her shoulder she muttered, "Now, if only JT would hurry up and get here."

"And Hippy Bob," I whispered back. "Maybe they're in the back. If they don't show up, I'll…"

There was a kind of disconnect between the music and the key Lucinda was singing in; the starting note seemed about half a note off. I turned around in my seat to glare at the audio guy at the sound board. He looked up from the sound board, to the stage—and then back down again. Then, furiously munched on his cuticles.

Lucinda could hold a long note all right, but it sounded like the atonal screech of a cat in heat. Earnest, shrill and disturbing—and like an alley cat after midnight, there was an urgency to stop it before someone got hurt, in this case—our ears and her dignity. With her arms open wide she warbled *"I---ee---I---ee---I."* I sank deeper into my chair. Patrice whispered, "Oh dear," and shrank down beside me. Shoulder to shoulder we suffered along with the captive audience. My neck retracted into my collarbone to the warbling of *"will always love yooooooooooooooo…."* No one walked out. Like any disaster we watched with the same morbid curiosity reserved for driving past car wrecks. I don't know if I had ever listened to a singer through squinted eyes, but it seemed to help. As she bleated, *"I---ee---I---ee---I---will always love yooooooooooooooo…"* the second time, amidst the tittering, I overheard, "Reminds me of that goat we found trapped on the fence. Remember that, Martha?" Martha responded, "Well, she better keep to teeth cleaning, bless her heart." That's one thing about the Southerners; they can be as mean as anyone, anywhere and cleanse their conscience with a "bless his heart."

Although curious about David's reaction, I didn't risk looking around for fear of making eye-contact with someone. I ducked through the door to the left of the stage and climbed the steps to wait in the wings. A volunteer mom rushed up and handed me a note. "You are Veronica, right? Someone asked me to give you this." I shoved it into my pocket as I nervously waited for the song to screech to an end. Lucinda made a small curtsy then a delicate finger wave to the crowd before prancing off to the wings.

"Quite a variety of talent we've had here tonight," I said; the audience had broken off into splinter groups and the room was abuzz with noise.

"This may be a good time for a drawing. Could you please raise my mic volume? Thank you, Audio Al. Let's hear it for our soundman!" I clapped frantically, urging the others to do the same. "Ladies and gentlemen, check your ticket stubs. Where's my volunteer mom?" A young woman stepped out from stage left carrying the fishbowl of tickets.

"Let's see who won a dinner for two at the Portz Restaurant, right here at the lovely Crowne Plaza." I looked at the gal beside me. She wore a red, white and blue sundress. "I like your patriotic outfit. What's your name?"

I pointed the mic toward her.

"My name is Wendy, from Beaufort."

"Let's hear it for Wendy from Beaufort," I chirped. "Could you please reach in and find a winner while I hold the bowl of tickets?" She looked nervous as she handed me another note. "Mr. Lindsey said to read this right now."

"Hmm, what do we have here?" I unfolded the paper and read it aloud. "The Bacardi Company invites you to enjoy a Cuba Libre drink at half price for the next fifteen minutes. Oh, I see the servers are already coming around with trays full of them. That was quick." No one was listening. "Back to the drawing..." Some of the older boys were shoving each other and horsing around, but I didn't want to reward their rowdy behavior with a comment. The polite and attentive audience that began the evening had degenerated into a feisty mob befitting a Monster Truck rally. My only friend was now looking at me with dismay as people scrambled over each other to get to the cheap drinks.

"Ladies and gentlemen, remember, don't lose your ballots," I pleaded. "You can only vote for one person tonight and we will collect them after the last act. We have ten more to go and the final seven will be here next Saturday night. Is this mic on? Anyway, Wendy, just reach in and grab a ticket for the dinner for two, compliments of your food and beverage manager, Mr. David Lindsey. Would you like to raise your hand and say hello, David?" I stepped out of the light and shielded my eyes with my hand. "David?" He was nowhere to be seen. Wendy drew a ticket and a teenager in front claimed the prize. He pumped the air with his fist and this caused more hoots and hollers. The evening was sliding away from me. In my hurry to get back on stage, I'd left the program and introductions on my seat. I totally forgot who the next act was.

Then, a loud wailing guitar riff shot through the air and silenced the crowd. I glanced behind me at the closed curtain. Another riff came from out of nowhere. The curtains opened and JT was bent over his Stratocaster guitar. Its piercing wail curled into a soulful blues lick. He stomped a boot on the wooden floor and sang out, "Something's got a hold of me, child—whoa, it must be love!" The song inspired a rousing cheer from the crowd.

Watching from the wings I was as energized as the audience. Suddenly I felt the note in my pocket. I opened it. *You need a little help. I'm on the program to go last— but I think I'll go next. Let's see if we rock this. JT.* What a sweetheart he was. When he saw the show was in trouble he jumped in, not waiting for his time slot. Now everyone was focused and the energy was palpable. Beyond relief, I thrilled to the music and stood in the wings clapping along with JT's rockin' blues.

The remainder of the show was an amusing quilt of home-grown talent. "Stick around for the announcement of tonight's semi-finalists, ya'll. We have a great magician to entertain you as our own John Martin, from the accounting department, tallies up your votes along with the votes of our three esteemed judges.

Tonight you will choose the top seven acts to continue on to the finals. Two weeks from tonight, July the third, you will determine the first time ever—our Island Talent Search Winner!"

CHAPTER 15

Backstage was in chaos. With a calculator on one side and a glass of Merlot on the other, John Martin whisked through the pile of three-by-five cards. It seemed easy enough; each paying ticket was worth one vote. The judges' votes would each cast twenty points and were distinguished by *pink* three-by-five cards. I was confident no one knew what the voting cards would look like, eliminating any chance to throw the contest.

"Okay, Veronica, we have the top seven acts here." The accountant handed me a piece of paper but before my fingertips touched it, David Lindsey snatched it away.

"Excuse me, John," he said, fidgeting like a bird on a perch, his neck thrusting out and back. "I must claim seniority over Ms. Bennett. I *am* management, therefore...let me have the—oh, dear, there's a problem, I see."

"Gimme that," I said, but he pivoted away just as I tried to grab the list. "Okay, we all know JT won, but who else?"

When David wouldn't answer I turned to John. "Who were the finalists? Please, John."

"Hell's bells," John batted the air. "I don't know the names. I only tallied the votes corresponding to the number on the cards. You need to look up the names. What's the problem, David?"

"No problem," David wiped his brow. "No problem."

Just then a kid from valet parking rushed into the room. "There's someone to see you, Miss Bennett." His tone was urgent. "He's asking for you to come out front, but I told him you were busy."

"Is he tall? Dark hair, short-trimmed goatee?" There was no response. I touched his sleeve. "Long eyelashes, named Bob?"

"Not quite. This dude's wearing baggy shorts, flip flops, and his hair is like blond dreadlocks."

"Hmmm, I don't know anyone like—wait..." I squeaked. "He's gotta big ol' backpack?"

Out of the corner of my eye, I noticed David whispering to the accountant. A few words surfaced like, "mistake" and "add a name." John set his wine down. "It's your world, David, I'm just trying to live in it. This whole contest doesn't matter a hill of beans. I'm only here because the GM told me to count up—"

I swirled around to face David. "What's going on? What did you say to John?"

Just then, my son tumbled through the door on the arm of a security officer. "Devin?" I gasped. "I thought you were coming *next* Saturday." I rushed to his side and we embraced. He whistled as he shook himself free of his captor, "Wow, Gestapo Island. What's up with that dude?"

"Sorry, Jerry," I said to the beefy security guy. A waitress slipped through the door and closed it quickly behind her, then leaned her back against it. The sounds from the ruckus were loud in the moment the door had been opened. Eyeing first me then David, she barked, "They need the results, the little dance kids are crying and people keep asking *us* who won. How long is this s'posed to take?" She turned to the security guy with pleading eyes. "The guys at the bar are slamming shot glasses, chanting *JT... JT...JT.*"

"I'll handle it," Jerry said, trotting toward the door.

The waitressed begged, "Can *somebody* announce the winners?"

"I'll do it—" David and I said, simultaneously. "Excuse us," he ordered as he pulled my arm, dragging me to the corner of the small room. "So? You have a guest to be staying *here?*" he whispered.

"Yes. My son."

"I'm just saying, it would have been nice to *know*. Did you arrange for a room?"

"*I'm* just saying I was going to handle all that next week. There's a little mix-up. I thought he was coming *next* Saturday." We both looked back at Devin who was slumped in a chair, yawning. When he saw us staring at him he shouted across the room, "Mom, can you hook a brother up with something to eat around here?"

David looked at me quizzically. "Brother?" I murmured something about him being a rapper.

"All I ate was pretzels and nuts for about a gazillion hours."

"Gimme a minute, Dev."

Turning around to face me, David hissed through a tight jaw, "*I'm* just saying, I need to know these things…"

"Gee David," I whispered, "I thought Ken was a good ventriloquist. You can talk without moving your lips too." Stepping closer, I got right in his face. "We were doing this contest together. What are you pulling?"

We were interrupted by pounding on the door. A chorus of voices shouted, "Who won? Who won? Who won?" It sounded like a mob scene.

David pulled a folded piece of paper from his pocket. "I made these flyers last night to advertise the finals." He passed it to me sheepishly. "I had two thousand printed."

It showed an adorable picture of Lucinda dressed in a cheerleader's uniform with a bubble above it saying, *Hi, everyone, don't miss the biggest event in Hilton Head! Come see me at the Island Idol contest finals, Saturday, July 3*rd*!*

"A couple thousand?" I choked out. A few more bangs sounded from the door.

"They're set to be delivered all over the island by noon tomorrow. She has to be in the finals."

Devin looked at John for the first time. "Why's everybody yelling, who won? Is there a game on?"

I walked back over to him and stroked his back. "I'll explain later."

"Mom, you are drawing a mad crowd out there." Devin cackled. "Why aren't you singing?"

Turning toward David, I put my fists on my hips. "What now?"

"I'm putting contestant number four into the finals," David said defiantly.

"Oh yeah? My kid gets a free room for five nights," I retorted.

"Ojay, okay" David said backing away.

I held on to his neck tie like a short leash. "However, no favoritism at the finals, David." I held on to his necktie. "Next time everyone gets TWO votes to make sure. One for their sister —or whoever—and *another* vote for the *best* act." I stuck out my hand. "That's how we do it." After a pause, he shook on it.

"JT will win, any way you slice it, Veronica." He sniffed. "So, it doesn't harm anyone to come back and see another show. Heh, heh. But, I can't get you a room till tomorrow. The hotel is full and I need to locate a room—"

"Near an ice maker? Mine is near the ice machine," I said, snidely.

Another bang came from the door and we both jumped. He pulled a handkerchief from his breast pocket and wiped his glistening forehead. Then, heading toward the door, he called over his shoulder, "There's a noisy ice maker on every floor."

"Go ahead and announce the finalists, David," I chirped, as he took long strides across the room. "You *are* management, after all. Pshhh."

He looked back at me with mild despair and seemed to brace himself as he turned the door handle. To no one in particular he announced, "Here we go."

"About time," John grumbled. "I want to go home and not pass through an angry mob, if at all possible."

I moved over to the chair beside Devin and rubbed his shoulders as we listened to the muffled announcement. David congratulated all seven finalists and gave their names in alphabetical order.

CHAPTER 16

"Hey, Mom, that taxi cost me bank getting out here. Dad gave me a Benji, or I woulda still been stranded at the airport."

"What's a benji?"

"Benjamin Franklin, hundred dollar bill. Don't you know your presidents? Anyways, I kept calling you, but I guess…"

"I couldn't hear my cell ringing with all the commotion for the talent show," I explained. "It's called the Island Idol Show. Did you notice the signs around?"

Devin barked a dry laugh. "That sounds lame."

"I have to agree. But, it worked out pretty good. Anyway, the hotel is giving prize money to the winner, and I'm helping out."

"The TV show is so phony and now they have to subject people to an even jankier version?" He yawned.

I stood up. "Let's find you something to eat." As we came through the door we almost bumped into Hippy Bob coming down the hall. He looked adorable. It was too late to suck back my thrilled expression, so I buried my face in his shoulder to hug a hello.

"Well, there you are." He stood back a step and looked me over with flirtatious approval. "I was looking for you, girl. You put on a great show." Then regarding Devin, "Oh, excuse me. Hey, I'm Bob"

"Bob, this is my son, Devin. It's so interesting you guys just met and yet you both knew to do the knuckle bump—and not shake hands."

"Mom, it's the fist-jab," Devin said, rolling his head. "Not the knuckle whatever you called it."

"Anyway, Bob, so—so you liked the show, huh?" I said weakly. "JT was awesome, wasn't he?" We pressed our backs to the wall as people were coming and going past us to the area we used as a dressing room. I wanted to leave the hotel property quickly before management assigned me another task. Like, fix the gardener's leaf blower or sweep the pool. "Say, we're just leaving to find something to eat. The coffee shop is closed. I don't know if we can get room service in my room—"

Bob turned to Devin and in a serious tone said, "Do you like ridiculously juicy, drippy, goo-running-down to your elbows burgers?"

"All the time," Dev grinned his reply.

Bob nodded, "Let's get. I know a place down the road, open all night."

I motioned to the crumpled backpack. "Is that all you've got for the week?" Devin nodded. "I'm staying two weeks, Mom."

"Oh, good. Then you'll be here for the finals, the night before the Fourth of July," I said, slapping him on the backpack.

"Hang on and follow me." Bob took my hand and I grabbed Devin's as we threaded through the crowd in the hall and out a side door to the parking lot.

I was trotting behind him trying to keep up with his long gait. Bob is so casual about everything he didn't react at being introduced to my son. Now a young dreadlocked, hip-hop, surfer was with us; nothing seem to surprise him.

"Great shortcut, Bob. The last thing I want to see is a contestant who didn't make the finals." Which was euphemistic for: or get stoned by the audience for the outcome. "Is JT still inside? Or Patrice?"

"They already took off," Bob called over his shoulder as he weaved us through the parked cars. It was unsettling with all the trucks screeching-out and rumbling past as they gunned toward the exit. Once inside the safety of Bob's truck, I wanted to just curl up and reflect on all that had happened. It felt good to have someone else at the wheel. As we rode along the dark highway, Devin leaned forward from the back seat and the guys discussed the merits of the Pacific Ocean versus the Atlantic.

This night had been exhausting. With barely time to take off my producer's hat—which was teetering on top of my singer hat—which barely covered my writer's hat—I now wondered when I'd last worn my parent hat? Actually, it was six months ago at Christmas. After burgers Devin would be back in my tiny room. I could already see him shoving my layers of clothes onto the floor and then stepping on them as he climbed into bed. No matter, I loved being his mom and desperately hoped things would be different this time.

******

"Veronica? You look like you're falling asleep," Bob smiled from across the Formica table.

I sat up straight and instinctively wiped my mouth with my wrist, in drool check. "Sorry, I just sat still for the first time all day, then...whew, I don't know."

"Mom, Mom, listen." Devin was dredging his fries through a puddle of ketchup and Tabasco sauce. "Bob has a couple jet skis and he said I could take one out for a blast around the island." His face lit up with the same enthusiasm that I'd seen when he was a little boy. My little slugger who swung the bat at T-Ball and ran the wrong way to third base was now nineteen years old with the same precocious grin. His hair was a wild tangle of blond streaks bound at his neck with a hair tie. His pale skin barely ever tanned, giving him an apricot hue with a sprinkle of freckles across his nose. His full lips always seemed to be peeling.

"Do you have any Chapstick?" I asked him. He pulled a tube out of his pocket and drew a line back and forth across his mouth. Then, he looked outside the dark window of our booth and said, "It's so, humid here. Just like in Kona, but it's 'Howlie-air.'"

I explained to Bob that Howlie was a derogatory term used to describe the mainlanders—people from anywhere else.

"It's weird to come so far," Devin said, "and then I get here and it's almost like home."

The word stung me. His dad's home was now *his* home? All I've got is a room key. He continued, "I could be, like, on the Leland side of the island and just be waking up from a monster long sleep. Straight up, it's not that different here."

"Wait till you see this place in the sunlight," I said.

Bob looked up from his burger. "You're going to have a great time in Hilton Head. We gotta show you some gators too."

"I used to be obsessed with alligators and dinosaurs. I had a dope collection. Remember, Mom?"

Bob looked at me.

"Dope means good," I explained. "Remember when the Superman movie came out and you loved everything Superman?" I touched Bob's arm. "Devin was always an inquisitive kid. When he was about five he asked me, 'When they made the movie *Superman*, did they only pick actors that could fly?' Then, another time, 'to get into China, do you have to have black hair?'" The laughter ran its course and I pulled him toward me in the booth we shared. I wrapped my arm around his bony shoulders and squeezed. There was nothing to squeeze, he was so thin he seemed to fold in like a chair, but it felt wonderful.

Dev wiped his mouth with his napkin. "Thanks for hookin' me up with the burger, dude."

I reached for my purse. "So, let's go back to the hotel, honey. I'm sure you're tired from the flight."

"So, *where* am I staying?" Devin asked.

"Since I didn't realize you were coming tonight, tonight you'll be in my room. I can get you your own room tomorrow."

"What?" He almost yelled before catching himself. "I'm sleeping in your room?" A couple at a nearby table looked up. He reined himself in. "Okay. Sure, that's chill."

As Bob paid for the burgers, Cokes and my hot chocolate, Devin stood up and stretched. He turned to face Bob and clapped his hands together. "I got an idea, bro. Since you said I could jet ski, maybe I could just go home with you now and stay at your place. Then I'll be already there in the morning, to, uh, do it."

"Devin, you *just* got here," I pleaded. "You came all this way to see *me*."

"You probably don't even have a car out here anyway, do you, Mom?"

I could feel my face flush hot and I resisted grabbing his arm to inflict the subtle finger nail injection. "You *just* got here, Dev.´ With measured words I said very, very slowly. "I don't think that's a...good idea. I'm sure Bob will find time during the week—"

Devin scowled. "Why are you talking like that? All phony?" Then he mimicked me by speaking in a higher pitch, "I'm sure Bob will find time..."

We walked toward the exit. Devin pulled Bob's sleeve and said, "You don't care, do you, bro?"

I shook my head and stomped ahead of them. As I walked I inhaled a lungful of Howlie air and willed myself not to cry. Why was it always like that? I loved Devin. I loved being with him and hearing his stories and his quirky candor. I was proud of his energy and zest for life, and his gorgeous blue eyes and everything sweet about him. Unfortunately, within the first hour of any contact, a spoiled child would peek out from the hood of his sweatshirt, a tormentor who seems to be obliviously insensitive or taunting me and doesn't care. He needs to *toughen* me up, he claims, that *I* am the drama queen getting overly emotional, and *nothing* is a big deal, and *what's* my problem?

Thankfully, it was dark and they couldn't see my tears as I waited inside the cab of the Escalade. By the time the guys got to the car it was somehow decided they'd drop me off and that Devin would go home to Pinewood with Hippy Bob.

CHAPTER 17

Dancing bears were performing on the stage of the Crowne Plaza banquet room. They tumbled into the audience in an angry display of claws and fangs— and devoured the entire front row. I awoke to the phone ringing on my nightstand.

"Hello?" I croaked. A grainy silence signaled that it was a long distance call.

"Don't tell me you're still sleeping."

"Uh, huh. Oh, hi Jack."

"Vee? It's already eleven, your time. I wanted to give you some good news, pretty girl. You aren't sick, are you?"

"No. Sorry, just a little bit groggy—it's nice to hear your voice, though."

"Get this. The shooting ran over and we needed another infusion of capital. Nissan's CEO is one of the partners backing *Pelican Island,* so to grease the money pipeline, my manager's sending me to a celebrity golf tournament that they're sponsoring. You'll never guess where I'll be in three weeks."

"Nissan-Palmolive's 22nd Annual Celebrity Golf Tournament in Hilton Head Island, July the eleventh?" I read off the advertising card the maid had propped up on the nightstand.

"Don't sound so excited, dear. Now, I know I behaved poorly in Sydney, but that was a month ago. I miss you, awfully." He paused as I tried to re-align the universe with my world here. Had I left Sydney *only a month ago?*

"You will be kind to me, won't you?" he continued. "Anyway, with a little effort, I think we can dash out more pages on the book during the week. I'm getting emails from Kendal Street Publishers. You've been cc'd on all this, so you know they're on the fast track to have *Jack's Back* on book shelves by Christmas. Our deadline is September nineteenth. Does that sound right? Anyway, the golf tourney should last three days and..."

As Jack spoke of tangible deadlines I shrank further down into the sheets. Had I squandered the opportunity, and dare I say, *privilege* of writing the famous actor's biography? Now, with the deadline for the manuscript looming large, its significance overshadowed entertaining my son, or The Island Idol contest-slash-sham of nepotism. Jack, someone I had allowed into the inner sanctum of my heart (and thighs), would be *here in three weeks.*

I couldn't believe what I was hearing. Jack Swanson was too large for this tiny coastal island—celebrity golf tournament or not. He rides into situations and takes over with a sense of entitlement he borrows from starring in seventeen action films.

I thrashed about in my pillows as he rambled on. Something about film schedules and the weather in Australia. Hearing his voice while lying in the dark room caused my pulse to race. The timing just wasn't fair. I had moved on, moved thousands of miles from the husky, sexy voice, olive skin and masterful, strong hands. Now he was coming back before the glue was set. Jack Swanson is a scene stealer whose innate charisma makes me feel like his leading lady in a steamy love scene anytime we're within arm's reach of each other.

I got off the phone as quickly as possible and rolled over to face the wall. Jack's arrival—in three weeks—would collide with another star in orbit—the congenial, Southern gent whose slow charm was as hot, sweet and nutty as pecan pie, Hippy Bob.

CHAPTER 18

I walked over to the other bed in my room and brushed aside a couple days' worth of clothes. Beneath the bathing suits and white shorts in four different lengths (mid-calf, to coochy mama), was my neglected legal pad of notes for *Jack's Back*. I tossed it on the desk and made coffee.

It didn't take long to realize why this project was on the burner *behind* the back burner. Jack Swanson was a fascinating man. While retracing his glamorous years in Hollywood I kept unearthing alleged affairs, real affairs, three wives (gorgeous actresses), women he was in pictures with, women he was *just* pictured with, and suspected dalliances. Lust's bit players, walk-on players who walked off after the wrap party—and then, there was always the mirror. His life was a playground of excess and now, writing about it put me on the teeter-totter. As his piano teacher, I was treated respectfully, affectionately, then passionately. Whee! I'm up high and Jack's on the other end of the board smiling with those perfectly sexy lips. This new thrill has me in the air with feet swinging off the ground. Whoops, Jack's turn to leave the see-saw and my turn to thud down with a jolt. The dust settles. I'm alone in the dirt.

According to Google he married the adorable Sally Benson in '95. I loved her movies. They look so happy in this picture with their baby. Whoops, thud. My board hit the dirt and I'm on the ground with a jarring headache.

A couple hours later I was pouring over pictures of Jack Swanson's roast at the Friars Club. For the caption it made sense to quote some of those people in the picture. However, in reading the *Daily Variety's* account of the evening, the funniest comments came from other people who were there, but not in the picture. What to do? Then the phone rang and yanked me out of Swansonville.

"Mom, this place is so cool." Devin started in, "The water here is like, 81 degrees. Okay, the waves are bunk, but I body surfed and they let me fire up the jetski."

"Did you meet JT?"

"He's chill. You should see all the guitars he's got hung up on the walls —but not *even* his bedroom. It's a guitar room. This place is sweet. I'm telling ya—these guys are mad rich!"

"Hey, shhh. Don't say that right now. Wait till we're alone. Is Bob around?"

"No, he's taking a shower.'

I added a spoonful of sugar to my voice, knowing I couldn't compete with the Tid-bit mansion, entertainment capital of South Carolina. "Your room here at the hotel is ready for you. So, I'll come get you now and we can have lunch together on the way back. Okay? Go ahead and ask Bob and JT if they want to join us too. Lunch is on me."

"JT is practicing guitar and Bob's in the shower. No hurry, Mom. I'm gonna take Becky for a run on the beach. You know, they never take her down to the sand? They said she likes the grass."

"Did Bob say it was okay to take her to the beach? If she doesn't go down there, there might be a reason, Devin."

"Come on, Mom. I gotta go," he barked.

"I'll pick you up in an hour. Have fun."

"Late," he said, and the line went dead.

******

When I got to the gate at Pinewood, I pushed the intercom. After a pause, I heard Devin day, "Who is it?" through the speaker. My God, he worked fast. He's like an invisible gas leak that escaped the kitchen, seeped under doors and now had permeated the security system at the mansion.

He graciously allowed me in and I parked. Immediately I sensed something was wrong. JT met me outside, but his normal carefree demeanor was replaced by a furrowed brow. I had never noticed him smoking before.

"Nice to see you, Veronica." He leaned down to peck my cheek. He tossed the cigarette butt on the ground and stamped it out with his boot.

"Are you guys coming to lunch with us?" I asked. "I'm buying at the Tiki Hut. Oh, and thanks for letting Devin stay over last night. He was excited to ride the jet ski... and couldn't wait..." I trailed off. "I guess."

JT looked to the Eastern horizon. "No lunch for me, thanks, ma'am. I'm going to stick around here and wait for Becky to find her way back."

Devin came running up and hugged my waist.

"Becky?" I turned to my son. "Back from where?"

Just then a shrill whistle rang out and we all looked toward the beach. The path leading down was lined with tall, feathery Pampas grass swaying in the gentle breeze. The German Shepherd ran ahead of Bob stirring up clouds of dust around her feet. She sprinted to JT's side with her tongue hanging out. Devin bent over to tousle her neck fur and was rewarded with a wet dog kiss. JT thumped his chest and Becky jumped up, her front paws landing near his shoulders as the two seemed to circle in a little welcome dance.

Eventually, Bob trotted up the path, panting heavily. He pulled a kerchief from a back pocket and swiped his forehead.

"Nice going, cuz." JT was still looking into the dog's eyes as he spoke. "Where'd ya find her?"

"She was just south of here. Finally she heard me whistle. I don't think she heard me the first fifty times. So I had to change direction and start all over again running south. The sound doesn't carry at all with the waves crashing."

"You call *these* waves crashing?" Devin exclaimed and rolled his eyes. "You ought to see Wiamiah Bay."

I pinched the back of his arm.

"Yow!" he yelped.

"We'll be going." I motioned to the backpack on the ground, saying, "Is that all you have?"

Devin picked up his meager luggage and knelt down to hug Becky one more time. "Hey, girl, where'd you go?"

I stroked Becky's head too, grabbing a little handful of neck fur and giving it a jiggle. Fortunately I was wearing sunglasses so they couldn't see my eyes. My lips were pressed tightly against my teeth. Once again, my voice demanded a sprinkling of sugar. "Again, thank you *so* much for your hospitality, guys." I forced a smile, and with a ripple of fingers waved as I headed toward the car. "Devin?"

"Thanks, bro," Devin said, bumping knuckles and shoulders with each guy. He got in on the passenger side and I slid behind the wheel.

"Put on your safety belt."

"Why, what's the danger?" He scoffed. "We're only going, like, five miles an hour."

"Look at me," I slid the sunglasses down my nose. "You are *definitely* in some danger."

CHAPTER 19

Instead of going to town and having lunch on the beach at the trendy Tiki Hut, I roared down the highway in the direction of Harold's Diner. "Why did you take the dog to the beach? You didn't have permission and you did it anyway."

"Dogs love the beach," he said while unwrapping a stick of gum. "You ought to see them in Kona. They all go in the water and..."

"You could have lost her," I blurted out. "This isn't Kona. What happened?" We went on like that for a few miles. I would ask a question and my son would mock my tone, asking me another question. Like, *why shouldn't dogs be where they can dig? Sand is perfect. Why are such a drama queen, it's no big deal.* Finally, I raised my hand and shook my head. "Enough."

We didn't speak the rest of the way to the burger joint and we hastily got out of the car.

We plunked down on a couple stools at the end of the counter. At Harold's there were only stools, with no room for tables along the narrow strip. The smell of bacon and onions filled the air and the hiss of burgers on the griddle was a warm welcome. Gimme some fried food; I was ready for greasy gourmet.

STARS or STRIPES 4th of JULY

Devin was busy reading aloud the signs plastered all around the place. "Look at that one, 'IF YOU DON'T LIKE WHAT YOU SEE—DON'T LOOK.'"

"Grab a pencil and fill this out," I said, handing him a paper strip that served as the menu. It had boxes to check beside the food items. "I guess we do it ourselves here. I'm going to have—a basket of shrimp with fries and slaw," I announced with some satisfaction.

The guy working the counter snatched the paper menus before I checked to see what Devin had ordered. He frowned slightly and said, "You need to print your name on the bottom. See here?"

With our menus rejected we dutifully followed his instructions and I had time to check Devin's order. "Devin, just get one or two things—are you kidding, you've got about five things checked off here?"

"Okay, give me another one." Devin pouted as he reached for another list.

The counter guy clicked his tongue, shook his head and moved down the row.

"Let's take a moment and read this thing," I said. "Now at the top, since you checked off burger, you can mark off what kind of cheese you want. Look. Lettuce? Tomato? There's even a box for chili. They serve big portions in the South even if it says half burger."

The counter guy overheard the comment and reappeared to correct me. Apparently, the half burger is actually a half *pound* of burger. The place was as famous for great food as it was for aloof counter workers.

We returned to a strained silence as we waited for our lunch.

"So, what did you and Bob and JT talk about?" I ventured.

"Nothin' really."

So much for riveting conversation. The golden basket of shrimp arrived and I dove in with gusto. "Did Bob mention he was studying to be a veterinarian?" I asked.

"Nope. I heard them talking about your talent contest, though."

"Oh really? That's great to hear. I didn't think JT was even going to show up. He sure doesn't need the money. Look how they live."

"Not really. They was talking about the money." Devin enjoyed correcting me at every opportunity. With a mouth full he said, "It's five thousand bucks, right?"

"Right. I'm sure he'll win. Even though there're a few good acts, like Ken and Casey. But he's the only one with real 'star' potential. For that kind of money you've got to be way talented." I stuck a straw into the chocolate malt set before me. I slid the remaining malt in the silver shaker toward him. "You want this?" He didn't bother with a straw, just tilted it into his mouth. The metal cylinder served as an echo chamber for the loud sucking sound.

"That noise would ordinarily be rude," I said, casting a sideways glance. "But in here it's just another kitchen sound, like a Mr. Coffee firing up. Anyway, I'm so happy to hear JT liked the contest. I never even saw him at the end of the night with all that was going on."

"I didn't say he liked the contest. He just told Bob the five-k was going for plane tickets. I asked him what five-k meant, that's why I remember it."

"Here." I handed him a napkin.

"Five-k sounded like cereal, but then I was thinking of Special K, so I didn't think he was using cereal to get tickets. Funny, huh?"

We fell into a contented silence as we ate. But something was gnawing at me. "Did he mention where he was flying?"

"Spain. I guess he's got some gig over there. But, those guys are chill. Can we go back there tomorrow?"

On the way out I noticed a stack of flyers for the Island Idol contest by the cash register. I had to admit, Lucinda looked hot.

******

Once Devin had settled into his room, I went back to working on Jack's biography. Taking out a calendar I calculated the number of days till his visit—twenty-one, versus the number of pages I needed to finish. Yikes, I needed to write ten pages a day. Clearly the pictures should be bigger. Maybe we could make the font a little larger, like the top line of the eye chart.

My cell phone rang and Bob was the happy distraction. He recounted the morning afternoon with my son commenting Devin was a funny kid. I swelled with pride at the thought of those two ripping it up on the jet skis. Best of all, he said to forget about the dog incident and that he was coming by the club tonight. Also, to reserve a double hammock for after the gig, which was, of course, a joke referencing our last stroll on the hotel grounds overlooking the sea.

The first week I was here I'd spent glorious afternoons reading in the hammocks that swung gently between the wild oak trees. Once Bob and I got cozy, we found it was perfect for two people, and was a fun challenge to find the center. Sometimes I tipped out and fell on my butt while trying to swing my legs up. Those first lazy afternoons on Hilton Head seemed to be eons ago, before life got complicated with the contest, mad crushes and mother-son bonding. Back then my only problems were wounded pride from Jack, and the writing deadline that was months into the future. After pissing away the last month, the clock ticked faster than the clacking keys of my laptop.

I hadn't caught up with Patrice, so I dialed her up.

"FACES Day Spa," she sang into the phone.

"This is Jo Jo the dog-faced boy," I disguised my voice. "Can I get a shave and facial?"

Patrice laughed. "Veronica, I was just thinking about you. You know how that happens? I heard your son is in town, but I must say right off the bat, I don't have my place ready for him to paint. I'm so sorry, but..."

"Oh, please stop, Patrice. He came in early or I wrote down the wrong date. Anyway, how could you have known when I didn't even know? Devin's having a great time."

"I can't wait to meet him. I heard he came by Tid-bit mansion last night. How did he get an invite and you didn't?"

"Long story. Maybe you can come by here and hang out at the pool with us? By the way, how did you like the contest? Were you so proud of JT? Was he happy about being a finalist?"

I could hear Patrice excuse herself from the spa desk and then a door shut. In a hushed voice she said, "Yes, I assume so. He didn't say much. After the show, I was looking around for him. He texted me that he was looking for Bob and needed to leave. I guess they came in the one car."

"That's weird, they don't seem to have their own cars." I said.

"Anyway, I found him and scooped him up and took him with me. We never did see Bob."

"He was with me, and Devin."

"All right, that's cute. JT and I went for a drink at the Tiki Hut and then went back to his place."

"You didn't see Devin and Bob come in last night?"

"I was behind closed doors and didn't hear anything but the music playing in JT's gynormous bedroom. I left about four. That's all I can tell you, girlfriend, without setting the phone lines on fire. You know, I might burn some little bird's feet."

Not to be outdone, I told her Bob was coming by tonight and we were going to spend some quality time under the stars in a hammock. Although I knew bringing him back to my room wasn't an option, with Devin in the vicinity. Those paranoid thoughts would keep me from any horizontal boogie.

CHAPTER 20

The moon hung in the night sky like a nail clipping. Bob and I tangled in the rope nest of the hammock until we were interrupted by a beam of light that flashed through the trees.

"The security guard is making his one o'clock rounds," I whispered in Bob's ear.

He put his hand gently across my mouth. The light swept again low through the trees. I heard the jangle of keys. He was getting farther away. I was fairly sure we were hidden in the farthest outpost of the hotel property, yet cringed at any chance of being discovered smooching a customer out back. Once it was quiet we rolled over on our backs and gazed up at the dark sky. Bob inhaled deeply and let out a contented sigh.

"So, next Saturday's the big night, huh?" He asked. His arm was wrapped around my back and he stroked my arm. "I've been seeing the flyers all over town. That chick on the flyer looks pretty good, but her voice left something to be desired."

"Uh, yeah."

"Too bad you can't enter. You sing so pretty. You're like my own little nightingale."

I turned my head and kissed his neck. "Hmmm, you smell like green apples. I'll save you a seat in the second row, next to

Patrice and Devin, how's that? Maybe I can come out and sit with you some of the time."

"Little darlin', I'm not so sure I can come that night."

"What?—why not?" In the struggle to sit up, my foot poked through a hole in the hammock, locking my ankle in place. "You know how important this is to me."

"Now, now, let's not get excited," he said softly.

I tried to keep my voice low. Unclenching my jaw slightly, I said, "Every time we talk on the phone you tell me your day, and I tell you my day, and my days have been filled with finding these contestants and it's all building up to the finals Saturday night—and, and, I've worked hard on this and, oh, forget it." I rolled away from him and almost fell to the ground. Still trying to regain my balance, I stood up and yanked the hem of my skirt back down.

Bob was thrashing about in the hammock now, too. He reached his arm out and tried to pull me back in. "It's just that I need to stay home with Becky," he said. "She needs eye drops and someone needs to give her medicine every few hours."

"Oh?" I said icily, "This is the first I've heard of it." I spun away and marched off before realizing my shoes were still on the grass. Grrr, I had to retreat to collect them, then, with my head held high, I marched off into the night once more.

Bob scrambled after me in an awkward lunge. "This hammock doesn't highlight anyone's grace, does it?" His foot was still looped in one of the swinging ropes. "Veronica, wait. I'll see if I can get someone to stay with the damn dog. I know this is important to you, but I hadn't figured it out. With JT out here performing, I just thought I had to stay home."

I froze like a statue in the dark. I didn't want to end the fragile summer infatuation so suddenly. The crickets chirped a warning as loneliness washed over me. Patrice and JT were now an item. If Bob and I broke off, I'd have no life beyond the gig. We had loose plans of jet skis, and barbecues, and kayaking around the wetlands. Sadly, I recalled my first week at the

Crowne Plaza. Bored out of my mind, I'd end the night talking to Mister on-and-on-on, Herb, the bartender. My only friend was David Lindsey, the needy Food & Bev Director. Maybe Bob was thinking the same way, because he rushed up from behind me and wrapped his arms around my waist. The humid air was easy to breathe and seemed to caress my skin. With his body now pressed against my back I could imagine us in a prom photo. His chin rested on top of my shoulder like an epaulette, as we stared toward the dark Atlantic.

"Vee, do you think your son could come that night and help out with Becky?"

"Probably," I said stiffly. "He's already expressed his opinion about going to the show." I mimicked his droll delivery, "Lame."

He turned me around to face him and pulled my arms up to wreath his neck. "I would never want to hurt you. Ever since you came into The Jazz Corner, I knew you weren't like the regulars. You have a style and grace that I find irresistible. Hell, I'd come into the club every night to hear you sing, but I don't want to look like a fool." He chuckled, "Actually, I don't mind being your fool. I just don't want to look like one." He smiled broadly and his words dissolved as he covered my cheek with soft little kisses. He found his way to my top lip and gently sucked it for an instant.

We broke away for a moment as if to find validation in our other senses. As our eyes locked, our rapid breathing was the only sound we heard. In the dim light I admired Hippy Bob up close. In the night shadows he looked like a brown-skinned Indian who belonged in the natural beauty of this landscape. With high cheek-bones and strong jaw he looked honest and earnest. He always spoke softly and his eyes, once on mine, never left my gaze. If a herd of buffalo crossed beside us, I felt Hippy Bob's eyes wouldn't waver. There was a power in his long gaze.

I stood on tiptoe, still holding my sandals in my right hand. He leaned down and kissed me with an urgency that was electric. We pressed against each other, trying to fill in every centimeter of space between us. An hour ago such kisses were experimental dalliances, a getting-to-know- you lip dance. Now, our mouths and hands ushered in a rising tide of passion and my knees wanted to buckle. He traced the line of my jaw with his fingertips and tucked my hair behind my ear. Leaning in close, resting his face against my hair, his breath warmed my neck as he spoke into my ear. "I don't think you've ever shown me the sweet place you lay your head."

"It's right this way."

CHAPTER 21

The following two weeks went by in a sunny whirl. Like a Pepsi commercial, my son and I rode jet-skis, swam, played beach volleyball—living large at Tid-bit mansion. Everyday, I'd wake up and give Dev a call to meet me at my room for a smoothie. A half hour later he'd be at my door. By then I'd had my coffee and assembled a well stocked canvas bag of towels, lotions, and paperback books for the day.

About noon we'd get into the car and pick up Patrice—who we discovered was a terrific cook. She would usually bring fresh baked brownies or cookies. Not to be outdone, we would arrange for the hotel kitchen for yum-a-licious take-out, usually a tray or sandwiches.

The guys' place led down to a private beach and their boathouse was like a dusty toy store. We found a couple of tandem kayaks and figured we'd plunk them into the Atlantic for a little row. That was a laugh, literally, since it was rough getting past the waves. The narrow fiberglass watercrafts spun in a circle facing us toward the shore. Again and again a wave would push us back to shore and we'd start over, laughing in the salty foam.

Devin loved it too and the chemistry between the five of us was amazing. I nicknamed him "Starfish," because out in the

ocean he was a rock star. My son seemed to thrive on the male
energy around him; when it was just the two of us, he was often
surly. Or perhaps it's just that people use "company manners"
outside of family. Either way, the days wore him out with all
the toys in the boathouse, not to mention his ability to body surf
for hours on end. Sometimes, just tossing the Frisbee to the dog
was all he needed. Watching him thrive in this wholesome
setting was all I needed. The guys even allowed the beloved
Becky on the beach—with supervision. I don't know how
Devin lost her that first day.

Lazy afternoons sailed by with Dev in the water and the
four of us adults playing cards and drinking pitchers of gin and
lemonade beneath the shade of a palapa.

"Bob, Patrice, JT," I said, breaking the contented silence of
sunning. "Let's all tell of an invention we made up at one time
or another." Undaunted by the tepid reaction, I launched into
my invention.

"Okay, I'll go first. My invention is rat-flavored cat food.
After all, why should we assume cats and dogs like lamb and
rice?" I was pleased with the round of groans. "Every cat I've
ever owned dragged a half-gnawed rat into the house. There is a
message there that advertisers are missing." I received a well-
deserved applause. "Thanks, guys. You're in the spa business,
Patrice, you probably have thought of a good beauty product.
What's your invention?"

She sat up and made a kittenish yawn with her stretch. "My
winning invention is teeth paint. Like nail polish. We could coat
our teeth a glistening, pearly white once and for all. The
beautifully gleaming coat would protect us from cavities too."

Like uncovering a conspiracy by the American Dental
Association, we all jumped in talking at once, indignant that this
product wasn't available *years* ago.

JT opened the lid to the cooler and passed around bottles of
Corona and a baggie of cold lime wedges. "That's a good one,
babe. Dentists just don't want to shit-can their years of drudgery

in dental school. Science came up with paint to protect the outside of a rocket to the moon, they damn well could come up with pearly white paint to coat teeth against coffee stains."

Bob jumped in with his idea to use Patrice's pearly teeth paint as bottom sealer for boats too. We all were rowdy supporters of the inventions so far.

Hippy Bob stood in front of us and I admired his tan, lanky body as he tried to sell us on his idea. A hangover lollypop for the nightstand. He acted out sleeping then reaching over with his eyes closed. "After a big night of partying," he drawled, "just reach over and stick it in your mouth. Suck it while your head is still on the pillow. You know, when your mouth feels like the bottom of a bird cage and your head feels stuffed with hay, and your eyes feel like two balls of butter in a dirt dish?" He narrowed his eyes, and pointed a finger. "That's your money maker, right there." We three nodded solemnly at the shared experience of heinous hangovers.

"By the time you stood up, you'd be good as new," I ventured to guess.

"Make it mint-flavored," Patrice said.

"Yeah," I laughed. "Call it Wake-up Sucker."

JT's invention could only have come by being last. He took Patrice's hand, looked into her eyes, lifted her palm to his lips and then kissed it gently. "I'd invent a way to bottle this fine lady's kisses." Bob and I groaned and yelled, "Cop-out!" The two of them kissed passionately, probably just to spite us, so Bob and I lobbed grapes at the back of JT's head.

One time the guys loaded two canoes onto a trailer and we took them to the wetlands north of my hotel. Devin stayed on the bank throwing the Frisbee to Becky as we launched the boats from the dirt bank into the muddy reeds. Our feet squished with mud between our toes and Patrice and I screamed, "yuck-tastic!" If Patrice wasn't so smitten by JT—following his every command, less the salute—I think she would have turned back.

Minutes later, there we were inside the slim boats with our feet hanging over the side. Bob splashed mine clean while JT did the same for Patrice, then we returned the favor. All the while we were chanting, "All limbs akimbo," which made it funny somehow. Once all our limbs were back inside, we rowed off toward the marsh.

Narrow waterways weaved through ten-foot tall grass which grew straight up in the marshy wetlands. We followed each other around grass walls and found ourselves clueless at intersections. Ducks and geese took flight as we swished past them; frogs croaked a bass line for the high pitched concert of whirring insects hidden in the grass. One could get lost in the grassy maze and that, I suppose, for the guys was the fun. Our wanderings became a race. JT beat us back and then it was Devin's turn to try it. Patrice exchanged spots with him, and with Becky inside too, JT rowed back out to the tall reeds.

Since we had to pass the Crowne Plaza to get back to Tidbit mansion, Hippy Bob suggested we drop off Devin. Maybe the legs-all-akimbo got things heated up, anyway, he had something to show me upstairs—he whispered that I had to come alone. Dev happily bolted out of the car almost before it came to a complete stop. Naturally I was curious as to what Bob had to show me. It was his tan line. An impressive band of white skin below his Indian-colored abs was well worth the trip upstairs to his room.

Even in the South Carolina humidity, he lit a scented candle and with a click, his iPod went to Al Green's greatest hits. Coaxing me to lie on my stomach, he massaged my shoulders explaining my shoulder blades must be sore—they weren't—from the unaccustomed motion of paddling. We rolled around on the bedspread for a few minutes, then without words gravitated to the shower. Although we'd made love before, taking a shower with Bob was more intimate. In the corner of the huge marble shower was apple-scented body gel that by now had become his signature scent. He explained I needed to experience the "forbidden fruit" starting from my toes up. It was a mix of good, clean, filthy-fun by the time his lips met mine. Then, we wrapped ourselves in plush towels and finished act three on his bed. By this time my inhibitions had washed down the drain and it was my turn to pleasure him. We were compatible in every way. Back and forth between athletic and slow and tender, I liked it best when he spoke softly— describing how it felt to be under me and under my spell. Sitting on his hips, rocking gently to the music I fearlessly smiled and our eyes locked. Oh, yeah.

Toward the end of the week they guys were especially sweet to Devin and said they'll miss him when he goes back to the islands. I announced that when he goes I can't be hanging out like this. Things were too good and I had to descend into writer's hell. Patrice and Devin were making sandwiches in the kitchen, and I was in the yard playing three-man ping-pong with the guys. Each of us held a paddle. The guys were at both ends of the table and I stood at the net. Once the ball was in play it was a fool's rush around the table keeping the ball in motion, all the while we laughed like maniacs.

"Seriously," I said breathlessly, "I have a writing assignment and deadline."

They seemed to find that hilarious. "I give her 'til Monday," JT snickered.

"You better not keep us waiting 'til Tuesday," Hippy Bob said, kissing my bare shoulder as he rounded the table.

They showed little curiosity about my writing assignment, so I didn't bother to fill them in. Patrice stood on the porch and sang out, "Shrimp po-boys, everybody! Starfish and I made our special sauce!"

"Come and get it, dawgs!" my son hollered.

******

Sunday, back in my room, I scowled at the desk piled with folders, clippings, printed off emails, and a tired, yellow legal pad—bent from suitcase rides. Because I write on the beach, the ubiquitous sand had dusted the pages and desk top. I squirmed in the little desk chair. A calendar was taped to the wall. September tenth circled in red: my deadline. Devin was exploring the hotel beachfront, I had a good job and social life, I should be able to pick this up and finish—I told myself. Self said, one summer isn't enough time to finish a hundred pages, while working, dating, raising my son, and producing a talent show. Self taunted me further by pointing out I'd only saved two thousand dollars. Not much to support me after September, either.

I listlessly arranged and rearranged the stacks, my throat squeezed tight. Filling in years of Jack's sexual exploits with co-stars was emotionally draining. I should have never, *ever,* gotten naked with him. I held a picture in my hand and gazed at the carefree smile as he squinted into the frame. On his arm was Shelly Max. The "It Girl" of that year. Easy for her to toss back the mane of curls. She had a hairdresser standing two feet outside the shot of the picture. Probably next to a make-up girl, standing beside the personal trainer who toned the friggin arms she had wrapped around Jack's neck. And Jack? His smile was starting to grate on me as *too* carefree. In the months I'd been writing his biography I'd hoped for an intensity he may be incapable of.

Tapping my pen against the blank page on the legal pad, to the tune of "Old Mc Donald Had a Farm," I sang, *Hopped in the sack in Sydney. Now I'm upside down.*

Geeze, readers want, and the publisher *expects,* all the sordid details—was I one of them?

CHAPTER 22

Tingling with excitement, I rushed up to the Admiralty Club, a free-standing banquet room on the hotel property. There it was. A sign reading: Bacardi Presents 4th of July Island Talent Search SOLD OUT. Wowie-zowie, it is here, it is now, and knowing what JT brings to the stage I knew it would be a huge success. Finally, someone had the presence of mind to drop "idol" from the title.

Inside the atmosphere was charged. The rum promotion undoubtedly fueled the friendly speculative buzz on tonight's winner. Some of the faces I knew but I smiled at everyone. A non-descript middle-aged couple waved me over to aisle seats. He raised his hand in a hello and she smiled sweetly. My mind raced trying to place them. Was it a spa customer? Had she been in a neighboring chair?

"Veronica, dear—how nice to see you." The woman hugged me close and smelled like roses. "You remember my husband, Ted?"

He turned to his wife, "Oh, Gertrude, no one remembers me, I just answer the door." They giggled as if this was a familiar joke.

"Thank you both for coming," I said. "Now, being a psychic, has anyone asked you about tonight's outcome?" As

127

soon as I blurted out the tactless comment, I regretted it. She didn't seem to take offence.

"I'm just here to have a good time like everyone else," she replied nonchalantly.

I leaned in. "You told me to watch out that I may lose something very valuable. I want to thank you for the advice, and I'm working on that now."

She looked away at first and then held my gaze, before breaking the moment with a crooked smile. Why did she have to be so cryptic? I considered pressing her about tonight's outcome, but remembered I got a freebie when I returned her cell phone and it's probably rude to sponge a reading. Anyway, everyone knew that JT would win.

The background music faded and the houselights dimmed. I took a deep breath and climbed the short staircase on the side of the stage. The mic had been adjusted for my height. I was nervous for some reason; perhaps unaccustomed to everyone paying attention. I held on to the mic stand and appraised the crowd assembled in the overflowing banquet room. "Thank you all for coming. We'll get right to the show, but first a few announcements. Tomorrow, on Independence Day, the Fourth of July, there'll be three fireworks displays. Bring a lawn chair to any of these locations: Shelter Cove Marina, Harbor Town Marina or Skull Creek." A huge applause and whistles cut me off.

"I'm guessing that excitement is also for tonight's winner—" Names were called out from the back accompanied by good-natured laughter. "Next Saturday in the Portz Bar, here at the lovely Crowne Plaza, the Hallelujah Singers will perform, along with their high-spirited," I looked at the card, "five-piece band, 'Juba,' it says here, it's a legacy of the Gullah culture from its roots in Africa to the present day. Also, July 10th, a week from today, the Crowne Plaza welcomes celebrities and star athletes to the Nissan- Palmolive golf tournament.

"Now, listen carefully. Tonight, everyone gets *two* votes for the Island Idol. Write down your first *and* second choice. The cards will be picked up by your servers after the last act. Bacardi Girls, wave your hands!"

The waitresses clad in Bacardi tank tops threw their hands in the air, to loud cheers.

"Your favorite act gets two points," I continued, "your second choice gets one point. Judges, please stand and wave!"

The three stood up from their front row seats as I introduced them. They turned and faced the audience with a wave and sat down. The crowd clapped a respectful "golf-clap" and I continued.

"Each judge picks only one winner," I explained. "That person gets five points. Our Food & Beverage Manager, Dave Lindsey, will announce the winner about ten p.m., awarding the Island Idol with $5,000, generously contributed by Bacardi, *the world's smoothest rum.* Or, maybe it just seems so after Earl mixes it up at the bar." There were more whoops from the back of the room as I looked down at the faces in the front row. "Are you girls rum and Coke fans? I personally like pineapple juice and Bacardi."

The blond in front pumped her fist in the air and shouted out, "Mai Tais!"

I signaled the tech guy and the room fell to darkness. "Our first finalist is from Buellton. He has been an active member of the Kiwanis Club and some of you may know him as last year's Chili Cook-off winner. Put your hands together for the tap dancing stylings of Ralph Jesse Bernal!"

Once off stage, I bumped into JT in the wings. He looked gorgeous in his black jeans, boots, and pale blue shirt. He had star quality you could spot from low-flying aircraft. "Hi. Oh, so glad to see you got here early," I whispered.

"Did you think I was going to flake out?" he smiled.

I motioned away from the stage to the three steps leading to the hall and he followed me. "I heard you had a lot of fans from The Jazz Corner here," I said. "It should be a good night."

"Oh, yeah." He looked down, adjusting his guitar strap. JT's confidant swagger wasn't an off-putting conceit. It somehow added to his smoldering sub-layer of charisma. He smelled of cologne, a dark masculine scent that was undoubtedly another reason for Patrice's mad attraction. It seemed that he was eager to spring out on stage and rock the house. Somehow I sensed tonight's performance might even top the last one, and I caught my mind lingering a little too long in JT fan land.

"Are Bob and Patrice out there?" I asked. "I taped-off two seats in the second row, but didn't see them. Did Devin's taxi get him to your place on time?"

"Bob came with me, so he's somewhere. Why don't you let him take your wheels?" JT asked.

"Because the hotel loaned the car to me—and someone might say something about my kid driving it. Plus—he could get lost."

JT flashed a dazzling smile. "Don't you worry, girl. Devin's with Becky now. Hey, you look like you could use one of those rum drinks you was talking about."

I motioned toward the tapping onstage. "I'm actually nervous for the contestants. It means so much to these guys. My heart goes out to each and every one of them. It's different for you, JT. You're talented and used to performing and being admired—" I stopped myself from adding a dozen more compliments. I needed to show objectivity. "But, for a dental hygienist, this is a huge deal."

He ran his hand through his thick crop of blond hair and grinned. "If you're talking about Miss Ample Chest—I don't think *she* needs to worry. The word around town is she's hustling up every family within twenty miles of the dentist's office."

"I saw her entire Jazzercise class on row two," I added.

"How could you know it was her exercise class?"

"They wore T-shirts saying 'Jazzercise votes for Lucinda.'"

JT chuckled, then cupped his hand around his mouth. "She's dropped those flyers all over. I heard she fills vending machines with condoms at truck stops, on the side."

"So do you think there are guys out there wearing condoms, that say: Condom wearers vote for Lucinda?"

JT whispered, "I saw guys wearing buttons that said, 'when you give 'em the love—wear Lucinda's glove'."

"What!" I almost shouted.

"I gotcha," he said laughing quietly. We shoved each other, laughing more. I leaned in, saying, "Anyway, I gotta run. The tap dancer is almost tapped out."

"Here's my intro card, sweetheart." JT pecked me on the cheek as he put it in my hand. "Thanks for getting Patrice and Bob VIP seating. Otherwise they'd be outside. Heck, she's later than me. The sign said the show's sold out."

*****

Backstage, John Martin, the accountant, was absently clicking buttons on his calculator. "How long do you think this is going to last?" He said, looking up. "I'm getting hungry. Why did I get here so early? I should have come later."

"John," I said, "let me get some fries sent back here for you. When the harmonica player gets off stage, I'll find a waiter." John seemed happy again. I checked my watch and took a seat beside him at the long table. "Last time, when the audience had just one vote, it was clearly a popularity contest. This way, David and I figured people would vote for their friend, and that's okay, but the *second* vote would be for someone else who might actually deserve it."

"Unless," the accountant said dryly, "they use the second vote for the worst act."

"Why would anyone do that?"

"Because, in a close race, you don't want to give a point to a close competitor. If my kid was out there, I'd vote for the *least* likely to beat her. You don't want to help someone good—maybe better—who might tip the scale away from your kid."

"How can you think that way?" I turned away in disgust and rose from the table.

"I'm a mathematician—remember? It's all in the numbers."

CHAPTER 23

Lucinda burst on to center stage. In a tight pink dress she looked like a flamingo testing the water, given the length of her legs and they way she extended them. There was the usual applause and the audience settled down to hear the familiar introductory chords to the song, "Crazy." If there ever was a karaoke standard, that was it. I stood in the wings with Ken the ventriloquist. With his puppet at his side, he was poised to go on next. Anticipating a train wreck with Lucinda's act, I scheduled the hilarious Ken and Casey to follow.

I groaned and turned to him, asking, "How many chick singers does it take to sing, 'Crazy'?"

"Okay." He played along. "How many?"

"Evidently, all of them."

I couldn't help but chuckle. "As a chick singer, I want to go on record: I've never sung that song without a request. It's a great song but it's a little over done."

"She sounds a little *under* done, if you ask me." The duck puppet said, bobbing his head toward me.

"Crazy for feeling so looooan—i—ly"

We exchanged glances. I couldn't know my expression, but Ken looked like he'd stepped in quicksand.

I mumbled, "I guess she got feedback that her last song was too ambitious and she went for an easier standard."

"Crap-tast-tic," the puppet said.

It was madness to pretend I was unbiased, but I tried. "I guess she has a wide vibrato, huh?"

"You could drive a tank through it," the duck observed.

As she sang, each note slid up to the proper pitch in a slow, painful rise. Just when she finally hit the right note, the chord had changed—because the song moved on—leaving a clash of epic proportions. Now our tired ears were in for another search-and-rescue mission as Lucinda explored the scale for the next note. I felt myself squinting for some reason, tensing up, anticipating the next horrific ledge this song would dangle from. People have pitch problems, okay. But it was hard to watch—a bit like Jessica Simpson and her dramatic facials, only on steroids. Lucinda clung to each flat note with the passionate expression of a silent film star. Unfortunately, what she lacked in talent, she made up for in volume; the warbling overpowered the room. And the parking lot. And the harbor. And the entire hapless island.

I stepped from the shadows to check the faces on the front row. "If this was a fight, I'd stop it," I whimpered.

"Crazy for ly…ing…Crazy for try…..ing, I'mmmmm…."

"Crazy for tryin', all right." Ken shook the puppet's wooden head and stared forlornly at the stage. "She's suckin' all of the oxygen out of the room." He looked at me.

"I'm so sorry you have to follow that, Ken." I whispered, patting his free arm. "Look, let's go out on stage together. We'll forego the introduction."

He shrugged, then nodded.

"As soon as the wail dies down, we race out there and you start your set." Watching Lucinda at the mic with her eyebrows arched, eyes shut and mouth in a perfect oval, made me re-think my profession. Such ghastly incidents set the vocal arts back a thousand years. "There may be fruit thrown," I warned.

"I saw orange slices on the Mai Tais," Ken mumbled.

Moments later, we ran out on stage. "Thank you, Lucinda," I shouted as I grabbed her hand, mid curtsy, and shuffled her offstage. "Now let's give a big welcome to Ken and Casey!" Thankfully, the ventriloquist team won back the audience. After that came the kids act. It was a brother and sister who danced adagio style with grace. The song was "Dancing in the Dark" and it was in homage to Ginger Rogers and Fred Astaire. The adorable duo also held the audience's attention.

A few more acts and it was time for JT to close the show with a spirited version of "Driftaway," the rock standard written by Mentor Williams and made famous again by Uncle Cracker. *Gimme the beat, boys, to free my soul—wanna get lost in your rock n roll and driftaway....* Generously, he encouraged the audience to sing along with the chorus, but the verses were solidly JT's own soulful Southern blues. The show closed with everyone on their feet cheering. I reminded the crowd to mark down their TWO favorite acts and that we'd be back after a fifteen minute intermission.

What an adrenaline rush! It was almost the end of the night and my first ever talent show was coming to such a thrilling end. With the room buzzing with energy, it was time to duck outside. The summer night was pleasantly without wind and as always warm. I was used to the humidity, which now seemed like Mother Nature's balmy moisture on my skin. As I walked behind the hotel following a path of lush foliage I left the din of chatter and the faint scent of cigar smoke.

With my arms crossed in front of my chest, I rubbed the tension from the tops of my shoulders and down my arms. It occurred to me Patrice and Bob would be looking for me. No matter. This was my moment to savor success. The initial irritation and dread going into the project had turned into a sentimental mush of pride for the contestants and deep respect for how hard they worked to entertain. Our Fourth of July bash had been a terrific boost for the island. The show was terrific.

Even Lucinda, bless her heart, had given it her all. With Bacardi paying the prize money, the hotel got positive press and plenty of good will in the community, not to mention plenty an infusion of cha-ching at the bar. So what if there wasn't any pay for me, I can't say that I blamed them. This hadn't been tried before and we were all surprised it sold out. At least I got two nights off work to run the show.

I paused a moment by the hammock to give Devin a call. He reported that the ice cream was great, and he wanted to go back to taking guitar lessons. Then, impishly, he asked, "People can't tell if you've been playing their guitars, right?" I chuckled and agreed, *people* couldn't tell, unless you de-tuned them into a different key. Apparently when I called he had been outside playing Frisbee with the dog. There were elaborate outside lights so he could play basketball too. As I clicked the phone shut I heard footsteps coming toward me on the path.

"Veronica? Is that you?"

"David?" I stepped out into the light. "Oh, hi. I needed to get away from the crowd for some air—nothing's wrong, is it?"

"No, no. Everything is keeno, slicko, sharpo," he exclaimed, then extended a one-armed squeeze. As we walked along the path he thanked me for all the work I'd put into the show. His wife and father-in-law had even called him a mover and a shaker. All week he'd been enjoying hero status at home. "I'm recommending to the GM that you get a bonus for all your efforts in making this the best Fourth of July we ever had," he finally told me.

"Aw, really? That's cool—I'll take it. Thank you, but either way, it was fun. So, we better get back. It's about time to award JT the big check, I mean—whoever wins the big check." We walked back toward the building swinging our arms and almost skipping with joy.

All of a sudden my bra was vibrating. I stashed my cell phone there when I didn't carry a purse. As David blah-blahed on, I discreetly flipped it open to peek at Bob's text message on the tiny screen. *Let's celebrate, baby! I want to ravage U 2nite. I got champagne.*

With no time to be clever, I sent back the response I always got from Devin. *"K."*

CHAPTER 24

When I returned to the building, I headed down the hall to the little room where I'd left our CPA, John, eating French fries. The door was locked for some reason, hmmm; I'd never noticed a lock on that little room behind the stage. Polite knocking led to pounding. I was getting annoyed. There was no time for this nonsense.

I grabbed a passing waiter and neither of us could understand how we got locked out. The waiter reminded me it was almost ten. I explained I needed to stay backstage and find David and John. He said he'd tell the audio guy to announce everyone return to their seats. Meanwhile, I pressed my ear to the door. There were voices arguing inside.

My face nearly got smashed when the door abruptly opened. David was as startled as I was. He gasped and clutched his heart.

"What happened?" I said.

He shuddered and looked past me.

"Did Bacardi back out?" I cried. "They won't deliver the check?"

He waved an envelope in the air. "It's in here."

"Then what's wrong? You're as white as Weber's bread!"

David's face was the classic tragedy mask—with mouth contorted, eyebrows in a frown. "I can never go home," he rasped.

"Tell me," I said as I gripped his arm. "Did the sponsors say he can't cash the check—now?"

David stuck a finger in his collar and yanked the fabric from his neck. "The winner isn't a *he*." Then, he dashed around me and disappeared down the hall toward the door leading up to the stage.

The soundman's voice boomed through the speakers. "The Island Idol is about to be announced. Take your seats, ladies and gentlemen. This first annual Fourth of July event is as hot as tomorrow night's firecrackers! As hot as Harold's Chili! As hot as the Bacardi girls in bikinis!" Everyone roared with approval. I froze in the hall.

The voice boomed again. "Now, everybody sit down in your seats and put your hands together for Kent Nasser, Bacardi Rum's regional manager, and our sponsor. Let's hear it for Bacardi Rum's Island Idol! He's coming to the stage to announce the winner!"

This thing had taken on a life of its own. Was I no longer in the loop? David undoubtedly was heading for the stage. The sponsor was already coming up to present the check. I was stupefied; as I stood in the hall. Should I dash out front and watch the end of the contest—the culmination of all my work? I eyed the open door to the office. I spun around and pushed the door open. John Martin was already packing up.

"Why was that door locked?" I hissed. "This is my contest and I don't appreciate being locked out at such a critical moment."

John looked weary but said nothing. Then, he went back to shuffling things into his briefcase.

"This shows me no respect— David didn't even apologize, he just—" I sunk into a chair. "Oh, my God. She won."

John's tone was flat. "Lucinda is the new Island Idol."

I wrapped my arms around my legs and rocked in the narrow folding chair. "I can't go out there," I gasped, "Ever."

"Veronica, there was nothing anyone could do. Even though second place gets just *one* point, almost every ballot gave Lucinda a vote. It added up that she got three more points than JT. Do you want to see the numbers or count them yourself?"

"This didn't happen," I whimpered into my palms.

"David argued with me. He did *not* want her to win. He invited her to join the contest and got the big idea to put her on the damn flyers because she's a looker. Believe me, the last thing he wants to do is face his wife and the G.M. when his friend, the lousy singer, won. But…" he shrugged, "she got the most votes."

John scraped a metal chair over beside me. The shrill sound caused me to cringe further inside myself. "I'm a trusted employee of the Crowne Plaza. Sworn to do the numbers, not cook the books—even for a talent show. I told David, no."

I sulked in my chair, staring down at my knees.

"We CPA's work with numbers without emotion. It's just shapes on a page, dear. I'm sorry." He stood up. "Thanks for the malt and fries."

A long spasm rose up from my solar plexus and erupted into a throaty gulp for air and an inevitable cry. My head sunk into my hands. "I can *never* face JT again," I sobbed. "Or Patrice or Bob, or anyone in this town. I hate this place. Why did I do it? JT, *poor* JT."

At that moment my bra vibrated. It was such a personal moment, to be weeping in front of a clinical accountant for one thing, and then to have my boobs shaken by an outside entity. On the second vibration I yanked it from my bra and flipped it open. It was a text. *I'll meet U at your room in 15, ok? Bob.*

John stood up and reached across the table. He shook a napkin out from his tray of dead food. "Wipe your eyes on this." I watched as he folded it into a triangle, looking for a clean corner. "Watch out for the salt. Here, this end is barely soiled."

There was a commotion in the hall. We heard a garble of sounds, probably audience reaction to the announcement. JT referred to her as "Miss Ample Chest," now she had another title. I didn't know and I didn't *want* to know how the community felt about this Fourth of July stink bomb.

The phone I was squeezing in my hand began to vibrate. I saw Bob had sent another text, *what's the room # again?* I texted back the answer.

John excused himself and I locked the door behind him. I dipped the napkin into his ice water and washed my face, then grabbed my purse and snuck out.

Having lived in the hotel a while, I knew my way around. I took the service elevator up to my floor. In my room I brushed my teeth and peeled off my clothes, replacing my finery with soft jeans and a white, sleeveless turtleneck sweater. I lit a couple scented candles and turned the TV on low.

A customer had given me a bottle of Merlot on my first night, it still sat on my dresser. Caving in to rudeness, I didn't wait for Bob, just poured a glass. The pity-party had begun. Sweet Bob was bringing champagne? Pshh. Little rich boy. He probably couldn't understand a level-four humiliation like this. I drank greedily and heard myself swallow. I felt like a drifter, hunched over a trashcan, guzzling cheap swill from a wrinkled bag, as I gripped the squat water glass filled with wine. A soft knock startled me. I opened the door and he stepped inside. Without a word I stood on tiptoe and gave Bob a kiss.

"Hey, little darlin'," he spoke in his soft Southern lilt. "It smells good in here." He set a bottle on the door.

"Thanks." We kissed again.

"I'm just glad to finally be alone with you." He looked adorable and so genuinely happy to see me; I already felt a little shiver of pleasure just being in his arms. His hands slowly rubbed up and down my back, then finally settled on my waist.

He nuzzled my neck. "I called Devin during the break. He's staying the night. He said it was 'chill.'"

"I might, I might as…well say this and get it over with," I stammered.

Bob kissed my shoulder and we lingered by the door a moment more. Then he slowly pulled back and held up the bottle of champagne. "Will this fit inside your little fridge for now?"

"Sure, I'll jam it in. Thanks." I motioned to my glass on the dresser. "Forgive me for drinking without you. Want one?"

"You didn't start without me. You forgot I was in the rum capital of the South for the last couple hours. Pineapple and Rum, Mai-tais, Cuba Libres."

"Oh, yeah. About that." I sighed and sank into the chair by the wall. "Did you see JT after the show?"

"No. He must have taken off like a hornet. Patrice and I looked for him, but…"

"Everyone used their second vote for the worst person. The thinking—I realize now—was to assure their favorite person would get the most votes. No one voted for second best. The worst act won. There, I said it."

Bob picked me up. With one arm under my back and the other supporting my knees, he lifted me like a groom crossing a threshold. I leaned into his chest grateful that, for at least a moment, I didn't have to support myself. My head rested against the stiff starched shirt and I inhaled his scent of smoke, booze and after shave. I met his gaze with, "Now, what are you going to do with me?"

He buried his mouth in my neck. "I think you know. Little darlin', you've had a long night. Now it's time to slow down and get Uncle Bob's special back rub."

I giggled, which seemed inappropriately juvenile, but I couldn't think of anything sexy or playful to say to match the mood. "I'm sorry for laughing. I guess 'Uncle Bob' sounded funny or maybe lecherous. Anyway, I feel shy."

"I thought we took care of all that shyness last time I was here." He grinned and looked at me with those half-closed, sexy eyes.

I looked at his shirt. "I relapsed. The shyness is back."

He gently rolled me out of his arms onto the bed, then switched off the lamp. "Shhh, we've got *all* night. I've been chasing you around this little island long enough. Just be still while I ravish you."

CHAPTER 25

From inside my deep sleep there was the distant sound of ringing. Hoping to silence it, I reached for a pillow to cover my head. That's when I touched a human and bolted upright. A slice of light intruded from the part in the drapes, and I recognized Bob's lanky, naked form on top of the covers.

"You better get that," he mumbled, as he reached behind for a handful of covers.

"Heh." My voice was hoarse. I tried again. "Hello?"

"Mom, don't get mad."

"Devin. What happened?"

"Mom, so when JT got home, I was upstairs watching a DVD, 'cause like, they said I could and…"

"Devin, just say it. What happened?" I was alert now. Across the room I saw the clock's digits glowing green in the dark. It was two-fifteen.

"So, I don't know when I fell asleep, but JT comes in a little while ago and he tells me Becky's gone. He's really pissed-off, Mom. I gotta get out a here."

"Uh, oh. Becky's gone?" I repeated the words and Bob jackknifed into a sitting position. I hushed him.

"I'll come get you. Did you leave the gate open? Did you look everywhere?"

Devin started crying over the phone.

"JT didn't hit you or anything?" I asked.

"Hurry, Mom." He sniffed. "No. He didn't, but, I can't hang here. It's harsh."

I hung up. Bob was swishing his arm between the sheets, fishing for abandoned clothes. He turned on the lamp and we both squinted at the room. Clothes were strewn all over the place. Crackers had spilled out of a box beside the champagne bottle lying on its side.

"Wow, that was a shock," I said, swinging my legs to the side of the bed and sitting up. As I rubbed my temples, I wished I'd taken an aspirin with a gallon of water after the ravish.

"This is serious," Bob said slowly, "if Becky's gone."

"Yes, I know, Bob," I said tersely. "JT has already intimidated my son. Devin's no saint, but I don't see why everyone assumes he did something wrong."

"I'm not everyone. I'm just saying it's not a good thing."

"I'm going to pick him up now," I told him. "And yes, I'm very aware it's not a good thing."

*****

This was definitely going to be ugly and I was dressed for it. My hair was a tumbleweed, dark make-up had smeared beneath my eyes, and I was in the nether world of half drunk and hung-over. I stuffed a couple pieces of gum into my dry mouth and aggressively chomped.

Bob got in my car and we silently drove over to Pinewood, arriving in the pitch-black at three-fifteen a.m.. This next hour was going to be the cringe-Olympics. Facing JT, after the debacle of the talent contest? *Gawd.* Facing Devin, as Bob and I arrive, clearly having spent the night together? *Gulp.* After frolicking intimately, Bob may side against me. JT was furious. Is he blaming my son for the lost dog?

Devin was going home in two days. Why did this have to happen? I slapped my steering wheel so hard it hurt the heel of my hand. The only other sound was the familiar sound of pine needles crunching below my tires, along with a deafening pulse beating in my ears.

I wished I could just hop on a plane and split this god-forsaken island, like I did in Sydney. Pacing in my luxurious hotel room, waiting for Jack to grant me a meeting to finish his biography, now seemed like a breeze compared to the Lucinda, JT, lost dog, Devin, and Hippy Bob jambalaya.

Taking a deep breath, my evolved self, "Alma," tried to soothe my primitive-reactionary self, "Freaka." It was exhausting hearing Alma try to coax Freaka off the ledge. *Just calm down. We just need to put up some lost dog signs.*

Devin met me at the car, opened the door and Bob got out and he climbed in before the engine was off. "Something's weird here, Mom. JT is all agro. I told him, dude, I'll make up some signs and plaster 'em all over, but he kept saying I don't understand. I told him I do understand, that once 'Sandy' ran away and …."

I flipped down the visor mirror and surveyed the damage. I looked like a depressed raccoon. "Oh, well. Just stay here, Devin. I'll be right back."

The parlor light was on. I braced myself and walked up to the house. The moon was half full and it was easy to find my way.

JT was sitting on the couch with his legs splayed. He was wearing the same great outfit he'd worn at the show, only this time, his eyes weren't twinkling. His cigarette glowed and I noticed there was a full ashtray on the antique table beside him. Under the circumstances, it was probably not a good idea to rebuke him for smoking in the house.

"Hi, JT. So sorry about your dog." I guess my voice lacked sincerity at this hour because he shot me a look of pure hatred. I dropped down on the closest chair. Bob called out he was making coffee. We sat in silence. The only sound was Bob clanging around the kitchen.

"I'm sorry that the audience voted for the worst act," I began. "You see, Ken and Casey had a lot of fans, as did you. The accountant explained that each of your fans didn't want to give the other good act—a vote. So, they threw it away on the worst act. Anyway, that coffee smells good. Do you think we ought to caffeine-up at this hour?"

JT's eyes were still focused on the carpet. He didn't look at me when I spoke. No wonder Devin wanted out of this place. In the middle of the night, with the smoke hanging above the antique furniture, it looked the parlor of handsome, over dressed, brooding, vampire Le Stat.

"How about," I began weakly, "I come back in the morning with some signs we can post around—"

"NO!" he barked.

Bob entered the parlor with a tray of dainty coffee cups and saucers. What was it with these guys and the trays? "It's half-caffeine," was all he said.

I reached for the elegant china cup and the small pitcher of cream." Thank you, so much." I ran a hand over the back of my hair and my fingers caught in the mass. The sound of my spoon hitting the side of the cup clanged as loud as a bell calling in farm hands.

JT produced a silver flask from out of the air and poured something into his coffee. "Want some?" he mumbled to Bob. Bob nodded. Now I felt both invisible *and* despised.

"Okay, no signs." I tried to take any amount of chipper out of my tone. "Should we...you don't think we should go out in the dark *now,* do you?" Gratefully, neither of them moved, they just sat brooding. The air was so heavy with smoke and bad vibes, the only thing missing was a Satanic ritual. I wanted to jolt them out of their stupor by yelling, It's *a dog, people!* But, instead, I offered, "After this coffee, we could go look around again. Do you have flashlights?"

JT just shook his head as he pondered the carpet threads. I was so anxious that I couldn't bear it any longer. I looked at my wrist, but I wasn't wearing a watch. "Okay, it's getting late. So, bye for now. Sorry if Devin had anything to do with it. I'll call in the morning and if the dog, I mean, Becky, hasn't been found, then I'll come back with Patrice and Devin and we can ask some others to help us and..."

"We have to find her ourselves," Bob finally spoke up. "No signs. We're keeping this quiet."

"Quiet?" I looked from face to face.

"Quiet," JT affirmed.

"All *righty* then," I chirped, then winced at my accidental homage to Jim Carey. I stood up, placed my cup on the tray and walked out the door.

Gratefully, Devin was snoring in the car when I trotted up for my quick getaway. We drove home and in a daze staggered to our separate rooms for a few hours sleep.

*****

From four forty-five to seven a.m. was a disconcerting fake kind of sleep, made disturbingly nostalgic by Bob's delicious scent lingering on my pillow. My dream was a spiral staircase heading down, a collage of last night's sensual love—then down more metal steps and a frightening sensation of driving lost, swerving, in the night fog. Spidery vines hung down scraping my windshield as my car raced down a path without headlights. Then, hot kisses on my breasts by an unseen figure, panting like a wolf. Repelled, yet drawn to my captors—shifty figures whose faces were hidden behind masks. Then, my hands were held above my head on the pillow by my lover holding me gently, and then the bed turned into a cot in a smoky dungeon of terror. Wolves were howling in the distance. Or, was it dogs?

CHAPTER 26

I'd been eyeing the shadows on the ceiling, trying to build momentum to roll out of bed, when the phone rang. It was Devin calling to ask if there was any news on Becky and should we meet at the coffee shop to pound food. I preferred to duck out of the hotel to eat. Neither David nor the GM had been around much since the contest. We somehow had been able to avoid seeing each other, and that worked for me.

I dressed quickly, grabbed my keys and we met in the parking lot. I directed Devin to the back seat and we jetted away from the Crowne Plaza. I punched in Patrice's number as we headed down the road and trying not to plead, I said, "Please meet with us. I know you probably want to get back to the spa, but—"

"It's closed today." Hearing her voice was a relief. I needed to process last night.

"Have you forgotten, it's the Fourth of July?" she said, then let out a sad little squeal, like a kitten yawning. "I never got a chance to tell you how great the contest was last night. Well, right up till they announced the winner. Then it really sucked. What in the hell happened?"

"I'll pick you up in fifteen. It actually goes downhill from there."

Patrice stood at the gate of her condo sporting a lime green and tan shorts outfit, jeweled flip-flops, and an awesome leather bag. She always looked like a magazine cover girl. I could imagine her running out of a burning building at three a.m. It would look like a Victoria's Secret shoot. God forgive me for that image. Once she was beside me in the Corolla, I filled her in on the last eight hours.

Patrice grabbed my arm. "So you think someone knew that JT and Bob would be gone?"

"Some jerk was an opportunist, and it happened on my kid's watch."

"Why would anyone want that dog? Besides, it would have to be a couple people, think how big the dog is. Huh?"

Devin piped up from the back seat. "Not really. Just wag a pork chop and a dog would run into an on-coming train."

"He's got his mother's wit," Patrice observed. "Back to the contest, Vee. JT didn't take it well."

I groaned and covered my eyes with one hand.

"Hey, watch the road," my passengers shouted.

"Which surprised me," Patrice continued, "because he always has such a, such a—?"

"Poised demeanor," I filled in.

"And, *doesn't* need the money," she said, shaking a finger.

I muttered, "So I had to twist his arm to enter the contest and he acts like I broke it when he lost."

"Where're we eating, Mom? I'm starving." Devin pounded the window. "Pull over, there's a donut shop,"

"Hang on, we're almost to the diner." I stepped on the accelerator. "I need real food. When we stop, Devin, honey, I want you to think of every detail of last night."

"Maybe we could call the pet detective?" he said as he bounced off the seat. "Like Jim Carey, huh? They got this show on TV called *Animal Psychic*…I saw it once."

"Wait a minute, guys. Listen." I slapped the steering wheel. "When I went to Gertrude the Oracle she told me I was in danger of losing something valuable. *This* is it!"

Patrice grabbed my arm. "It's not valuable to anyone else. It's only a dog. Hey, be careful and watch the road, you almost rear-ended that guy."

"Mom, slow down," Devin hollered over my shoulder.

"I hope this place is open on a holiday," I said.

"Yeah," Devin said, "Oh Mom, where are we going to see fireworks?"

I sighed loudly and I think everyone caught my drift; they got quiet.

We pulled into Harold's Diner on two wheels with gravel spraying all over. I directed them to go inside and order me anything. Next, I called Bob. I gave him the rundown on my reading with Gertrude. He'd never heard of her but listened politely. Gertrude's number was stored in my cell phone, so I gave it to him with a strong message for JT to get an appointment immediately. It was a long shot, but I wanted them to know I was taking some responsibility in Becky's disappearance, even if I had to rattle the spirit world.

Inside the coffee shop, Patrice was playing good-cop with Devin trying to jar his memory. I slid in next to her and stared across the booth at the last person to see the missing victim. He mentioned something odd. Cackling with laughter, Devin described a picture he saw hanging in a room upstairs.

"It was hilarious." Devin basked in the attention. "Because, who wants a gargantuan-sized painting of some old lady and the dog? It was the size of a movie poster. Becky is a straight-up, cool dog, but if you're gonna paint a painting, don't you want some smokin' hot babe next to her?"

"Did you ever see that picture, Patrice?"

"No. It was probably their Aunt Lila. Besides, I wasn't in all the rooms. Not that I wasn't curious." Then demurely, "It's just that JT and I hung out mainly in…well, some of the other rooms."

The waiter dropped off two plates of burgers and fries and a salad for Patrice. I thanked Devin for picking my food. He reached for a handful of fries. "They weren't home so I was looking in all the rooms. With the wind blowing it was like going through the haunted mansion. I even carried a candle around like they did in *Frankenstein*."

"What else did you see?" I asked.

"There was some suitcases lined up."

"Where?"

"In Becky's room."

"There's a *dog* room?"

"Yeah, Becky has her own room. It's like a low bed with those poles going up and a little bedspread thing stretched across the top."

"A canopy?" I offered and he nodded.

"She's got her dog toys in there. A bunch of 'em, and some trophies and more pictures of her."

"Are there any pictures of Becky with Bob and JT?" I wanted to know.

"I didn't see any."

"Devin," I leaned across the table. "Were the suitcases heavy? Like someone was packed? Or empty?"

"Hey, I didn't lift 'em. I saw about three in a row and they were in the middle of the dog room with a towel laid over the top."

"Would we assume someone was hiding the suitcases, by laying a big towel on top?"

Patrice slapped her hand on the Formica table, rattling our glasses. "What are you getting at, Nancy Grace? I don't like the tone of these questions. Devin, did you see any pictures of JT with any girls lying around?"

Devin cackled with glee. "Just the one with Brittany Spears."

"Come on, Dev. Be serious." I kicked him lightly under the table.

He lit up. "There was a big map of Spain on the table."

I sat back in the booth and closed my eyes. "I'm going to catch up on some sleep." Devin bounced in his seat. "Let's all meet at Harbour Town and check out the fireworks. Okay, Patrice?"

"Tiki Hut at seven—got it," she said.

"Mom, can I call the dog pound at least? I feel really janky about what happened. I shoulda never fallen asleep. I don't think I was asleep that long, anyway."

Patrice reached for his hand across the table. "It's a national holiday. Everything is closed. But we can definitely do that in the morning. Okay?"

"I'm leaving in the morning," he said softly.

I reached across and held their four hands in mine. "I know, and we all know, you wouldn't leave the gate open. Or, let anyone in. We just don't know why she would want to go with someone…some, stranger?"

Devin's eyes got big. "So, you think some tool jacked her?"

"Yup," I sighed, "I think some jerk took her on purpose."

CHAPTER 27

After lunch, Patrice stayed with me at the hotel. Devin hopped out before we even parked. It was his last day and he planned on being at the beach all day. We girls needed some alone time to catch up on the post contest activities, so we went to my room, put on swimsuits and headed for the pool. I needed to vent about Bob and my sexy explosion. I told her about how we nestled in each other's arms, before we were struck with after-glow interruptus: Devin's call. Hey—I held up my end of good times in room 521 last night.

Patrice and I found a couple of lounge chairs and dragged them to the most remote shaded spot around the pool. Patrice went to the bar and returned with Bloody Marys. We sipped and slouched in our side-by-side recliners.

"So," I said, adjusting my hat, "about last night—"

She lowered her sunglasses to the bridge of her nose and spoke slowly. "JT sure acted pissed-off for someone who didn't need prize money."

"Un-hum. What happened when the contest ended? I was backstage. Oh, and spare me the details of Lucinda accepting the check. What happened when you saw JT?"

"We talked on the phone immediately after—it was a mad house in there. Anyway, we agreed to meet at his place. Then, while I was driving over, he called and changed his mind. He said he was in a bad mood and just blew me off, basically. Said he'd see me tomorrow. I told him he was terrific in the show and I was sorry about what happened. Neither of us could figure out why he didn't win...."

I filled her in on 'why bad things happen to good acts' and as we chatted softly, across the pool a woman seemed focused on us. I'd noticed her scanning the area near the lifeguard stand and now she was walking in our direction. As she was wearing a sun visor, tube top and shorts, it was hard to place the face. It was the swinging hips balanced on three inch platform sandals that looked familiar.

"There you are, Veronica." She pointed at me from eight feet away.

"Oh, hi." Then, I blurted out. "What are you doing here? How did you find me?"

"I went to the front desk. They rang your room. You weren't there and I thought to myself, Lucinda, where would I be on this pretty day? So I came outside and asked the lifeguard if he's seen you. Wow, here you are." She raised her glasses up and swept the frames to her head.

Her eyes fell on Patrice. "Excuse me for barging in. I'm Lucinda."

Patrice extended her hand and congratulated her on last night.

I managed to croak, "Yes, congratulations."

"That's why I'm here, to thank you. Remember when I heard you singing at the piano bar, the first time we met?"

"Yeah," I said.

"And I asked you to help me prepare for the contest?"

"Uh huh," I said, reaching for my drink.

"You told me I could do it myself, and by-golly, that's what I did. Can I sit down?" Without waiting for an answer, she dragged over a chair.

I was never so glad to be wearing sunglasses. My dad used to say that watching me listen to a conversation was like watching TV with the sound off; all my innermost thoughts cross my face. Holding on to a rigid, pleasant expression is hard.

As she positioned herself in front of us, my cell rang. Patrice and Lucinda made small talk as I combed through my purse for the phone. It was a brief conversation. I turned my attention back to them. Patrice waited for a pause in Lucinda's stream of words and asked who called.

"Bob said no news on finding her."

"Nothing?" Patrice moaned. "Maybe we'll grab Devin and have our own search party. Huh?"

Lucinda perked up. "Uh-oh, is someone missing? Can I help?"

I batted the air. "Our friend's dog got out last night. We're all pretty upset that we can't find it."

"Dr. McWalters has a patient who died and left all her earthly belongings to her pooch. Swear to God. Can you believe it?"

"Really?" I said. Are you talking about Leona Helmsley, the New York hotel owner? Is that *his* patient?"

Lucinda shrugged.

Patrice added, "It was in all the papers."

"Maybe that's who it was." Lucinda nodded. "Anyway, Veronica, I brought you a gift card for a complimentary teeth-cleaning. You can use it *anytime* you want to. You were so nice to me. And everyone here at the Crowne Plaza was so sweet. David Lindsey, and Mr. Nasser from Bacardi, just everyone. They gave me a big ole bottle of their best dark rum, even. I have a gift card for David Lindsey too. Have you seen him?"

Patrice's phone rang and she moved away from us.

"No, I haven't. But thanks for the card." I flashed a toothy smile and hoped it passed her professional eye. "What do you plan on doing with the money, if you don't mind me asking?"

"Savings. I already deposited it in the ATM this morning." She positively radiated joy. "Isn't it hard to believe all this excitement is over? Last night seems so long ago. Are you having a contest next year, too?"

"Last night seems like years ago to me, also. Hey, I'm just a temporary employee here at the Crowne Plaza. Next year is up to them. If you'll excuse us." I stood up and then caught myself being a dismissive bitch. I reached for her hand and looked her straight in the eye. "Lucinda, I'm glad that your dream of being a singer came true." With that, we exchanged a long hug.

"If there's anything I can do," she squeezed my hand, "to help you find the missing doggie, let me know."

Patrice raised a palm in farewell and Lucinda was gone.

"Bad news, girlfriend," Patrice said, slipping back into the beach chair. "JT and Bob don't want to party tonight. Gosh darn it. There're so many places to see fireworks and dance. But, they're staying home. On dog watch, he said. I offered to come by—well, I didn't offer but let a hint float around."

"The hint sunk?"

"Something like that."

"It's probably because I'll be with Devin and they don't want him around. I don't care about seeing either of them anyway." I sniffed. "Enough drama. Dev and I can stay here tonight. Seen one Roman candle—seen 'em all."

"Heard one whistling Pete, heard 'em all," she said, glumly.

"Smelled one snail, smelled 'em all." I stared at the bottom of my glass.

"Stepped on one sparkler and burned your bare foot, stepped on 'em all," she added.

" Hey." I pointed toward the bar pool. "Look, they're already setting up a barbecue over by the cabana. I'm not going anywhere."

Patrice said, "I thought you wanted to get out of the hotel so you didn't have to see David or the GM."

With my eyes closed and facing the sun, I stretched and it felt good. "I'm staying right here. Devin can cruise around the hotel tonight. He's made a couple of friends in the maintenance department. But, you go have fun. Forget the tid-bits, you know plenty of people at Harbor Town. Just go to the open party on the wharf."

She answered with a shrug and signaled a passing waiter.

CHAPTER 28

It was six-thirty a.m., and Dev's flight out was at eight. My son and I have always begrudged the morning hours and we grunted to each other while fumbling around in his room collecting his things. Finally, Devin zipped up his bulging backpack.

"I found your wet swimsuit in the bathroom," I said wearily. "Stick it in this plastic shower cap then into the outside zipper part." As he did that, I checked over the list on my small note pad. "Were you able to write a quick thank you note to the hotel for getting you this nice room?"

"Mom, I thought you had to pay for it."

"I did, but we got a discount. I don't know. It's just a nice gesture. Never mind now, it's time to leave. We can do it later." I opened the single drawer in the little desk and removed a sheet of hotel stationary.

"Where's my shells?" He stomped his foot.

"They were in that glass and I put them inside this." I handed him a bulging Fritos bag. "I'm guessing you're the only one taking shells to Hawaii, but, I understand. Nature's treasures are...do you have everything?"

He grunted a response and we walked out into the hall as the heavy door clunked behind us. I had dreaded my son leaving, but now at 6 a.m. sentimentality was a burning emotion.

We drove to the airport in silence and, after checking in, we plunked ourselves in two of the five chairs in the little snack area. I pulled the hotel stationery and a pen from my purse. Devin scrawled out a few lines of gratitude and stuffed it into the envelope as I dug for change to use in the vending machine.

"Some airport, huh?" I gestured to the bored cashier filing her fingernails as she stood behind the only counter.

Devin looked the area over. "It's even dinkier than ours in Kona. The baggage claim is outside though. There are like big straw umbrellas; it's kind of a random courtyard. You've never been there but you ought to come back with me—I mean one of these days."

"How long do you think you'll want to live in Hawaii?"

He shrugged.

After scanning the ceiling for a less emotional topic, eventually I stood up. "I'm going for some of those little mini-donuts. Want anything?"

"Gatorade," he called out as I turned away. When I returned with the goods, he said, "Yeah, Mom, you should really watch the junk food." Then we stared at the tile floor. "Be sure and text me as soon as Becky shows up. Thanks for not—like, like going psycho on me."

"She'll turn up. She had a good life there. I bet someone found her and just took her in." I shoved the half pack of donuts toward him and he popped a couple in his mouth. "Dev, I'm sure glad you came. We had fun, didn't we?" I patted the top of his hand. "What was your favorite part of this trip?"

His eyes squinted in thought. "One time, I think I told ya, I was walking along that long driveway out to the main road. So, you know where that first little bridge is? I stopped there and saw a mega-big alligator just lying on top of the water real close to the edge."

"I've seen him there too."

"Yeah? So, this one time there was this big mama turtle and about five little turtles about so big." He held up a mini-donut. "They were swimming around near her in the sun and I'm thinkin', look out! I was afraid the alligator was gonna open his mouth and suck 'em all in and eat them. But, he never did. It was a peaceful little swamp—and those turtles weren't even scared to swim near his big ole long alligator snout. So, it's stuff like that I like about this place."

I crunched the cellophane donut wrapper and swept the snowdrift of powdered sugar away with the flat of my hand. "Good story. I'm going to try not to worry about you when you're in Kona. I'll take a lesson from the mother turtle and know that the baby turtles can swim around dangerous water and not get hurt. Like fall off their boards when huge waves are breaking."

Devin grinned, causing me to lean in for a sitting hug. I wiped a runaway tear off my cheek and we both squirmed with embarrassment.

"Love ya, Mom. Thanks for having me out here, and also for the dough-re-mi," he said, patting his pocket.

I walked him to the passenger inspection line. We embraced and I let loose a long sigh of loss. "I love you, Dev, and I'm proud of you. Keep up the studies, okay?"

He extended a thumb and little finger, with the others tucked in, and shook it in the Hawaiian tradition of 'Hang loose.'

I turned away and headed for the glass doors leading outside. The morning air was fresh as the sky a pale lavender. The dark green palms bent gently in the wind and I stopped for a moment to hold this picture in my mind.

I didn't want to go back to my room. After the sugar and coffee I was useless for sleeping yet too melancholy for writing. Even the airport in Hilton Head was in a beautiful place, so I decided to leave my car in the lot and just take a walk. I hadn't been in that particular plantation, although they all seemed about the same to me. I followed the exit signs out to the one main road, turned right, and then trudged along the gravely soft-shoulder of the highway.

By the sound of all the whistles going on above me, the birds were having a convention. I cawed back to them, causing a break in their chatter, but they quickly resumed. I tried to join in with my friendly peeps and whistles but lost interest before long.

I figured it was best to stay along the main highway to avoid getting lost. There was a blast of loud intrusion over the nature sounds. Devin's plane took off, so I guess it was eight-ten. I kissed my fingertips and sent a wave toward the small aircraft.

Eventually I came upon a strip mall in my aimless wandering. The little business district had a laundromat, donut shop and hair salon. Something seemed familiar about the little free-standing stucco building that housed a dentist and real estate office. Odd, given the fact that I'd never been over on this end of town, with the exception of two airport runs.

Dr. McWalters, Dental Care, the sign read. That sounded familiar. I snapped my fingers—it was the name of the dentist that Lucinda worked for. Without giving it a thought I walked up to the door and opened it.

A pudgy middle-aged man wearing a white coat stood at the counter shuffling papers. He looked up with surprise, and I think we startled each other suddenly eye-to-eye.

"Oh, excuse me," I stammered, "I was just passing by."

"Well, come on in," he invited. "Take a card, if you'd like. I'm Dr. McWalters."

"Hello." I raised my hand. "I was taking a walk and noticed your sign. Actually, I was given a certificate by a girl named Lucinda to have my teeth cleaned here. So, well—now I know where to go."

"My hygienist Lucinda? Oh, she comes in at nine. I get here early to go through the mail. I could see if we have room for you this morning."

"Don't bother, my certificate isn't on me. I left my car down the road."

By that time he was running his hand down a book. "Yesiree, I guess I could take you now. Don't worry about the certificate, I trust you. What's your name, dear?"

Boy, dentists in this part of the world sure seemed friendly and available. My dentist in L.A. generally waits a couple months before calling me back to even *schedule* an appointment. Maybe there's little interest in dental care on the island and he's drumming up business. Regardless, it felt rude to turn him down at that point, especially when he was pushing a clipboard toward me.

"You sure you don't mind?" I said, eyeing the form and picking up the pencil.

"Not at all, Ms. Bennett." He read my name upside down. "I think the best way to build up a practice and find new patients is to let them get a feel for our services. Oftentimes they switch over to our office." He led me down the short hall and into a room with the chair facing the window. "However, I can see by your address that you're just visiting from California."

He led me down the hall and secured a paper bib around my neck. Then the good doctor jacked up the chair with a foot pedal.

"Are there any other dentists on Hilton Head, sir?" I asked. "Just wondering, because it's a pretty small place."

"There is one other dentist on the other side of the island. My colleague, Dr. Cortez...."

I suppose he'd had a few cups of java too and welcomed someone to chat with this early in the morning. He droned on a bit about the location of the other dentist compared to his location and I tuned-out, distracted by the wretched sound of scraping. My bottom teeth were being gouged by some evil tool. After I sat up and spat into the circular bowl, it seemed to be my turn to respond to whatever he was blabbering about. "Well, that's good that there're enough patients for two dentists. Hey, by the way, did you ever have Leona Helmsley as a patient?"

He stopped and jutted his head back. His eyebrow raised an inch or so. "Why do you ask that? I assume you mean the woman with the Helmsley Hotel fortune. But, uh, she's from New York."

I twisted around to see him. "I guess I thought she came here, because of something Lucinda said. I hope I'm not breaking any rule about confidentiality, but she said ya'll had a patient who left her fabulous estate to her *dog,* and I just assumed it was Leona Helmsley. Her story was in all the papers."

Dr. McWalters, chuckled. "Incredible as it may seem, there's more than one eccentric millionaire who passed away without heirs. My patient, Lila Lee Honeywell—interesting name isn't it—she died and left her considerable fortune to *her* best friend, a very fortunate German Shepherd. She lives—I mean to say, she used to live over at Sea Pines Plantation, which is actually closer to Dr. Cortez's office, but she came here because she was referred to me by—"

"Oh, my gosh. Did you ever see her dog?"

"As a matter of fact, I did. Now lay back, Ms Bennett, and open your mouth. We haven't begun the top teeth."

"What was the dog's name?" I insisted. "Do you know?"

"Open wide." He wedged a cotton roll between my molars. "That'll hold your mouth open. Let me see. The dog would always accompany Miss Honeywell...a well-behaved shepherd. They'd come in together and sit in the waiting room until it was time for her to go back. Anyway, her driver would take the dog for a walk during Miss Honeywell's appointment. She got her teeth cleaned quarterly. 'Just like the seasons,' she would say. Does this hurt?"

"Uh, huh."

"Almost done here. She was such a lovely person, we bent the rules a little bit. Everyone knew she didn't go anywhere without that dog. Let's see. Becky was the dog's name. I remember because her Christmas cards would have a picture of the two of them, signed Lila Lee Honeywell and Becky."

Jackknifing up from my reclined position, I garbled the words, "You don't happen to have one of those cards still around, do you?"

"Goodness no." He chuckled. "This is July. Now lean back and hold your mouth open for me. Bite down on the cotton rolls. That's it. When Lila Lee passed away about a year ago, she left her entire estate to that pooch."

"Wah dode yo saw?"

"Don't try to say too much, Ms Bennett. The cotton rolls." His fingers were back inside my cheek. "Now, lay back in your seat, thank you. There, there. Miss Honeywell had no heirs, you see. I heard the bank hired some caretakers to look after her estate for as long as the dog's alive. After that, her entire estate goes to PETA. No reason to get up just yet. Open wide."

CHAPTER 29

I jumped in my car and sped down the road in the direction of FACES Day Spa. I had too much energy to call ahead; I needed to step on the gas. Besides, some twisted part of me wanted to see Patrice's face when I told her. I walked into the spa and was greeted by the luscious scent of cinnamon aromatic candles. At ten-fifteen it was probably too early for customers; anyway, it looked pretty empty.

She was standing behind the counter alone. "JT hasn't even called me today," Patrice sulked. "I'm going over to Tid-bit mansion to do a little hound-hunting," I whispered back. "Want to come?"

"I'm wearing this." She opened her arms to reveal a black sleeveless top and white pants. "A bit much for plodding through tall grass. Should I go home and find a hound hunting outfit?"

"Knowing you, you probably have one. Just come as you are. Can you leave now?"

"Sure, I'm the boss, remember?" She retreated to the stock room and I heard voices. She returned with her purse. Another woman followed her to the front counter and bid us good-bye.

Once outside the door and crossing the parking lot she said, "I can't concentrate. Glad to leave. Isn't that awful? Did you talk to Hippy Bob today?"

"I haven't spoken to either of them. Let me unlock your side of the car. I'll fill you in on the latest, then we're heading over to Tid-bit mansion cause there's some 'splaining to be done."

******

As we rolled up to the gate, I announced, "Patrice and Veronica, amateur hound hunters, have arrived." After that pass at levity, our car crawled down the familiar tree-lined path and the eerie foreboding of last night's dream returned. In the rearview mirror I watched the gate swing shut and heard the shrill sound of metal slamming. The statuesque live oaks with drooping moss had once been welcoming. Now it all felt spooky as if the trees had secrets.

As the car rolled up to the parking area I could hear the familiar clank of metal horseshoes hitting a stake.

"Sounds like they're amusing themselves," Patrice noted. "Are you going to bust them for lying? Maybe we shouldn't bring it up since they're so sad about losing Becky. I don't know what to do. That dog probably isn't even theirs. JT blew me off last night. After all the buildup to the talent show and it turned out weird and he hasn't called—"

"Hush, we're here now. Let's just see what happens."

We got out of my dusty Corolla. From the short distance I could see JT on the porch. He was extracting a long gray stem from the barrel of a rifle. He had a pile of rags and a can of WD 40 beside him. Bob was pitching rusty horseshoes. They kept at their tasks as we crunched up on the dry pine needles.

"This is definitely a little-house-on-the prairie scene." I planted a neutral expression on my face as I eyed the gun JT was wiping down. "Any sign of Becky?"

"Ladies," JT nodded.

He leaned the rifle against the step and turned to face us. In the morning sun, he was dressed in shorts and a sleeveless tee-shirt that emphasized his bronze, muscular torso. Patrice trotted over to the porch and gave him a hug worthy of a soldier returning from war. As they faced each other talking softly, Bob and I were left stranded on awkward island. How embarrassing to have been intimate only two nights before the line in the sand was drawn—by the paw of a *dog*.

"Bob, how are the veterinarian studies going?" Searching for a clue to their true selves, I immediately winced that I didn't show more patience. The comment hung in the air like a challenge.

Bob tossed a horseshoe, avoiding my eyes. "Good, good. Being on-line I can drag it out longer than I should. But I enjoy learning about science and animal behavior." The shoe rang loudly as it struck the post. "It doesn't seem to be helping me with this one, though."

"For me that's the weirdest thing of all." I drew a semi circle in the sand with the point of my shoe. "You all loved Becky so much and she was such an obedient dog, why in the world would she leave?"

JT spun around. "There's no reason she *would* leave."

Patrice hung on his side like a barnacle.

"Then what happened?" I said, looking to each of the guys.

"She's been stolen," JT stated flatly. "Because somebody thought they could shake us down for the prize money. We were both at the Crowne Plaza Saturday night and some jackass with a bright idea probably jumped the fence and took her."

"That's shocking!" Patrice clutched her throat.

Cautiously, I said, "That clears Devin of *losing* her."

"You could say that." JT pushed his sunglasses up on his forehead and met my eyes. "But Devin was asleep when I got home." JT reached in his shorts pocket and pulled out a package of Kools. He lit two and handed one to Bob, who accepted it with a short nod.

Stepping into the shade of the porch I stood next to JT, meeting him head on. "Do you hold me responsible because I asked Bob to come?"

No one spoke.

"Now, now—" Bob threw his hands in the air as if being frisked. "No one's blaming anyone. I was there at the show because I wanted to be with you, Veronica, and support JT. Let's not miss the point here. Whether Devin was asleep or not, this thing happened."

"If your theory is true," I said slowly, "then it must be someone who knows your situation. That Becky is no ordinary dog. In fact that she owns this place."

Patrice dropped her arm from JT's side.

JT blew a smoke ring into the air. We watched it turn into an oblong form then disperse into white ghostly shapes. "I got a call about nine this morning. Some dick-wad wants ten thousand dollars by midnight tomorrow."

"No!" Patrice gasped.

My hand flew up to my mouth as I tried to stop a squeal. They didn't even deny that Becky owned Pinewood. Patrice just shook her head.

"So," Bob said, "that's why we were pitchin' shoes. There's no point in searching for anything but money." He dropped into a lawn chair and exhaled a plume of smoke.

"Have you called the police?" Patrice and I tumbled over the same words.

JT shot back, "We're handling this ourselves, I told you that."

Struggling to keep my voice calm, I faced JT. "When you talked about finding Becky yourselves, okay, but this is different." I took my hands off my hips, aware I'd slipped into mother-mode. "There's a criminal element to it now."

Patrice piped in, "One of the state troopers' wives, Gloria, is my customer. I can call her at home and we can keep this all quiet, if you want."

"Girls, girls, thanks but we can handle this on our own," Bob finally spoke up, bending down to pick up a horseshoe. He flung it into the air from about fifty feet and it ringed the rusty stake.

"You're paying the ransom?" I choked on the words. "I'm sorry, but it doesn't seem right. Bob, what do you think?"

"We've got about two thousand here in the safe. I need to find the rest."

Patrice stood up. "Do you have any idea who's behind this?"

"Are you going to pay it first," I said, looking from one guy to the other, "then try and get it back once the dog's returned?"

"That's all we can do, Veronica," JT said bitterly. "If the police make a report, it will come out we couldn't do our job and we'll lose our contract here."

"As dog sitters?" I pushed.

"As *caretakers* of the Honeywell estate," he corrected me. I plopped down on the porch step. We hadn't been offered anything to drink and I hadn't eaten much all day. I felt faint. "This seems like a bad western."

"I suppose you girls see us as the villains too, huh?" Hippy Bob said. "You see, that's why me and JT never went out. We had to stay here twenty-four/seven."

"What about the night we met you two?" Patrice directed the question to JT.

He looked off in the distance and spoke offhandedly. "That night Becky was at the vet getting her regular check-up. He kept her overnight to take pictures or some damn thing."

"What about those implants they put in dogs and cats so they can be found?" I was excited. "She must have that tracking device?"

"Again," Hippy Bob explained in a slow patient voice, "we can't go to the vet or the cops or anyone because if it's discovered she's missing—we lose our contract. We get paid at six months. If she checks out healthy and the estate is in good shape, then Miss Lila's bank figures we done our job. In between it's just a small stipend to live on." His eyes clouded over. "We're not too exciting now, are we, ladies? We meet women sometimes and they assume things."

JT spat on the ground, then turned to face us. "So mostly we just stay out here and keep to ourselves."

Patrice's arms crossed her chest as she hugged herself, even in the warm sun. "We didn't assume anything. You said this estate was left to you and your—wait a minute. Are you two even cousins?"

JT cleared his throat. "No. Just friends. Lila Lee Honeywell is nobody's aunt. Just an ol' lady who left all her earthly belongings to her dog. A dog that is very rich, and very gone. One of us should've been here guarding Becky. Somebody saw us both at the Crowne Plaza Saturday night."

"I need to get something to eat," I sighed. "I was up at five getting Devin off to Hawaii." I pulled my keys out of my pocket and turned toward the car. "Patrice? You coming, or—what?"

She looked at JT and then to me. I could see the dilemma played out on her face. Judging from her body language, she'd probably overlooked all of JT's lies. Now, he needed quick cash and everyone knew her business was thriving. I couldn't take her checkbook out of her purse and drive off. She's an adult. It was insane not to contact the police.

"Go ahead, Patrice," JT said softly. He planted a kiss on her lips. "I'll call you later, babe. I got to get my head wrapped around what's going down here. Okay?" As his hands moved up and down her back, she clung to him like a mountain climber on the side of a rock. When she finally released her death grip and turned toward the car, he gave her ass a little pat.

Hippy Bob came over to me, wrapped his lanky limbs around my limp frame, and gave me a full body embrace. My arms hung at my sides. We said nothing. I hid my face so he couldn't know how good that hug felt.

CHAPTER 30

The Corolla rolled slowly out of Pinewood's tree-lined driveway. I couldn't help wondering if it was the last time I'd be up here. The trees rustled overhead as birds carelessly darted in front of the windshield. Neither Patrice nor I had spoken a word or turned on the radio. I had just pressed the button for the gate to swing open when she said, "I'll be honest with you. I'm going to lend JT the ransom money. Or, at least part of it."

"Oh my gosh, Patrice, that's too much," I exclaimed. "Can't you just offer...less? A couple thousand, maybe? I'm the one that feels guilty about having my son on watch when it happened." I pulled the car out on the highway and we picked up speed. "I feel like, well, maybe they could ask some of their friends."

"You heard him," she responded, "they always kept to themselves. They've only lived here less than a year. It is *so* not fair. He is so talented." She started rambling about how JT would come to the spa to get his pickin' finger acryliced so he could play guitar, but other than that, how they would just stay home with Becky. He was so gifted blah, blah, blah. I don't know what this had to do with the kidnapped dog. I tuned her out as I drove, then interrupted her passionate rant. "Then we came along, and things, and what? We wrecked everything?"

"I'm not exactly saying that," she said, pouting.

"Hold everything." I fumed. "I'm not apologizing for talking to them at The Jazz Corner that night. They were flirting too. When I told JT about the contest, I thought for sure I was doing him a favor. Who knew he wouldn't win."

"That fecken' Lucinda," Patrice said.

We both had just finished reading a novel by Irish author, Marian Keyes, and had taken up cursing like the Dubliners. She rolled down the window and stuck her head outside, which was out of character for her to abuse her perfect hair.

"Put your head back inside," I ordered. Her shoulders were doing an up and down thing. "Wait, are you crying?"

She ignored me and kept her face to the wind, eyes closed like a hound.

I kept talking, though practically shouting above the wind. "Patrice, I'm the one who should be coughing up the money. I insisted Bob come and hang with me that night. It was *his* duty to stay and guard the dog, but I guess he couldn't tell me that. Hey, I'd worked hard getting that show together. I figured it would be a night of celebration. Naturally JT would win, we'd all do shooters at the bar, I would be toasted as the clever girl who everyone would thank for years to come and..." I shook my head. "You're right. Shyte, that fecken' Lucinda."

Patrice ducked back inside the car to say, "I couldn't even look at her at the pool the other day. She put her five grand in the ATM to *save*, pfff."

"Actually, she did offer to help any way she could," I said slowly, tossing her a sideways glance.

"As *if*," Patrice scoffed.

I pulled the car into the Sunoco Mini-mart. I cut the engine and started fueling. "While the gas is filling up, I'm getting something inside. Do you want anything?"

Patrice shook her head. Her eyes were red from the wind and tears.

"Not even a Slurpy?" I smiled, poking my head back in the passenger side.

She merely looked away.

A few minutes later I climbed into the car with a small bag of Fritos and carton of chocolate milk.

"I've got an idea. Here's what we do. I'll call JT and *insist* he get a reading from Gertrude the Oracle."

She looked up. "I thought you already suggested that, and they blew you off."

"Now that there's a ransom to pay, they may take it more seriously. Gertrude has to know *something*. She has her spirit guides. We got nothin'"

Patrice nodded slightly, "Gertrude might have a clue if we should pay the ransom. The ladies in the shop say she's really, *really* good."

It was good to have my friend back in the conversation. I nodded vigorously, saying, "She didn't know a thing about me and told me to be careful not to lose something very valuable. I thought she meant my mother-son relationship. All along it was Becky."

Patrice bounced in her seat. "So that proves right there she is dialed in on the doggie vibes, doesn't it?"

"They need to ask about the ransom first," I said. "Look, if Gertrude says to pay it and that we will get our money back—I'm okay to chip in." Then, meekly, "There's a plan to get it back, isn't there?"

"JT said that they need to put the ransom money in the mailbox out on the road. After the dog is turned over, then Hippy Bob, whose car will be stashed in the bushes, can follow the car and get their ten grand back."

"When did he tell you all that?" I asked.

"When you walked ahead to the car."

I started up the engine and pulled out of the filling station. "If Gertrude predicts the guys will really get the money back, then—this sounds wild—but I'll ask to borrow Lucinda's prize money."

Patrice clapped like a two-year-old in front of a birthday cake. "You would do *that*?"

"She *did* offer to help any way she could, didn't she?" We both let out a wicked laugh of comic relief.

Patrice wiped away a tear. "And, you know where to find her—at work. Thank you so much. I'll say, you've got guts, girl." Then, counting on her fingers she added, "They have, what? Two thousand? Lucinda has five, you pay one and I'll pay two. There's the ten thousand! Stop the car and call right now, Veronica. There's no time to waste—they need to get the oracle on the case."

We parked on the side of the road at Patrice's insistence. After a brief conversation, I snapped my cell shut and turned to face her. "Okay, Hippy Bob took the number and promised JT would call as soon as we hung up."

"Wow, I guess I feel better," Patrice sighed. "I was ready to write a check. I'd probably regret it by the time the ink dried. Vee, thank you for figuring out we needed an impartial third person."

"Uh huh."

She yanked on her long fingers, making a popping sound. "Isn't it weird how the guys didn't even deny they were just pet sitters?"

"How 'bout that?" I clicked my tongue in disgust. "They aren't even cousins either. That also explains the one car between them, pfff."

"Let me call the shop and check on things," Patrice said, "Then we'll go to breakfast." We were still sitting in the car applying makeup in the mirror side of our visors when the phone rang.

We both yelped, then laughed at our responses to the predictable sound. I flipped open the phone. "Hello, JT?"

Patrice grabbed my arm. I listened a moment and snapped my phone shut.

"Well?" she said.

"He got an appointment with Gertrude the Oracle at one-thirty today."

CHAPTER 31

Back in my room I had a restless sleep. My head was floating an eighth of an inch off my pillow—I was that tense. I kept seeing the back of Devin's dark-blue, Billabong backpack as he got smaller and smaller inside the airport. When he vanished among the other travelers, I frantically searched for his speck in the crowd. That scene was interspersed with a meeting with Kendal Street Publishers. Just as I was turning in the manuscript—after a year of writing Jack's biography—my agent morphed into Lucinda.

"Aghh!" I sat up in bed. It was two-thirty p.m. and I'd slept only an hour. Dully, I counted ahead the number of hours before I needed to get up. I actually missed talking to David Lindsay. Since the debacle at the contest, I'd only seen him once across the lobby. How weird. I wondered if he caught hell that night, after fecken' Lucinda won. Oh my gosh...if I was going to borrow from her, I'd better get on it. I groaned and stretched across my comfortable bed. I flicked my cell phone back on, my voice mail had four messages. The first was from Devin. "Hi and I don't know why I need to call, but I said I would when I changed planes." The second was from my literary agent "checking in with your progress." If that weren't cringe-worthy enough, the next message was from Hippy Bob. He spoke in a flat tone, reporting that JT had been strongly advised by Gertrude to pay the ransom. According to her, the dog would be returned safely and the money recovered. Hmmm—there was good news and bad news.

I scowled at the clock. Why did I promise Patrice I'd borrow from Lucinda?

Here was my plan. Go by my bank and withdraw half of what I had—a meager one thousand bucks. Next, shake down the dental hygienist. If she agreed, then pick up Patrice's contribution, then deliver the eight grand to the fake cousins all before my gig at eight. Grrr. Delivering it made me a complete patsy. Maybe someone could pick up the dough at the hotel.

I swallowed two Excedrins and jumped in the shower. By letting the water beat against my skull, I willed the little pain-numbing molecules to work their magic. Selecting an outfit was a challenge, but I think I covered it with a pair of gray slacks that were comfortable enough for a long day and night ahead. The white linen blouse looked business-like, suitable for an IOU proposal and unassuming as we withdrew large amounts of cash from Lucinda's bank. This was probably a better choice than ski mask and pistol while I stand behind her in the teller's line. Underneath my blouse I wore a lacey peach camisole suitable for crooning ballads at the hotel. I squirted myself with Tuscany perfume and strung some silver hoops through my ears. A six-pack of Five Hour Energy Drinks was sitting on my dresser, leftover snacks from Devin's room. I peeled the tab off one and downed the tart elixir.

I picked up the phone on the nightstand and dialed the number printed on Lucinda's card. My legs felt so weak, I plunked back down on the bed.

"Dr. McWalter's office," a female voice announced.

I swallowed. "May I please speak to Lucinda, the dental hygienist?"

"May I make an appointment for you? Or," she sounded snarky, "is this a *personal* call?"

Why does everything have to be so difficult? "It *is* a personal call," I matched her tone exactly, "from one of your *patients.*"

A moment later, Lucinda chirped a hello into the phone.

"Say Lucinda, it's me Veronica. I wanted to say thanks for the teeth-cleaning gift card. I don't know if Dr. McWalters told you I came in—"

"Oh yes, he told me," she gushed. "Actually, he recognized you from emceeing the contest."

"Gee, I guess that makes both of us famous," I chuckled, "Or, notorious."

"I'm still on cloud nine," she said, in a breathy voice. "How 'bout you?"

"Cloud nine's a stretch. Maybe, cloud four. Anyway, I'm in the neighborhood and hoped we could meet for coffee on your next break."

"Oh, did you take someone to the airport?"

"Something like that."

"Let me see. I can take a break in half an hour. Is that okay? There's a little donut shop next door—"

"I know," I said. "That's perfect. See you there."

CHAPTER 32

Two empty cartons of milk and two half-filled Styrofoam iced tea cups sat in front of us. Perched in my seat with my elbows planted on the Formica table, I had come to the end of the story. I was nervously spinning the waxy paper boat that held the maple bar crumbs. "Boy, Lucinda, you really can be quiet when you want to be. I'm used to seeing you bubbling over. Heh, heh, you know, with charming enthusiasm, I mean."

I stacked the three sugary napkins and restacked them. She let out a sigh and checked her watch. Like a yawn it was contagious and I checked my naked wrist.

"That's really a-MAY-zing, Veronica. I didn't know there were such mean guys just walking around here." She shuddered. "So, your friends won't go to the police? What if there's a fight?"

"They seem to have a good plan to retrieve the money. The dognappers just need to get the cash first—then they'll release Becky."

She gave me a quizzical look. I decided to elaborate.

"I think they're going to mark the bills. They assured me we'd all get our money back."

I was making up stuff at this point. How did I get so involved? Maybe in a tiny corner of my mind I thought

180

Lucinda's prize money actually did belong to JT. Or, dreaded the prospect of Patrice putting the spa on the line by paying it all herself. Lucinda interrupted my dark thoughts.

"I've heard of that fortune teller, but never went to her. I'm Christian, you know, and we don't believe in that stuff."

"When I went to Gertrude's house," I explained softly, "she was wearing a cross and had a big picture of Jesus hanging in the living room. I don't know how the psychic connection works, but the time I went to her she was right-on accurate."

Lucinda rocked back in the folding chair and her eyes perused the ceiling. "I remember that sweet dog, Becky. I can just see Miss Lila in the waiting room reading People Magazine, her dog lying on the floor at her feet. She was so well-behaved." She turned to me and covered her mouth with manicured fingers, suppressing a giggle. "I'm talking about Becky. Well, Miss Lila was also well-behaved, don't get me wrong." She lowered her voice. "Being a medical office, it was a no-no for dogs to be in the waiting room, but we let it slide. I just knew that shepherd wouldn't run off. Miss Lila positively doted on her."

"Hmm," I said, drumming my fingers on the edge of the table, like I'd seen my son do a thousand times. God, it was an annoying tick. I withdrew my hand quickly.

Lucinda ran her fingers through her long tresses. "Now Miss Lila is gone and poor Becky is in the hands of some— scheming bubbas."

"Patrice's money is wrapped up in her business. She can't liquidate her assets that quickly to come up with the cash. It was so fortuitous that you happened to come up to us at the pool. I could tell you were really a pet lover when you offered to help."

More silence.

I pulled two pieces of paper from my purse and slid them across the table, routing around the crumbs. "I wrote out an IOU for five thousand, in case you agreed." I dug a pen out of my purse and pushed it toward her, then looked at my watch again. "The banks back home close about five."

"Oh, what the heck." Lucinda grabbed the papers. After a quick glance at the single sentence, she signed both. She folded up her copy and tucked it into the pocket of her white smock. "I guess we better get over to the CBSC."

"Huh?" I said.

"Citizens Bank of South Carolina."

I jumped up and hugged her. "Thank you so, so much. So—can we go together? Now?"

She frowned and my giddiness hit a wall. "What is it?"

"I have one more patient," she explained. "Maybe if Doctor doesn't have someone else waiting for me—he'd do it. Was it yesterday that he did your cleaning?"

I nodded. "The days are such a blur, it's hard to believe it was only this morning I met your doctor. He was very nice. Again, I can't thank you enough, Lucinda. I'll just be waiting in my car. As you saw on the IOU, I gave us three days to get our ransom back. I can't be sure, of course, when we'll get it back—but Gertrude assured us the dog will be returned and we'd get back the ransom money."

"Honey," she lowered her chin and looked up at me, "I don't believe in that hocus pocus. I'm doing this for Miss Lila. I know she's in heaven now looking down from a cloud and would want us to do everything we can to get Becky back to her own yard. Isn't that funny? When Doctor mentioned he had a patient who left all her money to a dog, I never put two and two together."

We left the donut shop. She held the door open for me and we stepped outside to a furnace blast of late afternoon heat. "Don't get me wrong about the money. I need it too. I'm using it to invest in my career. A few singing lessons and I'm making me a demo. I'm calling it, 'Lucinda Star—Rising in the Carolina Sky'"

"It's a little bit long—but, yeah. Okay, good luck with that," I choked out.

She shook her head and whispered, "In the country when someone dies, their hound just goes to a neighbor or someone offers to take it. I never gave that shepherd another thought."

Declining her offer to wait in Dr. Mc Walters' office, I stayed in my hot car waiting for Lucinda to finish her last appointment. Immediately I called Patrice with the good news. Patrice was less worried about the safety of her two grand than she was the safety of her boyfriend.

"What if they get in a shootout," she wailed. "It gets so dark on that road, a shot could go off and no one would even hear it."

"Did he tell you the exact plan?" I insisted. "I mean, more details than just Hippy Bob follows the car that stole Becky?"

"No," she moaned. "He clams up when I ask. I can't say that I blame him; this is all new to us."

The phrase, 'can't say that I blame him' seemed to pop up a lot when JT was involved. I, on the other hand, could easily blame him. "Listen, if these guys were straight with us in the beginning, none of this would have happened. We still would have gone out with them. We *still* would have liked them, or in your case—loved him, maybe. We aren't gold diggers."

"Right," she sniffed. "We aren't gold diggers. We're only shallow when it comes to their hot looks."

"Exactly my point. Had we known they had a cush job and the *only* requirement of the job is that someone stays at Pinewood, well, that would have been okay too. There are plenty of things to do over there."

Patrice laughed, "If I ever let him out of the bedroom."

"How about all the watercraft toys in the boat house?" I reminded her. Patrice and I went on and on like this until Lucinda appeared in the window of the dental office. She waved frantically, inviting me inside, but I shook my head, pointing at the phone. Every few minutes I started up the engine to blow cool air over me. "Ay, yay, yay, I can't believe how things have deteriorated," I moaned. "And here we are joking about hanging out with the guys."

"What could they do?" Patrice snapped back. "They didn't want to tell us they were pet sitters because they really like us and didn't think we'd still be into them. Who can blame them? I own a spa and you're a glamorous singer."

"Whatever."

"Admit it, Vee. We were pretty impressed with the Cadillac Esplanade and that mansion on the sea. Maybe they'd been dumped before— after telling the truth. They didn't, like, *lie* exactly, they just let us think—"

"Thank God Gertrude could fit in an appointment with JT so quickly." I interrupted because her tone was getting testy. "Without that reassurance, I would never borrow the money. I really need my savings for when this gig ends." I was mumbling to myself at this point. "It has to support me while I finish the book."

"Gertrude was the deciding factor for me too," Patrice said. Then she started to recount stories her customers had relayed to her regarding the psychic's prowess. After so many retellings, I knew them by heart. I pretended to listen.

"Hey, it looks like Lucinda is coming out. I gotta go now and follow her to the CB."

"Aw, you're sounding like a local, Vee. I'm going to hate it when you leave."

"All right now, Patrice, you round up your two thousand, swing by my gig and pick up our six thousand, and then drive it over to the guys. Got it?"

"Got it," she said.

"Do you think we should get a receipt, or IOU?" I said.

"I know what you mean, but…" she groaned. "I feel weird asking."

"*Weird*? I feel weird still caring about those big fat liars. I have a signed IOU from Lucinda; I'm going to have to pay her

back. I'm insisting we draw one up for JT and Bob too."
Without waiting for a reply, I continued. "Make sure we each
get a signed IOU. You sign for me. After they sign the IOU, put
it in the envelope with the eight thousand," I said sternly.

"I'll use one of those big padded envelopes," she sighed.

I was getting anxious. "What about marking the bills?"

"Let's leave it up to JT," she said. "I'll be by about eight."
Patrice was blabbing on and I wasn't listening. I watched
Lucinda get into her car and pull around in front of mine.

Patrice wouldn't get off the phone. "JT said the exchange is
at midnight and he insisted I get away from there long before
then. He is *so* darling. He sounds just like a cowboy. How'd he
put it? He goes, '*Little darlin' I don't want you anywhere
around these parts when this goes down.*'"

"Yeah, darling," I muttered with dripping sarcasm. "Gotta
go." I hung up as I wheeled out of the parking space behind
Lucinda's car and headed into town.

CHAPTER 33

What's love got to do...got to do with it? Whaaat's love got to dooo...got to do with it?

I finished up the old Tina Turner song with a little more angst than usual I suppose. Anyway, it was followed by generous applause. "I can see there's time for a couple more songs and then I'll be taking a break—just till tomorrow," I told the audience. The waitress circled by with a long-stemmed glass of wine. She dropped a napkin on the table beside me and set the glass down. I cupped my hand over the microphone and whispered to her, "You know I can't drink in here."

She just winked and swung her head toward the back wall. "It's from the boss."

David stood up in the back of the room. He made a little salute-type gesture and smiled. I reached for the glass slowly, counter to my instinctive reaction—grabbing it like a hose in a house fire. Reminding myself to sip like a lady, I mouthed a *thank you* in his direction and played an instrumental medley of Disney tunes. That was the good thing about being a pianist. Times to tune-out were covered by instrumentals.

It was twelve twenty-five and the dog caper was supposed to take place at midnight. Hippy Bob said he would text me as soon as it went down. For some reason he didn't trust the phone lines. I told Lucinda I'd call her in the morning; she seemed satisfied with that.

"Disney tunes—ah, those old songs bring back memories," David said, dropping down in the seat closest to me. He plunked down a white ceramic coffee mug. (Management always drank their cocktails from a coffee cup.) "Especially Zippity Do Dah. You can't find the music for the *Songs from the South*. Good for you, for dragging out the more obscure hits."

"I'm either a musical genius, or that tune is so easy a five-year-old can fake it," I said. "Seriously, you do know your music—that sound score is out of print." I lifted my glass. "Thank you for the Chablis, David."

Then addressing the audience, I spoke into the mic, "Thanks for coming out tonight. Remember, you've got to make the good times, because the bad times come by themselves." I played a little then, turning back to the mic, "My name is Veronica Bennett and I'm here all week. I'll close with a song you'll remember. Made popular by the Jackson Five and written by Clifton Davis. *Never can say good-bye, never can say good-bye...Even though pain and heartache seem to follow me wherever I go—I always try to hide my feelings, but they always seem to show—*"

A smattering of applause followed. When I swung the boom stand and mic away, I checked my watch again. It was exactly twelve-thirty-five. I flipped off the sound system and turned my attention back to David Lindsay.

Avoiding each other since the talent show took energy. It was awkward for me and I can only assume the same for him. In my first week on the job he was nutty, spontaneous and candid. We had so much in common, both having been road musicians. A traveling entertainer has an affinity for one who shares this unique life experience, and we bonded. Once the talent show got into the mix (another music term), I felt he'd taken advantage of me. Hired to sing and play piano should have been enough. My spare time was meant for writing.

The waitress came by our table. She shook a piece of paper and waved her arms around quibbled about some schedule change. As the customers ambled toward the door, I just watched as David dealt with her. He had to concern himself with the minutia of bus boys, bartenders, bar-backs, waitresses' work stations, work hours and work whines. A heavy wave of sorrow came over me as I realized how much he, as a talented musician, gave up. At the piano everyone likes you; but it doesn't pay the bills. David was not suited to be a clipboard carrier.

The Chinese say, *It's no good to bury the hatchet if you just keep digging it up.* Watching David wrangle with the waitress, I knew. It was time for me to forget where I buried it.

"I got your son's thank you note," he said, clearing his throat once the waitress stomped off. "I went ahead and ordered you another glass of wine. I hope you'll stay a moment."

I nodded.

"Devin seemed like a nice young man."

"Thank you. He really had fun. I can't believe he left yesterday morning. It seems like so long ago."

Karen reappeared and David handed me the glass from the round cork tray. "Last call," he said with a smile. "By the way, I took care of your son's two week stay. Your credit card is on file, so make sure you didn't get charged for anything beyond incidentals."

"Oh my God, David! Thank you. I was just grateful for the employee rate."

My cell phone startled me as it vibrated against my breast. I bent down to discreetly slide it out of my bra. A text had come in. I excused myself from David and as I walked in the direction of the bathroom, I heard him say, "Don't keep your cell in your bra. It could lead to, uh, cancer having something as powerful as that next to tissue."

"Thanks," I said, hurrying off. It was a weird exchange for many reasons. Just around the corner I paused in the hall and opened the message: *Becky here. $$ back 2morrow. Have lic.#. C U in a.m. Hotcakes @ 10. Luv, Bob."*

My heart was beating so loudly, I could hear it. I jumped in the air a little and then called Patrice.

She answered on the first ring. "Isn't it wonderful? They just texted me."

"Yeah," I sighed in relief. "Maybe this whole thing will just be just another crazy story next week. Did they find out who did this? What do you know?"

"Oh, not much. They must have some James Bond fantasy thing going on, because they refuse to talk on the phone tonight."

"Whatever. They'll tell us why in the morning. Did you get the text about breakfast at ten?"

Patrice sang out, "Hotcakes."

"We'll get our money back—thank God. I really chanced it—big time. Hooray, Becky's home. I need to text the good news to Devin and get back to the lounge. David just bought me a drink and wants to have a heart-to-heart."

"I wish I could sleep," she murmured. "I've been at the shop all day doing inventory, then came back home to fill out a gazillion order forms for our suppliers. I guess there isn't anything we can do now. So, see you tomorrow."

CHAPTER 34

As much as I didn't want to, I returned to the lounge. Whatever David had to say couldn't take long since it was already almost one a.m. As I got closer I heard someone on the piano. David Lindsay was playing "Piano Man," the song Billy Joel so aptly penned about lounge singers' lives. *It's nine o'clock on a Saturday, the regular crowd shuffles in....*"

I sat down at a table in time to join in, "*and they sit at the bar, putting bread in the jar, sayin' man, what are you doin' here? La la-la-lah, la-la-la-la-lah...*"

"I love sitting here with a glass of wine and listening to you," I said, as he dazzled me with clever chord progressions.

"This song almost makes me cry," he said forlornly.

"Me too," I agreed.

His voice was earnest as he sang, *and the waitress is practicing politics while the businessmen slowly get stoned, and they're sharing a drink they call loneliness...*" I joined him for the last line. *But, it's better than being alone.*

He closed the cover over the keys and came around to my table. "Veronica, there aren't words to thank you for all you did for the talent show. The GM was happy for all the business it brought in, the PC was triple what it would have—"

"PC?"

"Our pouring costs were outstanding even for a Saturday night. Bacardi was happy to sponsor the event since it was well-attended. One can't be sure, you know, as it was the first time."

I nodded. "How about the outcome? Was anyone happy about *that*—besides Lucinda?"

"Lucinda worked it. She got all the neighbors, her dental patients and the bubba-vote. Folks just voted for her because they said they would. She's a very likeable girl."

"I didn't realize she was bringing in a big—uh, fan base."

David bounced in his seat. "That's why I put her picture on the flyers. She offered to drive them around and drop them off at every gas station, diner, boat rental, you name it, all over the island. I confided in you that she has a condom route for the restrooms along the highway, right?"

I finished my drink. "So, that doesn't mean the girl can sing. I guessss I should be glad there wasn't a lynch mob out to get us for the *least* talented person walking off with the grand prize. It was so weird that John predicted she'd get all the throw-away votes and win. What about the GM, the sponsors?" I realized then his wife may not have known he encouraged his dental hygienist to enter.

David scoffed. "Hey, if they don't care, why should we, huh?" He looked more serious than I'd ever seen him. "The bar made money. Bacardi gained good will. And that, my friend, is exactly why I left the music business—those kind of inequities."

"I thought someone might arrest her for obliterating 'Crazy,' as it's such a revered country standard."

David smiled for the first time all evening. "And, most folks don't know Willy Nelson wrote it. Okay, I'll speak to the mayor about an ordinance forbidding Lucinda singing 'Crazy' this side of the Mason-Dixon Line." A worker was vacuuming the rug near our feet. We waved him away. David picked up my glass and his mug and walked toward the bar. "Don't go," he said. "I have one more thing to say."

He returned with a couple of bottles of cold water and sat down. We sat in the stillness of the empty lounge. It looked so small when empty. The room was like a shell on the beach. It needed a living organism to come alive. High tide would be tomorrow at eight, when the guests and my piano music would return, and the shell would move and live again.

"Veronica," David clapped his hands, jolting me out of my reverie. "I'm offering to extend your contract beyond Labor Day. But, just so you know, it's pretty close to hurricane season and we kind of empty out."

"I can imagine."

"Still, if you don't mind playing to a smaller house, we'd love to have you through September. We'll only have entertainment Thursday through Sunday, so the pay would go down accordingly, but with fewer guests in the hotel we could move you to a better room. What do you say?"

"Thank you, I'll think about it. Hurricanes, huh?"

He beamed at me. "Ah, you've handled bigger things than a swirl of water. Don't tell me you're scared."

"I've noticed they don't refer to it as 'Swirl of Water season,'" I cracked, then we hugged.

"You deserve more than that," David said, "but it's the best I can do. You understand, right?"

"I understand. I appreciate the offer. Good night, David. Oh, and just a thought, maybe you could fill in for me one of these nights—just to keep your chops up."

*****

Morning couldn't come early enough. I bounced out of bed and spent at least an hour getting ready. The weather was gorgeous and I wore a bathing suit under my clothes in case we went to the beach. I must have changed ninety times trying to find the right top to fit over the bathing suit. Finally, I left early to escape the boredom. If Patrice was ready we could pick up a coffee on the way.

When I called she said she'd been up since dawn and was happy to get going. As soon as she got in the car I started to relax. We were in this together. I didn't know what I would have done if I had to go over there alone. "Sorry I couldn't talk last night, David and I had to clear the air and then afterwards I was too depressed to call you back and risk hearing an entirely new flavor of depression."

"Well, I for one think there's no reason to *be* depressed," she chirped. "I've accepted JT as he is—a talented, big-hearted, hunky, fake cousin, dog sitter. Becky is home. We're getting our money back and summer isn't even half over yet. I'm glad you're wearing your suit too." She reached over and snapped my strap lightly. "I'm wearing mine. What a beautiful day." Patrice pulled a plastic bag from her purse. "I even brought some steak scraps for Becky."

"Were you a Girl Scout, or what? You're always pulling some food out of that purse of yours." I searched the road ahead and didn't see anyplace worth stopping. "One thing about South Carolina, there isn't a Starbucks on every corner. In California they'll have two in the same block, not to mention Peet's Coffee and the Daily Grind. Where do ya'll go?"

"We just stop at the mini-marts I guess." Patrice touched up her already perfect makeup in the visor. "Coffee is coffee."

"Well, that's a refreshing attitude. People have a sick reverence for hot bean juice where I come from. Anyway, there's a Sunoco Mini-mart on the way." A few miles later we were getting coffee inside the gas station's convenience store.

The only other person inside was a man next to us filling a giant Slurpy cup. Since he was an older gentleman I thought it was kind of cute and nudged Patrice. He seemed to notice I was staring at him.

"That looks good," I said with a cheery smile.

"Oh, yeah," he beamed. "My wife's out of town and when she leaves, I have one of these Big Gulps almost every day. How are you doing today, Miss Veronica?"

The surprise had to show on my face. "Excuse me, do I know you from the Crowne Plaza?"

"Last time I saw you, you were hosting that talent show over there."

Patrice stepped back and looked over from the condiments. "Do you come into FACES Day Spa?" She asked the man.

The gentleman wore shorts and a fishing cap, which was regulation retiree uniform. Some folks just have a generic look, I assumed, as I paid the clerk for our coffees. I glanced over to tell him to have a nice day, but the man took a long draw from his frozen drink and turned to Patrice.

"Oh no, I've never been in a spa. Don't worry about not recognizing me. Most people are so set on seeing my wife Gertrude that after I open the door they just pass me by." He waved his free hand, saying, "I'm Ted."

"Oh, then we've never met. But I've heard plenty about your talented wife." Patrice pointed at him with her free hand. "I'm Patrice, by the way. My customers at the spa have told me about readings they've had. Very impressive. Oh gosh. This is, well, you've already met Veronica."

As the two of them ambled toward the cashier, she tapped me on the shoulder. "Veronica, did you realize this is Gertrude the *Oracle*'s husband?"

He slapped some coins on the counter. He walked toward the door, pulled it open and held it. "Ladies?"

Then, with a nervous giggle, she added, "I said oracle, but that may not be what she likes to be called. Sorry,"

"Gertrude is a 'sensitive,'" he said.

"Enjoy your Slurpy," I cut in, waving good-bye. There was a strange sound and I looked up to see a V formation of geese overhead. "Check it out," I said, pointing to the eastern sky. All three of us stopped and gazed skyward. It felt good to inhale the morning air and I had time to think a moment. I called out, "Excuse me, Ted—"

He began crossing the lot but paused for a moment with his hand on the door handle of his sedan. He turned toward me with, "Yes, dear?"

"Did you mention—your wife, Gertrude, is *out* of town?"

"She always spends the Fourth of July week with her sister down in Florida. It's Irene's birthday and the two of them have a tradition. I don't go anymore. She'll be back day after tomorrow, she tells me."

Patrice gasped. "She's been gone all week? Did she take her cell phone with her to do readings in Florida?"

Ted smiled. "Goodness no! A vacation is a vacation. It's turned off and on the dresser. Her regulars know not to call around the fourth." Then, he opened the car door and eased in behind the wheel. "Girls, girls, get out and enjoy this beautiful day that God blessed us with." He sucked the straw of his Big Gulp.

Then, standing completely still, and probably looking and sounding like robots, we said in a monotone, "Bye...Ted." He backed out, the car lurched forward and he was off the gravel and onto the highway.

Patrice flung her hot coffee at a nearby trash can. It fell inside but not before splashing onto her white shorts leaving a huge tan stain.

CHAPTER 35

While I waited behind the wheel with the engine running, Patrice went back inside the mini-mart. A moment later she returned with a bottle of water and a roll of paper towels. Her stained outfit was the least of our worries.

She opened the door and strapped herself in the seat. "Don't say a word. I just can't deal with anymore bullshit about that fuckin' liar."

"Liars—plural! I *have* to say a word, because we were supposed to be headed over there." I ripped out of the parking lot and merged into traffic. I was breathing raggedly and driving the same way. Patrice was rubbing her shorts frantically and spilling water all over her legs and car seat in the process. I reached behind and threw her a towel from the back seat. "Here, use this. So, let's still go over there and not let on that we know. Okay?"

"Slow down, girl!" Patrice shouted.

I had come up too quickly behind a big van and almost climbed up his fender before I heard his horn blast. I pumped the brakes, which jarred us into mini-convulsions. "Sorry."

Patrice's shoulders were shaking and she held the towel over her face, her head bowed.

"Don't cry, Patrice. These losers aren't worth it." I whacked the steering wheel with the palm of my hand. "That's it. We're going to the police. Forget their story. It'll just be more lies. Let them tell it to the cops."

"No, I want to hear what JT says," she said, jerking her head up from the towel.

"Why? There's no explanation. Gertrude's been gone all week. Can't you see? They were playing us, so we'd come up with the money." In a snarky imitation of Bob's voice, I added, 'Gertrude strongly advised we pay it.'"

Patrice wailed into the pillow, "I feel like such an idiot."

"Now, where's the police department?"

"I'm not sayin'," was her muffled reply.

I pulled my car off the highway and rolled along the gravel-paved shoulder. "Where is the police department, and I mean it, Patrice. These guys have our money."

It was almost ten. The car rolled to a stop. Patrice was doing that thing where she looks out the window and clams up. Just then, my cell phone made a whirling sound, indicating a text message. As I dug around in my purse to find it, Patrice looked back at me with pleading eyes. "Who is it?"

I read the message. "What kind of lizards are we involved with?"

Patrice grabbed the phone from me and read the words on the screen out loud. *Bring swimsuits, it's beautiful here-Bob.*

"Aghhh!" It was my turn to growl. I peeled her fingers off the phone and snapped it open and dialed 411. "Hilton Head, South Carolina. Police Department, please."

Patrice snatched the phone away and held it over her head. "No! We're going over there and playing it cool. We want to get our money back—let's see what they say."

"I'm not that curious," I hollered, grasping at the air above her. "Give me back the phone, I'm serious—"

"Give them the chance at least to return it," she hollered.

Since we were confined by our seat belts, it was a very unfulfilling cat fight. In trying to grab her thin wrist, I tipped the bottle of water over and it spilled on the seat. Now we were both wet. We reached for the towel at the same time and clunked heads. "Ouch!" we moaned together, then instinctively batted the air like dueling kittens.

I threw the towel at her. "Okay. We'll do it your way. We go to the cad-pad and leave in one hour. No matter what they say."

"Cad- pad?" she said, "How do you think of these things?"

"I'm a writer, remember? *Tid-bit mansion* has lost its luster. Now, it's more like—Perpetrator Palace."

She clucked her tongue.

"Liars Lair?"

Patrice was not amused. She rolled down the window and stuck her head outside, an act I'd seen several times by now. Maybe it was her way to get out of the car and still have transportation.

I slapped the steering wheel and stated the obvious. "Those guys *knew* we'd help pay if Gertrude said to."

She swung her ponytail back inside and said, "Let's not let on we know JT never saw Gertrude."

"This reminds me of the scene in *Pet Detective* when the woman gets mean and threatens Jim Carey, 'how would you like me to make your life a living hell?' And he calmly replies, 'Thank you, Lois, but I'm not ready for a relationship right now.' Why did I get into a relationship? When I came here, that was the last thing I wanted."

"Me too," she squeaked. "Especially not with a client."

We just sat in silence. It was dreadful listening to my head thumping, so I flipped on the radio, which was tuned to a country station.

Patrice scowled at the dashboard. "I can't believe they're playing *that* ancient song."

"*Sometimes it's hard...to be a woman....*" Tammy Wynett warned from the tinny car speaker. Then, the chorus, "*Stand by your man.*"

I looked at her. "You are taking it *w-a-a-y* too personally."

The message in the music proved too powerful for my friend. She swiped the air with the wet towel and the tears started flowing. "Why couldn't JT have been just a garden variety louse? You know, cheater? Why does he have to be a Hall of Fame liar-thief?"

Cars were whizzing down the highway. Every time a truck passed by, I held my breath and leaned toward the center of the car as we rattled from the vibration. Finally, I stuck the key back into the ignition. "Let's get out of here. It's jive dangerous."

"Danger?" she said drolly. "That's how we roll."

I laughed at the sardonic wit that somehow surfaced through her tears, then made a mental note: it's 'a must' in a best friend to make inappropriate jokes when the shit hits the fan. I took a deep breath. "All right. Let's take it one step at a time. They *claimed* the money would be returned. We will be delightful right up 'til then." We high-fived in agreement.

The mansion was about fifteen minutes away, but this time I drove slowly.

"I hate them," Patrice seethed.

I didn't remark on the fact that she was applying mascara. I just bobbed my head in agreement. "Say, have you ever noticed that all the crimes on the nightly news are committed by men? Everything from war, to crooked politics, to murder, to gang violence. It's *all* men. If they had to limit the news to crimes by women, they wouldn't have a show. Maybe a little embezzlement, a little child abuse, some shoplifting... but not an hour's worth of crime."

"Um hum," she murmured.

"I mean, think about it. Some brilliant network head should come up with an, *All Men Are Pigs* TV station, and they'd have twenty-four hour programming."

Patrice flipped the visor up. "Who knew there would be enough to say on a twenty-four hour *weather* channel?"

"They have sports all day, news all day, a game show network," I added.

"A food network, a cartoon network," she added.

"A Men Are Pigs Network would need a charming host. I know who could get that job. too." This train of thought felt good, dispelling my rage. "Remember, Patrice, don't let on. Let's just have a few drinks and go along with lying happy horse-shit."

"After we get the ten grand back," she shook her finger, "then, we can bust their balls."

"Whoa, this is a whole new side of you, Patrice." A sideways glance verified that snapping sound was her cracking her knuckles.

"Why did you say *ten* grand? We only lent them eight."

Patrice let out a huge sigh. "I didn't want to leave them with nothing to live on. Lucinda leant five, you one, and me the other four thousand. Okay, you got that? Now don't say a word to me about it."

When we reached the entrance I pushed the button without announcing anything. The gate swung open.

"Act normal, Veronica," she whispered. "You look mean."

"You can't even see my face. I'm looking straight ahead out the windshield."

"Yeah, but your knuckles are white on the steering wheel." She reached over and stroked my arm. "I can see the veins in your neck popping out. Sorry I turned into a psycho, by the way." Patrice pulled the band out of her ponytail and fluffed up her hair as it fell gloriously around her narrow shoulders. Then she whispered, "I'm leaving my sunglasses on."

"I'm drinking a vat of gin," I said.

"Since I'm all wet, I might just wear my bikini anyway." She snickered. "Seriously, I've lost three pounds in three days. Besides, I just got a wax and spray tan."

We stopped talking. Becky was bounding up to the car with the guys close behind.

CHAPTER 36

Becky sprang up on the car door and when I opened it she scrambled to get in. I laughed in spite of the dusty paws on my thighs. The loveable German shepherd was a joyful distraction.

"No kisses, Becky." Although it felt wonderful to hug her thick neck, I gently pushed her head to the side avoiding direct face licks. Patrice came around to my side of the car and knelt down to pet her. Becky made a creaky little happy whine as her wagging tail slapped the car door.

Once we were both out of the car, Becky did a little dance, bowing and leaping, back and forth between us. We showered her with praise and I was relieved for it took the sting off the awkwardness of the situation.

"Hello, gorgeous," Bob said, approaching me with a smile. "I gave her a bath this morning. She was looking pretty shabby last night."

JT walked directly to my friend and planted a kiss on her lips. "Are you girls hungry? I hope that's a swim suit strap, the beach is waiting." It was hard to tell if Patrice squirmed away or her body rippled with pleasure.

Bob extended an arm and drew me in for an embrace. "Country bacon is sizzling and the batter's just waitin' to be poured."

"Sounds good," I managed to say.

I understand why directors pick criminally handsome men to play villains in soap operas. Hippy Bob's long hair must have been just washed. It was still damp around his shoulders, and his long bangs caught amber glints of sun. His olive skin was supple, clear and gently tanned. Some people you'd meet in a bar benefitted from dim lights, but Bob's rugged good looks were even more stunning in the daytime. Being dressed in long shorts and tennis shoes highlighted his shapely calves. One could easily imagine the fake cousins on center court at Wimbledon.

"What a night," Bob exclaimed. "You girls are a welcome sight."

"I can't wait to hear everything," I blurted out while stroking Becky's furry spine. "We were so worried about you guys. But, this big girl is back. What a huge relief. I texted Devin and told him as soon as we heard last night."

JT just smiled.

We all migrated to our usual place, the huge front porch. The table outside was set with cloth placemats and napkins. A yellow pitcher of syrup was set on a yellow saucer. Now that I realized that their place belonged to an old lady, the knick-knacks all made sense. Why else would two straight men have a hive-shaped bowl for honey?

"It was quite a night," JT said, as he pulled out a chair for Patrice. "Shall we eat right quick? Or, would you girls like to go down by the beach for a mimosa?"

Patrice and I froze, then cast quick looks at each other for a cue. Hippy Bob nuzzled my neck. "You aren't in any kind of hurry, are you?"

I started to shrug and it turned into a spastic twist of indecision. The tall grass seemed to wave me down to the beach. "A mimosa can't be a bad thing, I s'pose. Uh, but you said breakfast is ready. I don't want to mess up—"

JT disappeared into the house. After a couple minutes of small talk he reappeared with a tray holding a glass pitcher of orange juice, ice bucket, bottle of champagne and four glasses. A little bottle of Maraschino cherries anchored down the cocktail napkins. "We're off," he said.

"Our rockers," Hippy Bob added, as we headed away from the house. "To the beach, Becky. Go girl!" He threw a tennis ball down the path.

We trailed behind her, each of us cupping a hand over our mouths to avoid the sand her paws stirred up.

I tapped Bob's shoulder. "I thought Becky wasn't allowed to go to the beach. You usually put her inside."

"Oh," he called over his shoulder, "it's fine with us. We just don't want anyone else taking her down."

"It's fine with me, if it's fine with you," I mumbled, thinking back to the big upset when Devin lost her for a few hours at the beach. Tall palms swayed on each side of the path and for a moment it felt like a carefree summer day; we were four kids with a dog, just heading to the ocean.

A weathered wooden table and four chairs were set up at the base of the hill. The tide was out and the hard, wet sand was gray and shimmered for what seemed like a quarter mile before it joined the small waves. We found seats under the large green tattered umbrella shielding us from the July sun. Patrice slid off her skinny T-shirt revealing a hot-pink bikini top that emphasized her golden tan—among other assets. Instead of sitting at the table with the rest of us, she pulled a towel from her large tote and laid it on the back of a beach recliner facing the ocean. Although the temperature was already in the 80's, I wasn't taking anything off.

As JT poured the drinks, Bob finally got to the point. "Okay, here's how it went down. About ten to twelve, JT walks down the road to the mailbox. Oh, and we can't thank you enough, ladies. That was a very classy thing you did, lending us the ransom. JT and I been talking about it all morning. We were really stuck. I don't want to think about anything bad happening to 'angel fur.'"

He made a little whistle and Becky trotted to his side and sat down. He caressed her head lovingly while we watched. Patrice laid on her side facing us, as JT picked up the story.

"I got the ten grand in the padded envelope," he explained. "Each thousand is in a paper clip. I've got a key for the pedestrian gate since I have no intention of opening the main gate in case the wise guy wants to drive in to my place." He passed me a glass. "Veronica—we thank you. We salute you."

I took the drink from him. He did the same little salute to Patrice when he passed her glass over. I blurted out, "Let's not forget Lucinda—who chipped in half of the money." Immediately I regretted the reference, as it recalled the inequity of the talent contest. My foot was in my mouth and I chased it with an icy drink while my stupid words just hung in the air.

JT ignored the comment and took a large gulp from his mimosa. He finally looked in our direction. "Like I said, I put the dough in the mailbox. By that time my eyes were pretty accustomed to the dark, but dang, it was pitch last night, mega-dark."

"Did you have any weapons on you?" Patrice asked.

"All the guns around here are rifles, so I couldn't carry one. But earlier in the day I stashed one next to that live oak by the gate. I had a knife in a sheath on my belt and I was carrying a flashlight. So anyway, I'm on the other side of the gate and as soon as I close the metal hatch to the mailbox, this light hits me, nearly blinding me. The asshole had parked just south of the road and he popped on his brights as soon as he saw me. I was kinda blinded for a second, you know. I guess I was expecting someone to drive up. It was majorly quiet. So, next I hear Becky barking like crazy in the distance."

My heart was racing as I pictured the empty road at mid-night with an evil stranger approaching.

"This dude was coming from the car, naturally, and he was back-lit." JT paused to light a cigarette. He continued. "Becky's bark was unmistakable, though, and I had her leash in my pocket."

"Bob, where were *you*?" I squirmed with suspense.

He reached across the table with the champagne, already refilling drinks. "I'm down the road in the other direction, off in the woods. I borrowed the gardener's little Toyota truck for the night. It's small and fast."

"The guy looks kinda thick," JT continued. "Older dude, maybe a hundred seventy-five pounds and about five-ten. He's already walking up with Becky on a leash. She's goin' all ape-shit, barking and yippin', he tells her to shut up, and then says, 'put your hands out to your sides like you're walking a tight rope, 'cuz, man, you are. Any quick moves or …blah, blah"

Patrice was off the recliner and over to our table in a streak. "Or, *what*?"

JT ran his index finger around the rim of his glass in a slow circle. "He said he'd shoot the mutt. Then he laughed. He told me to get over to the other side of the road as he counted the money. The lights were plenty bright and it didn't take long."

"Since the lights were bright," I said, "you got to see his face, huh?"

"Did he have a gun?" Patrice asked, her voice barely above a whisper.

"I couldn't tell," JT said. "I couldn't see his whole face, only the side. First he tells me to turn around. I say, 'no way, you dumb ass.' Because I pictured him just taking me out, execution style. If he points a gun at me, at least I can run like a jack rabbit or throw my knife. Maybe whistle for my man, Bob. But then he says, okay—sit down then, but no fast moves.'

"So, we're across the highway from each other and I can only see his face at an angle for about thirty seconds while he counts the money. Then, just like that," JT snapped his fingers, "he bends down and unclips the leash on Becky's collar. Then, the asshole high-tails it back to the truck.

"The car with the lights on was about a hundred yards to the south." JT jerked his thumb over his shoulder, as if to indicate the spot. "I saw the dude run down, get in the driver's side of the car with the headlights on, and he makes a U-ee, and peels out. The whole thing took about three minutes. As far as I know, he was alone."

Bob broke in. "He was driving a black, or dark Ford Forerunner. JT was holding Becky and checking her out and I chased the mo-fo down Highway 15 with two loaded deer rifles on the seat." With that Bob stopped talking. We were focused on him and no one moved as he gravely looked off to the distance.

I held my breath. "Go on," I pressed.

"This is the hard part to talk about," he said, his neck sinking a bit between his shoulder blades.

Patrice and I leaned in. I felt sick. I croaked out the words, "You shot him."

"No." He shook his head slowly, his elbows were on the table and he dropped his chin into his palms.

JT stood up like an alpha male taking charge. "The truck had something pulled over the license plate. Maybe a cloth or tee-shirt, anyway, he didn't get the number and the truck outran him."

"So, we go to the police now," Patrice stated.

"No," JT said, calmly. "We can't. If the executors of the Honeywell estate know about this, they won't *pay* us. "

"Or," Bob said, "renew our contract. Don't worry girls." He patted the air with his palms as if to calm us. "You'll get your money. We told ya'll, we're getting paid, finally, after six months. Our contract is up on the tenth of July. Friday, Becky goes to her semi-annual check-up with her vet. Then the bank dude comes over and does a quick inventory of the property and estate." He rubbed his thumb across his fingertips. "We get paid Saturday—*you* get paid Saturday—right off the top."

"That seems so unfair," Patrice moaned. "I mean, thank you for paying us back, but you've worked all this time and to have someone, just….just?"

"What happened, happened," JT said. With one hand he bent a match inside the matchbook and struck it. He lit a cigarette and blew the match out. "Don't get me wrong—I'm not letting this dirt weasel get away with it. But, we need more time to figure out who he is."

"Are you staying on here?" Patrice's voice was small, making me wince from the eagerness. Then she must have caught herself because she added, "I mean, I wouldn't blame you if you decided to leave this job."

"We've already told the bank we want to re-up another six months." Bob blew a smoke ring into the air, then winked at me.

"Bob's bringing Becky into town this afternoon to see another vet," JT added. "Under a fake name, just to make sure there's no surprises. But, she's acting normal so far."

Patrice looked directly at JT. "So…we get our money back on the tenth?"

"You girls are the first to be paid, Saturday, July tenth. Four days from now."

"Just out of curiosity," I said, swishing my drink around the glass, "what did you think of Gertrude the Oracle?" I took a long sip.

JT didn't miss a beat. "She was quite a trip. Nice lady though."

I caught Patrice's eye and discreetly tapped my wrist. She slipped her t-shirt back on and brushed sand off her legs.

I fished around in my purse a moment then pulled out my cell phone. "Oh, this text message just came in." I turned to Patrice. "It's Lucinda. She wants to know if everything went okay. She's expecting me to pay her back—today."

Patrice was putting her sandals on. "I thought you had three days. It's only been two." She put her empty glass on the tray along with mine.

"The problem is," I said calmly, "that we won't have the money tomorrow either. We need to go explain *something* to her. I don't want to make this call on the phone, so you'll excuse us?"

The guys stood up, then exchanged glances.

"No breakfast, ladies?" Hippy Bob asked, sounding thoroughly wounded.

JT let out a long whistle. "Whoa, that was quick."

"Another time, just not today. But thank you." I smiled and turned away. My face felt hot. I herded Patrice in front of me as we quickly climbed the hill, back toward the car.

CHAPTER 37

"Just keep walking," I ordered Patrice, under my breath. "Don't stop. I mean it."

We were practically jogging to the car in our hurry to leave the Cad-pad, and we made it without looking back. We waved out the open windows as we backed up. Then, after a wide turn, we were headed to the gate. "Don't say anything until we are out on the road," I said through tight lips.

Patrice grunted in agreement as she adjusted her seatbelt, then she tipped the rearview mirror down to look behind us. "Bob's just standing there talking to the dog. JT is going toward the house with the tray."

The gate was already open by the time we reached it. I barely felt my foot smashing down the accelerator as we pulled out of the driveway and soon enough we were speeding down the highway.

"Slow down," Patrice begged. "Where are we going at warp speed, anyway? Gertrude won't be back for a couple of days. We can't even ask her advice." She groaned as she massaged her temples. "Ohmygod, I almost forgot Lucinda. You have to face her now, don't you?"

"Not necessarily," I said. As the trees whizzed by the window, a sign caught my eye. I slammed on the brakes and pulled off the road, gravel flying as the car ground to a stop in front of a little roadside tavern. The sign read, *Curley's Brew and Cue.* "How about a beer?" I asked. "I'm too nervous to drive."

"Here?" Patrice said, recoiling.

I pulled up between a rusted pickup truck and a motorcycle, and slammed the shifter into park.

"I thought you had to go see Lucinda, what about the text?"

"Ah, I just made that up to get out of there." I cut the engine and opened the door. "Come on. We need to figure out a plan. I can't drive *and* brainstorm."

"That's a fact. I take it you don't believe the guys?"

"You mean the fake cousins, who—according to Devin—have suitcases stacked up? Who *claim* they'll be paid a chunk of money at the *end* of the week? Bob? The veterinarian student? *Online*? Pshh, what a crock. How about your honey, JT? Did you hear him say Gertrude is a nice lady?"

She started to shake her head. So, I got out and slammed the car door, leaving her inside. I stomped up to the wooden steps surrounding the front of the tavern. Glancing over my shoulder, I could see that Patrice was coming, as I knew she would. Still, I wasn't exactly thrilled about going into some bubba bar before noon. I wished there was a giant roadside trampoline so I could jump off my tension, bouncing my way out of my own skin. I wasn't sure there was a drink inside that would relieve my anxious heebie-jeebies, creepy-crawly skin and shallow breathing. Driving like a lunatic wasn't the answer. Something had to be done and I was sick of waiting for their next lie.

*****

Through her ties at the Chamber of Commerce, Patrice was able to make some discrete inquiries. The Mutual Bank of South Carolina handled the Honeywell Estate, AKA Pinewood, formerly Tid-bit mansion, currently Cad-pad. Patrice claimed that we were lucky Miss Lila's bank was local and not in Charleston or Savannah. It was hard to place that factoid in the *luck* column of recent of events.

I held the bank's address in my hand. It was four o'clock. Despite the heat, I was dressed in a tan pants suit. I checked the mirror for the last time, grabbed my keys, and walked out of the Crowne Plaza mumbling.

Deciding it would take too long to get an appointment, or be too disappointing if no one would see me, I drove over, equipped with only adrenalin and a few lies of my own. As I made the drive into town, I vaguely recalled Bob and JT arguing over some forms that needed to be faxed to a bank, but that seemed like weeks ago. I should have paid more attention. The whole thing was a disaster. I should've never lent them the money in the first place. Instead of interrogating bank personnel, right now I should be learning new songs for my gig or working on Jack's book.

As I walked toward the bank's entrance, my cell phone rang its happy tune.

I reached into my purse guts, pulled it out and trying to shut it up, I accidently answered. "Hello? Oh, hi Lucinda. Yeah, I'm glad to talk to you too. Listen, I'm driving in to a—" I snapped the phone shut. Long ago I learned you can always get rid of a caller if you hang up on yourself.

Only a few people milled about inside the bank—which I took to be a good sign. A uniformed security guard smiled at me when I entered—good sign number two. Instead of waiting for a teller, I went directly to the carpeted half of the bank and sat in an upholstered chair in front of an empty desk. People were walking around and speaking in hushed tones. I reminded myself that my voice tended to carry. All my life I've been hushed by well-meaning hateful people.

"How are you today, and how may I help you?" a middle-aged lady wearing a pants suit wanted to know.

"I'm very well, thank you." I fixed an earnest and what I hoped would appear sincere expression on my face.

"Are we here to open a new account?"

"Actually, I'm here to inquire about a job," I said, clearing my throat, "that may be coming available at the estate of one of your bank's clients. May I speak to someone who handles the Lila Lee Honeywell estate, er, account, please?"

She squinted slightly. "A job with the branch here, you mean?"

"The Lila Lee Honeywell Estate is handled by this bank. May I speak, please speak, to one of the managers?"

The request sent her off to a hushed conference by the back wall. Soon, a gentleman, typical portly, good ole boy, pulled out a chair and seated himself in front of me. "Howdy." He extended a meaty hand. "My name is Randy Randalson."

I shook his fleshy mitt as he pumped my hand a couple times. Distracted by the red-neck bank manager, I said the first thing that popped into my mind. "Is your first name really Randy? Or, is it a nickname for Randalson?"

"Naw, it's just a nickname that stuck, Miss. I've had it since grade school. Between you and me, the name's really Carl." He shook his head with mock disgust. "And, your name?"

"My name is Veronica Bennett, and, ah don't mean to take up mucha yer tiiime." I heard myself accidently mimicking the soft Carolina accent. I tend to slip into regional dialects from time to time and it always surprises me to hear it come out. It's an involuntary response to copying songs, but in conversation it's a rude linguistic burp. If he'd been English, I might have blurted, *don't mean to be a bother, really old sport, but—*. As my mind wandered in this direction, I swallowed hard and hacked out a couple dry coughs.

"Can I get you a little cup of water, Miss?"

"Thank you," I rasped.

By the time he returned holding a teeny Dixie cup in his huge hand, I'd had more than enough time to be embarrassed. All these minutes in the carpeted section of the bank and I didn't have the decency to open a new account. "Mr. Randalson," I started off, "I understand that Miss Lila Lee Honeywell's estate uses caretakers. Are you familiar with the Pinewood Estate over in Sea Pines Plantation?"

"Yes, Ma'am. I handle the trust."

"Well, my friend told me there's a position opening soon for a new caretaker or caretakers. So, I came to talk to you about that possible opportunity." My leg started to shake and I put my hand on my thigh to try and squash the nervous energy from sprouting out of my kneecap.

He leaned back in his chair and it creaked with the strain. "First off, the job calls for a couple of caretakers, because it's several acres—"

"I have a partner."

He smiled in a patronizing way. "It's a bit more compli-cated than that. I don't know who told you about the Honeywell Estate, but there is more to it than just mowing the lawn. There is an animal to care for and it's actually—"

"Is the job for caretaker open *now*?" I said, breathlessly. It occurred to me that maybe the guys were about to be fired.

"I'd have to check on the date, but the fellas doing that job *are* leaving, so your source is correct. We've been screening applicants and running background checks all month. We've settled on a nice retired couple from Buellton to take the post." For a moment we both just sat there looking at each other. "I'm sorry if you made a trip all the way down here. We coulda told you over the phone, Miss."

I couldn't get up from the chair. It felt like I suddenly weighed a thousand pounds. It took high-voltage restraint not to snatch him by the lapels and beg for answers. If I walked away now, I would never know the real circumstances of the mysterious Pinewood Estate. "Do you mind if I ask when the new couple is starting?"

"Let see. The current caretakers completed their contract. So, I believe the couple's moving in tomorrow. The fellas came in the other day and got traveler's checks, I remember that. Nice fellas."

"I see," I squeaked.

He cleared his throat. "Oh my, you look disappointed, dear. Being a caretaker isn't a job for a woman." He opened a couple of drawers. "Here, take this." He handed me a tissue. "Have you seen the classified ads? They come out on Tuesdays."

I shook my head and willed my eyes to absorb the tears forming.

"Would you like to open a savings account? I can include free checking?"

"Actually, I don't have any money to save right now. When I do, I'll come back though."

*****

I scurried back to my car under skies that threatened rain, and called Patrice. She answered on the first ring. "What did you do with the IOU you got from the guys?"

"You could say hello," she hissed.

"Where is the IOU for the eight-thousand?" I persisted. "I mean ten-thousand."

"Veronica, I don't want to tell you. You'll get mad."

I sighed into the phone. "What? Are we ten years old? You're a business woman. You own a successful spa that you built from scratch. Don't tell me you didn't *get* an IOU from the guys. A *signed* IOU."

"I didn't know how to ask JT to sign it," she whined. "The ten grand was supposed to be paid back the next day, Vee. It seemed stupid to ask a good friend to sign a piece of paper. Remember, we thought Gertrude OK'd it," she lowered her voice, "at the time."

"*Geeze,* Patrice." I wanted to bang my head on the steering wheel, when I spotted Randalson come out of the bank walking past my car. He caught my eye and shot a hand up in a wave. I did the same.

"I knew you'd be mad," Patrice whimpered. "Let me go outside to talk." There was a pause and I heard a door opening and closing in the background. She lowered her voice. "What did you find out at the bank?"

"Nothing good. Gotta go." I clicked the phone shut and bolted out of the car in the direction of the portly banker.

CHAPTER 38

I caught up with Mr. Randalson and almost mowed him over. He was moving slower than I'd realized. "Mr. Randalson, excuse me."

"Miss Bennett, isn't it? Are you still looking for that newspaper?" He did a little head slap. "After you left, I knew I should've gone over to my desk and grabbed you the classified section."

We were standing on a sidewalk that rimmed both the shopping area and bank. His attaché case in his hand suggested he was leaving for the day.

"Sir, do you have a moment?" I touched his arm. "I have just a couple questions to ask. Please?"

His expression was stern, but I could tell he was conflicted. "I've told you all I can about the Honeywell Estate, dear. We can't divulge information about our clients."

Just then, it started to sprinkle. I searched from side to side. I needed office space. Where was a donut shop when you needed one? It was now or never. Ignoring the shoppers that were parting around us, I kept him there blocking the narrow sidewalk. "Regarding the caretaker job—could you at least tell me what it pays?"

He shrugged. "Again, that would be bank business that doesn't concern you since we are no longer taking applications for caretakers. This job has a certain amount of, what can I say, confidentiality attached to it."

A woman pushing a child in a stroller weaved around us. "Okay, well enough. But, Sir, please, just a moment of your time. Are you aware of any unusual occurrences going on at Pinewood this last week?"

He nodded.

"Thank you. Did the caretakers who were working there get fired, because of a—a, strange occurrence?"

He pursed his lips and tilted his head to the side, like a judge considering the evidence. "No, ma'am, it was only a six month probationary period. Two months ago they opted to move on once this contract ended. Do you still have your mind fixed on getting that job?"

"No." I put my hand on his sleeve. "But if something *was* to go missing while—a caretaker—was on duty, well, should that theft be reported? Just say?"

The banker squinted, then shifted his weight from one foot to another. "I've got a question for you. Have you ever noticed the tallest building in a big city?"

"Yes, sure," I said.

"Which businesses occupy most of these tall buildings you see in a big city?"

"I don't know, hotels?" I guessed.

He stepped a little closer and lowered his voice. "They are *insurance* buildings." He drew little quotations marks in the air. "They handle *occurrences*. My advice to you is to leave well enough alone. Estates, just like people, dead or alive, have insurance companies. Thefts are reported. Insurance companies have the responsibility to pay those claims."

Beads of perspiration dotted his forehead. His folksy demeanor was gone. "So, you don't need to concern yourself with the goings-on at Pinewood. Got it?"

I nodded.

He turned around and shouldered his way through the crowd.

Walking back to my car was like a moon-walk, where gravity had shifted. My feet were heavy, my shoulders slumped. Each step aged me a few years; I was no innocent ingénue. A few steps more and I was well past being a trusting girl with a ready smile and a few thousand bucks to lend a summer boyfriend. By the time I turned the key in the ignition I was ready to pack it all in and drive directly to the convalescent home. When the car backed itself out of the lot, I tried to recall where I'd seen a cemetery.

My singing gig started at seven. If I went straight back, I'd have an hour to eat. It was either that or confront the jerks at Tid-bit mansion on my way home. Involving Patrice was useless. I had to go solo. I splurged on Devin while he was here and now I couldn't afford to lose half the money I'd saved, let alone pay back Lucinda. The thought of returning her calls seized me with humiliating fear and dread.

As I drove on, Randalson's words played back in my mind. *Insurance companies have the responsibility to pay claims.* That would include ransom claims. Naturally, the bank wouldn't do anything to lose a multi-million dollar account. The trust could go on for years. Even if the insurance company didn't pay the ransom note, the bank would—just to keep the status quo. As my windshield wipers smeared the rain, I tried to calculate all the money the guys might have racked up. It made me sick to my stomach.

The sky had turned charcoal in a matter of minutes. The wind whistled along the highway, its invisible current trying to blow me off the road. All I knew was that, if the banker was right—the moments were ticking down. The new caretakers were moving in tomorrow. That left only now—to face the thieves.

CHAPTER 39

I pulled up to the familiar old gate. Flinching from the rain pellets, I rolled the window down a third of the way and hit the buzzer.

JT's voice came through the metal box. "Who's there?"

"It's me, JT. I'm passing through this way. May I speak with you guys for a minute?"

"Bob's still at the vet's with the dog. You want to drop by after work when he's here?" This wasn't part of the ill-conceived plan.

"Gee, could I just speak to you a minute?"

The gate swung open, permitting me one final roll down the oak-lined entry of the Honeywell Estate. It was eerie how each trip here became progressively worse. This time there were no sparrows chirping. Lightening split the sky, followed by a roar of thunder and the tinny patter of more rain pelting the roof. I entered alone to confront a thief.

Instead of parking in the clearing to the side of the house, I brought the Corolla up to the porch. I left the keys in the ignition. *You get more flies with honey than vinegar, you get more flies with honey than vinegar,* I chanted softly. At this point, getting the money back was all that mattered.

He met me on the Carolina Room porch and held the door open as I rushed in from the storm. I was holding a magazine over the top of my head so my bangs wouldn't frizz up. Once inside the familiar yellow kitchen, I smelled coffee.

"Want a cup?" JT held his mug up in the air. It was odd that we had dispensed with all the happy horseshit hugging and predictable round of compliments that normally began our visits. Maybe because I said I needed only a few minutes, or maybe he was tipped off by someone.

"Thanks," I said. "Coffee sounds good."

"You shouldn't be out." He secured the screen door tightly as I stood dripping in the assigned area of the porch. "Come on in." He motioned toward the kitchen area. "And, take an umbrella when you leave," he said, eyeing the wilted magazine on the floor beside me. "Didn't you hear the hurricane warnings, girl?"

He moved to the counter and poured me a cup.

"A little cream and sugar, thanks, and, yes I heard about it. It's surprising how dark the sky becomes—and so sudden." We stood there for a few moments, neither of us friendly enough to sit, I suppose. "JT, I guess you know I need to pay back Lucinda. Is there a chance we could get the money before Saturday?"

"Sure," he said. He left the room for a moment, and then returned with a light blue business-sized envelope. Probably the linen stationary of an old lady, I thought to myself. He stood before me, opened it, and silently counted the bills inside. Relief washed over me. I had to refrain from giggling-off the nervous tension. He licked the flap and sealed the envelope. "Thank you, for the loan." His smile was unpleasant.

"Sure," I said, and my voice sounded ordinary. I eagerly took the envelope and then flushed with embarrassment for what I was about to do. Avoiding his eyes, I forced myself to open the envelope and count the bills. I flipped through the hundreds, ten in each paperclip. There weren't enough paperclips. "Uh, there's only five grand here."

"That's what we borrowed from you and Patrice. As far as Lucinda? You, me, and everyone on this island knows that prize money was *mine*. She don't like it? She can come to me herself."

I gasped. "Are you serious?"

"I'm as serious as a heart attack."

The electricity seemed to falter and the lights flicked off and back on. Instinctively, I looked to the window. What a time for a blackout. When I looked back at JT, his stare hadn't wavered.

"Have you no *ethics*?" I asked.

He shrugged. Then he lit a cigarette, shook the match, and jauntily flopped onto the window seat. In the dark, chilly kitchen, alone with this man for the first time ever, JT took on the aura of a seasoned sociopath.

"How did you get this job as caretaker, anyway?"

He answered simply, "It's not important."

"Ethics *might* be important to a bank running background checks. What *is* your background? I know what you are not. You are not Bob's cousin. Or Lila Lee's nephew. Or, even a caretaker, for that matter. You term is up." My voice got louder and I couldn't slow down the words. "I happen to know the new caretakers are moving in tomorrow."

JT made a hissing sound like air escaping a tire. "It'd seem you'd have enough to do singing your little songs at the hotel. Bob tells me you fancy yourself as a writer." He emitted a malicious laugh. "So, are you a *mystery* writer? Is that it?" He waved his hands in front of him, like a palsy victim. "Whooo…crime fighter?"

"I don't know how you did it—but I think you scammed us—and probably the bank and the insurance company too." I stepped closer to the window seat where he sat with his legs splayed open. He might have been sunning himself on the beach, judging from his leisurely posture. This infuriated me even more; I felt my bottom lip quaver. "I also doubt that dog was even kidnapped. To think you even tried to blame my son. But, I guess ripping-off people beats working."

He appraised me coolly. "You two got your money. Lucinda can kiss my ass."

With the blue envelope pressed to my chest, I ran out the door into the pounding rain.

CHAPTER 40

The road was slick with a rain that pounded clear horizontal stripes. The windshield wipers swung back and forth like a sad metronome ticking off my remaining minutes on this stinking island that had ripped me off—body and soul. My tears blurred the treacherous road as I tried to navigate while sobbing. When I pulled into the hotel's circular driveway, I defiantly used valet parking. For employees, it was a capital offence.

There was a half hour to go from drenched and depressed to a care-free girl, singing with a smile. I shuddered at the thought of the eight o'clock crowd rolling into the piano bar, looking to *me* for entertainment.

Dripping into the lobby, I stepped around a huge cardboard sign on a tripod: *Welcome to the Nissan-Palmolive 22nd Annual Celebrity Golf tournament!* With all the drama, this event had slipped my mind. For years the biggest golf event of the southeast took place in Hilton Head the weekend after the Fourth of July. Still, I found it difficult to care. Without an umbrella, my hair had been rained on, dried, and then rained on again. Judging from my reflection in the windows, the top of my head was frizzy, like the back of a sheep.

"Veronica?" A familiar voice called out. I glanced back and Jack Swanson leaned in and kissed both my wet cheeks. "Darling! How wonderful to see you."

Instinctively, I wiped my face with my hand.

"Vee, you aren't wiping away my kisses—are you?" He put one arm around my shoulder and ushered me around the corner away from the registration desk.

Once we were alone, I buried my head in his chest, gripping his back like a rescue raft in an angry sea.

Jack gently peeled my fingers off his back. "Oh, dear. You aren't okay. Can we go somewhere and talk?"

I nodded once and with one hand on my back he guided me to the elevator. "Will this get us there?"

I nodded again.

We stepped inside and I pushed five.

He murmured, "My, my. You must have seen an alligator. I've never known you to be speechless."

Once inside my messy room, I cleared piles of clothes off the only chair and sat him down. He immediately looked relaxed, the way his arms spread wide across the back of it. I'd forgotten that quality Jack had, always comfortable with himself. It must have come from being on so many movie sets. Wherever he was, he looked like he belonged.

Dressed in a black windbreaker over a tan v-neck jersey, he surveyed the room. His hair was longer than I'd remembered. He pushed back some wayward strands in his trademark hand sweep across his head. I'd forgotten Jack was older, as crow's feet don't show up in emails. Fortunately, his brand of masculine good looks just made him seem, well, experienced.

"Where did you get those cool boots?" I asked. "You just flew in from Sydney, didn't you?"

"It's about time we got to me," he chuckled. He stretched out his long leg modeling the footwear. "This is ostrich hide leather. I went to one of those animal preserves in the outback and bought these in the gift shop."

"That doesn't sound real PC. Your outback tan looks terrific, though."

"And, might I say, you are a sight for sore-eyes yourself."

"Really, you wouldn't believe the day I've had."

"When do you get to escape Alligator Island?"

"My contract ends Labor Day, but I've been offered the chance to extend through September. I plan to hide out in my room until October."

"Do I dare ask how *our* book is coming?"

I pointed at the desk. "Okay. It needs a little more time. I think I can. I, I...."

"Come here, Vee, and sit on my lap. Don't say a word. Just let me hold those wet curls against my shoulder. See? It's waterproof." I fell into the nest he offered and for a few minutes my cares seemed to dissolve.

"There, there, isn't this nice?"

It was, and after a brief respite, I called the bar and told them I'd be a half hour late. As I picked out clothes, I filled him in on the last twenty-four hours, including the fact that I was dodging Patrice and Lucinda's calls. It couldn't last long, since they would most likely show up at work despite the storm.

After my quick shower, he riddled me with questions. As horrid as it was, recounting the saga was somehow liberating. I sat in my robe while applying make-up. A twist of my tangled hair was secured with a tortoise shell barrette. I chose a basic black dress for the night, knowing Jack's preference for a classic look, and a little midriff-brushing silver sweater. In the back of my top drawer was an envelope and jewelry box inside. I took out the opal and fastened the chain behind my hair. Then, grabbed my music bag and motioned with my head toward the door. "So, that's the story. The creeps have flown away with Lucinda's money." I didn't add, as well as our dignity— although he may have guessed as much. "I have to repay it."

"Darling, no one is flying anywhere," he said. "The Hilton Head airport was closed a few hours ago. I came in through

Savannah. The hotel sent a car. Due to hurricane warnings, all planes on the island are grounded. To go anywhere they would have to take the interstate 95 South to the Savannah airport. How long ago do you think they left?"

"Hmm," I said as I slumped down on the bed. "The bank closed at five. I confronted JT about five-forty-five. I left the cad-pad at ten after six, drove here and it's seven-ten now."

Jack rubbed his chin and I heard the sound of scratching. "I just came in on the only road. There was only one lane open on the north side, and the other side of the highway looked like a parking lot. There's a good chance they're still in that line."

I sniffed. "That doesn't do me any good."

"Your boss, what's his name? The one who insisted you do his little Island Idol contest. Is it David?"

"Yes."

"Do you suppose he's still in the hotel?"

"I'm sure of it." I felt my heart thumping with new dread. "The F & B manager has to be here when the VIPs come in to register. Why?"

A private smile crossed his face. He swung his hands together in a thunderous clap. Then he jauntily walked around the bed and picked up the phone. "Please put me through to the Food and Beverage Manager," he said into the receiver.

I tapped his arm and whispered, "His name is David Lindsay—what are you doing?"

Jack pressed his finger to his lip and shhh'd me. "Ah, Mr. Lindsay. Jack Swanson here. Yes, yes, everything is as it should be. Thank you, sir." After a pause, he said, "It's no bother at all to autograph those posters. What? Oh, don't worry about the storm. I can actually use the rest tomorrow. Say, I understand you had quite a talent show here last weekend. Your staff told me it was your idea." Jack nodded and rolled his eyes skyward as he listened. He pointed the receiver in my direction and I could hear David's tinny voice gush with hyperbole about the Island Idol contest.

I snorted with disgust and moved to the chair.

"Congratulations, David," he finally said. "As you may have heard, I just wrapped a film in Australia called *Pelican Point*. The song that was to play over the closing credits was just a simple guitar and voice. He was a local bloke in Sydney. Now I'm told there was a mistake in the release documents. I'm in a rush to find another song to complete the bloody editing process. It's a long shot that you might know a guitarist, but we're in a crisis to finish. I'm looking for a male voice singing to guitar. It's an Indy film, which means artistic, low budget." He chuckled affably. "Frankly, it's easiest if we just go with an unknown."

I jumped up from my seat and Jack swatted the air in my direction.

"David," he spoke into the phone slowly. "Does anyone from the talent contest come to mind? Oh? His name again was? Oh, yes? This JT Barton sounds interesting. Perhaps he has a recording of a song that just might fit." Another long pause as Jack nodded at the phone.

"You say you have his phone number on file? Would you be kind enough to give him a call and explain my situation? Terrific. One more thing. The airlines lost one of my bags. I need to return to Savannah early in the morning to identify it. Oh, thank you, but I'd rather drive myself. Here's a thought, ask what's his name—JT—to meet me at the Wingate Hotel coffee shop. Yes, it's next to the airport. Good. I'm sure it's a bother for him to drive to Savannah, since he lives in Hilton Head. However, if he has a demo and wants to submit it, he needs to get it to me then and there. Otherwise, I'm flying out." Jack murmured a lot of uh-huhs, then said, "Tell him to meet me with his demo at nine. Thank *you*, my man. Call me back to confirm if he's available. No doubt he'll be grateful for your referral. Wasn't it your idea to find the talent, the Island Idol? If this JT is all you say he is, then it's time for him to be recognized."

CHAPTER 41

"All right, darling, we've got our sting in place," Jack said, dropping the phone in its cradle.

Naturally, David was ecstatic to be involved with the star-making machine once again. Within half an hour the Savannah meeting was set. Jack was so clever to have David present the idea.

There was a narrow strip of carpet between the dresser and the wall at the foot of the beds in my room and I paced the nine steps back and forth thinking how glad I was that I'd never dropped Jack's name to anyone on Hilton Head Island—as tempting as it was to brag about our affair. Now JT and Hippy Bob were contacted by the Food & Beverage Manager of the Crowne Plaza, all very up and up. How freakin' perfect.

Jack propped up the pillows behind him and leaned back on the un-made bed. A mischievous grin crossed his face and he clapped his hands together. "Now what shall we do with them?" Rubbing his palms like in a melodrama, his voice lowered to a growl. "Tie them up and throw them into the Savannah River?"

"Duct taping them to a telephone pole may take too long," I said, joining him on the bed. "Although that's tempting as well." He scooted over and lifted one arm. I snuggled in and pressed against his body. We sat quietly staring at the blank wall. The reality was just settling in.

"Veronica, I can't tell you how thrilled I am to come to your rescue."

"Again," we said at the same time. We both remembered the time I'd got myself out on a limb, actually a twig of a limb— a year ago. It was how I came to be writing his biography.

I turned to him. "I could thank you with sex, but it seems so cheap."

We laughed heartily and rolled over together. Lying on our sides, facing each other, we gazed into each other's eyes and then fell silent. He had a way of looking at me that felt like a kindly inspection; the way a mom looks at her child wearing frosting on a chin.

Thin horizontal lines creased his forehead. Wrinkles that may now cast him into roles playing *sidekick* of leading man. But beneath the dark brows, his eyes danced with life. Jack's deep eyes drew me in. I was a thirsty person leaning over a well. Not knowing how far to lean inside, how precarious it is, I was willing to fall all the way down recklessly whirling toward his will. His passively seductive will. Passion rose into feverish kisses that seemed to channel the lightning storm's electricity.

He pulled back a little to look at me, and then whispered, "Hold that thought. If I am to continue being the hero in your dramas, it calls for a hot shower and a few hours sleep. Mmmm, I'll find you later, you sexy minx."

I rolled off him and we calmed ourselves, replacing urgent squeezes with my nails gently stroking the inside of his arm. The windows rattled with the force of the storm and my head buried into his neck—wanting to burrow forever. "This weather is a shame. All the golfers just arrived," I murmured.

He stood up and brushed his hair back with the palm of his hand, then tucked in his shirt. I sat up and hugged his waist. Leaning my head against his soft belly, I noticed it was different from Hippy Bob's six-pack abs. But Jack was fifty-eight, and with that came a few pounds. At this moment he was my strong, masculine, soft rock. I brushed aside some renegade tears, careful not to look up. "Jack, I have to go play now. I'll be back about twelve."

He gently unclasped my hands from his waist. "We need to get an early start in the morning. I'll call downstairs and get a car."

"I have a car—"

"Vee—you make a very bad criminal."

"Oh, right. They know my—"

"I'll get us a wakeup call at seven. We'll leave at seven-thirty and be in Savannah by nine." He fumbled in his pocket and pulled out a little cardboard envelope. "I'm in penthouse G." He stroked the side of my face with his fingertips as he straightened up to his full six foot-two inches. "Now, don't get all teary on me. We haven't gotten Lucinda's money back yet."

"I know, but you are *helping* me. It means so much."

"It's raining. Can't golf anyway." He smiled and rubbed his chin. "Hey, I might get a chance to recycle some of the idiotic lines I memorized for *Pelican Point*."

"Really? Tell me one."

Jack narrowed his eyes and jerked his head back as if smelling month-old Roquefort cheese. "*Punks like you have a place in this world. I just haven't found it. But you can help me look!* Then, I pick up the guy and dunk him head-first into the toilet. It's not Shakespeare, but the kids like it."

CHAPTER 42

When I arrived at the piano at exactly five after eight, both Lucinda and Patrice were already there. Seeing them seated together was odd, until the volume of laughter and empty glasses betrayed an allegiance all too common in bars. Either, A) Patrice had forgiven the buxom hygienist for winning the talent contest, B) She was running interference for me since she knew we didn't have her money, or C) She was blasted and didn't give a rip. Acting pleased to see them both, I sat down on the piano bench and began with, "Here's That Rainy Day." *Maybe I should have saved those leftover dreams...funny, but here's that rainy day.*

My friends absolutely decorated the piano bar with their friendly Southern charm and hottitude. As locals, they knew tonight was the beginning of the celebrity golf tournament and even rain wasn't going to keep them from seeing who'd show up. The buzz of the evening was focused on a Monkey; a member from the vintage pop band, specifically, adorable Davey Jones. Still a 'tid-bit' with a dark tan, Davey seemed to have a constant stream of table-hoppers wishing him luck with the tourney.

Apparently, this night brought out a swarm of single women. A few times I overheard Jack Swanson's name pop out of the din of conversation. I'd smile at my secret, feeling my face flush with pleasure.

By the end of my set there were two full drinks in front of Patrice and Lucinda. Patrice slipped away and came back with an empty coffee cup. I watched as she poured one of her Cosmos inside, then furtively passed me the cup.

"Don't tell anyone," Patrice slurred, "but Lucinda just told me about her second job. It's hilarious."

David had already blabbed the top-secret information, but I acted surprised when Lucinda leaned in close. At that point, the Highway 15 truck stop/gas station condom route was described in detail. With dignity, the dental hygienist earnestly proclaimed that it was still in the health field.

"Lucinda, you are so right," I agreed, with a wink to Patrice. "And, by the way, I'm so sorry I wasn't able to get back to you earlier. I didn't want to bother you at work." Averting my lying eyes, I knocked back my cocktail like a sailor on a two-hour pass. "I'm glad to report that I have your money upstairs. Thank you so much for trusting us. I'll be right back."

Patrice leapt from her seat. "That's awesome!" She turned to Lucinda and jabbed her in the side with her elbow. "We helped pay the *um-hum*, too. Boy, I can really use the money. My quarterly taxes are due."

I leaned in close to Patrice. "Not so fast. You'll need to lower that thumb back into your fist, then wrap it around another drink. We only got half."

"What?" she gasped.

I stood up and reached for one of the cocktails in front of Patrice. Then set it on a different table. "I'd hate to see you ruin your eye-makeup with tears. You're pretty, uh, *animated,* my friend." I kissed her cheek and whispered, "I'll explain later." Turning to Lucinda, "I'll be right back with your—envelope."

I was back in a flash and watched Lucinda demurely slip the blue envelope in her large purse, without counting it. It made me wonder why I counted the money in JT's presence;

how that whole ugly scene would have been postponed had I just dropped it in my purse, thanked him, and left. He would have been gone by the time my shift ended—left town with our ten grand. Now I feared him too, a witches brew of toxic emotions.

As I played instrumentally, fairly ignored by the increasing conversational din, I recalled how blasé JT was about the money thing. Imagine, just now, me telling Lucinda, *JT won't repay you, and said, kiss my ass.* I started to get steamed, recalling his words; *she can come and talk to me if she wants to.* Just another lie. They were clearing out tonight. Not only that, what part did Bob play? Did he go along with the scam? Was it the plan all along? Did the insurance company pay the same ransom?

The night ended with a sing-a-long. When the crowd gets unruly, I can either ignore them and just improvise blues tunes, or jump in and become the counselor for camp buzz. Feeling the energy in the room, I invited them to sing along with, *Say it's all right? Say it's all right. It's all r-i-g-h-t—to have a good time, whoa, it's all right.*

That song always works with the drinking crowd because it has a great beat and they get a chance to sing the words only seconds after hearing them. It became a tequila-inspired spiritual, when they raised their arms into the air, with fingers rippling on, *Whoa, it's all right.* Then everyone chimed in loud on the chorus, "it's all r-i-g-h-t, to have a good time...It's all right."

******

Once in his room, Jack and I celebrated his homecoming with a sexy romp. Having downed enough drinks from the coffee cup Patrice kept filling up, I eagerly jumped into the arms of the lover I'd scorned only a month ago. It was welcome home, tension relieving, infatuation rekindling, no-agenda, enthusiastic sexual play.

"I see you're wearing the opal," Jack said, once things had calmed down. He fingered the pendant and it fell back into the hollow of my throat. "Nice to see you wearing our little souvenir from Sydney."

"This is the first time I've worn it," I confessed.

"This is the best time to wear it." He kissed my neck, near the sparkling gem. "I'll always remember this moment; you dressed in only an opal."

In the morning our wake-up call sprung us out of bed. Instead of drowsy 7 a.m. zombies, we were warriors ready for combat. He made a little pot of coffee in the room, and by the time I'd spruced up the Styrofoam cups with cream and sugar, we were set to go. Jack had rented the only vehicle available, a large SUV. Armed with nothing but the keys and bad intentions, we discreetly zoomed down separate elevators and met in the parking lot.

Being more familiar with the area, I insisted on driving. I put on Steely Dan's Greatest Hits and we sang along for about half an hour. Jack called the Wingate to reserve a room. I stifled a laugh hearing him request a room on the third floor, "with a view of the parking lot." After repeating himself, I guess he felt the need to explain, saying he had a nice car and felt better seeing it from the window.

He hung up and turned to me. "That's for you, my dear. With the curtains drawn you can sneak a peek from a safe distance."

I pulsed against my seatbelt with excitement. "What will you tell them? Do you have a gun on you?"

"No, I can't take a gun on the plane."

I remembered when Patrice asked JT the same question; back when he was one of the good guys. JT told her that there were only rifles around the place. Maybe he had his own pocket-sized revolver, though. In my mind, he began morphing into one of those slick villainous soap opera stars, shedding skins of deceit hourly. Surely, he wouldn't pack heat to meet a potential buyer of his music.

As I sped down highway 95 toward Georgia, I wondered if JT and Bob were fans of Jack Swanson. They seemed to be the type to like action movies; at least they'd know his name. Since David had been the go-between, it was hard to gauge how big a deal this fake opportunity was to JT. One thing for sure, he was a confident SOB, and his ego would assume his time for recognition was here. The sting was great. It's the *what do we do now?* that Jack wouldn't discuss. He just tried to calm me. "Just stay safe in the room and I'll fill you in on the ride back."

"You don't know what the guys look like," I objected. "How will you recognize them in the coffee shop at nine? Just watch for two guys in their thirties, carrying a CD case? Jack?"

Apparently I was cutting into his nap time. He opened one eye. "Most people can pick me out of a room. Don't worry. I'm closing my eyes now."

CHAPTER 43

I watched Jack saunter across the parking lot toward the Wingate entrance, and then disappear inside. The light sprinkle of rain hit the roof as I scanned the parking lot for creeps. The weather had cleared up and we'd made good time.

A few minutes later, Jack returned. Leaning through the car window, he spoke softly. "After I deal with the punks, we'll hit the road and get some breakfast on the way back, okay?" He lowered his sunglasses and wiggled his eyebrows in a comedic lascivious exaggeration, adding, "Better yet, just wait in the room and we'll get room service, huh? Anyway, I'll see you in less than an hour."

He pulled a cardboard key folder from his pocket and handed me one of the keys. "Room 333, doesn't that sound lucky? Come on, give me a smile. That will do until the real one comes along." He tousled the top of my head like you'd do a five-year-old spaniel, and then became serious. "Now listen to me. See that palm tree there that splits at the bottom, by the green truck?"

I nodded.

"There's the side door of the hotel. The elevator is just inside. No reason to go through the lobby, you go right in at the side door, after I go in through the main entrance."

"Got it." I laid my hand on his arm, which was resting on the ridge of the open window. "Thank you for everything, Jack. If it doesn't work out that they're carrying cash, well, then, I understand. We did our best. Really, I can't tell you how grateful—"

He looked at his watch, kissed me on the cheek, and then walked away as my words petered out.

It was eight-forty-five. I wished to God that I had a recording device. Where was a Radio Shack when you needed one? I couldn't imagine *how* Jack could make them hand over five thousand dollars. But, we had come this far, and one way or the other, the drama would be over in an hour. The part about not seeing it, or *hearing* it, was the pisser. Maybe I should... maybe I *could*? I looked at my watch: it was now eight-fifty. The parking lot had about forty cars scattered about—nothing out of the ordinary. JT's Escalade wasn't among them. It probably belonged to the estate and had to be left on the property anyway. Who knew what those guys were driving? I *hated* to passively wait in the room. Why should I miss all the action?

With a bolt of inspiration I climbed over the seat, then again over the farthest rear seat, and ducked down in the small suitcase area. I took off my little zip-up sweatshirt, wadded it into a pillow, and lay down on the floor beside the rear window.

Curled up into a ball for what seemed forever almost had me dozing. Then I heard muffled voices outside. A loud click signaled all the doors unlocking at once. There was a flurry of sound: men talking, getting in the car, doors slamming. The weight of it all shook the car. In my tight rectangle cage, I flipped to my other side and wiggled into a more comfortable fetal position. My spy quarters were protected by the high back seat. Hippy Bob's familiar voice spoke from the back, only inches from my head. Barely breathing, I strained to hear, but most of the conversation was taking place in the front seat. Bob only added extraneous, *yeah mans,* from time to time.

Jack was saying something about not having enough time to hear all the cuts on his CD to pick the best one. JT turned the CD player on, and "Ricky Don't Lose That Number" came through the sound system. When it clicked off, I heard JT compliment Jack's taste in music. Then, he stuck in his own CD of original songs.

Whatever they were saying in the front, I couldn't make it out with the music blasting. Hearing JT and Bob's congenial voices made me want to gag. They were giving Jack the double-whammy sales pitch on JT's talents.

A funky bass line weaved a pattern of low notes, accentuated by drums beating out a tight eight-bar groove. Next came the signature "chuck-a-chuck" of JT's percussive attack on the guitar strings, striking chords into a catchy and soulful melody line. The mix was so clear you could hear his palm slap the body of the guitar. His high tenor voice pierced through with a haunting melody. *I try and imagine—t—r—y and imagine, my life without you....*

Someone turned the volume down.

"You sound like John Fogherty," Jack commented.

Get on with it, Jack. Tell them to hand over their travel dough, and let's hit it.

"Yeah, people always compared me to Credence when I was a kid growing up." JT sounded wistful. "But, I guess it didn't do me any good. There already was one a him and I wasn't 'bout to go into a tribute band thang."

Jack asked, what was a tribute band? From the back seat Hippy Bob explained a tribute band played only the songs of a specific act; that it made up the whole show. He told him that there were a bunch of tribute bands, from the Beatles to the Rolling Stones, including Credence Clearwater."

Who cares? My leg's falling asleep.

Jack told JT to start the music over; he wanted to hear it without everyone talking.

I'm going to scream. Could it be that Jack actually cared about this song?

Someone rolled down a window and I snuck a breath of fresh air. Although my heart was pounding with fear, it wasn't the fear of being discovered. The music was pretty loud, and honestly, they seemed rather absorbed. The song started again.

When it ended, Jack said, "This is good stuff, man. *Pelican Point* ends with all the main characters either dead or gone from Australia. The closing credit song needs to be a plaintive cry of melancholy and resignation. Let's hear it from the beginning again."

Now my shoulder is falling asleep. I'll show you a plaintive cry of melancholy, buster.

JT asked Jack if he wanted to hear the next cut. Thank God, Jack said no. I'd heard JT's great songs before, this time I could only think of reaching down his throat and plucking out his vocal chords.

"Are you doing all the finger-pickin' too?" Jack asked.

"He does it all," Bob crowed from the backseat.

As JT's rock-solid vocal stylings pierced the air, Jack occasionally interrupted to question a lyric. Then he asked where they recorded the demo.

"Nashville," JT replied.

Jack turned down the music to say, "Do you know what they call pot in Nashville?"

"Nope," the guys answered.

"Writing tobacco."

They all laughed like hyenas. Did the power of music override our mission? I twisted out of my fetal position and flipped on my back. Then sat up, bumped my head on the roof, and made a yelp. Their three heads turned toward the back of the car and everyone started shouting.

I shouted, "What's going on here? Did you forget why we're here?"

Jack pointed an angry finger. "You're supposed to be in the room!"

JT glared at me, then looked to Jack. "*You* know *her?*"

Bob grabbed my arm. "Babe, I'm so happy to see you. I never got to say g'bye."

"Babe?" Jack grumbled from the front seat, leering at Bob.

I shook my arm loose and shrieked over JT's song—now on its third playing. "I can be anywhere I want to be." As I flung my arm out in exasperation, my knuckles hit the window. "Ouch! I'm here now to get back the money you stole from me. Pay me the money, JT, before you fly away—on to your next scam."

JT and I broke into a shouting match, each trying to drown out the other. My mantra was, "I won't be your victim," while he repeated, "I was *going* to pay you. Geese, chill out. "

Someone stopped the music. JT opened the door to get out and Jack yanked his arm back inside the car. "Not so fast, pal!"

JT swung with his free right hand, clobbered Jack in the face, and took off running. I screamed, feeling helpless in my pen. Holding his nose with a hand and dripping blood, Jack ran after him. JT bolted toward the trees surrounding the lot. Jack was no match for the fleet-footed athlete, but he kept running just the same. In a moment, I lost sight of both of them.

Hippy Bob sprang out of the backseat, jumped in the front, and slipped behind the wheel. He reached across the seat pulled the door shut, then started the engine up, crept along our row, peering between the cars. Jack was running down a parallel aisle, looking between the cars, too. Bob swerved toward the trees as I sat cross-legged, gripping the back of the seat for balance.

Bob slowed down and lowered the window. He beeped the horn three short blasts, and then, with his head out the window, he whistled three shrill bursts of the same length. This may have been some code among creeps, because the disheveled JT surfaced from the thin grove of trees. As the car slowed, Bob reached over and opened the door. It swung open and JT hurled himself inside. He slammed the door. Bob gunned it and we were careening through the lot toward the exit.

CHAPTER 44

As Bob whipped around the parking lot, I unwedged myself from the cargo pen and tumbled into the backseat. Jack was long gone and even the Wingate had disappeared as we tore down the highway. Tossed around during the crazy exodus, with relief I finally cinched myself into the middle seatbelt.

Bob shouted, "What kind of a cluster-fuck was that?"

JT answered by loudly thumping the dashboard with his fist. Anything I wanted to say stuck in my throat. My body stiffened with dread.

In a silent storm of tension Bob drove about two miles, then the traffic stalled, forcing us to slow down to a roll.

"Oh, this is fucked!" JT slapped the dashboard again, this time with the palm of his hand. I winced at the possible damage to our rental car. The three of us craned our necks to see what the hold-up was. The car edged along when JT turned around to regard me for the first time, then turned to face Bob, like I was too loathsome to warrant eye-contact.

"So, what's up, Veronica?" I watched his angry profile. "Are you a *stalker* or some shit like that? Waiting all night in Jack Swanson's car? Is that how *desperate* you are?"

Wow. He assumed I was a Jack Swanson groupie. An uninvited pang of sympathy rippled through me. Ten minutes ago, he was on the brink of the biggest break of his career—and now? I stared straight ahead, stunned into silence.

As we crept along I noticed orange cones blocking our lane. Two officers were conversing with the drivers in front of us. After a brief exchange they waved the car on and we were next. A jumbo-sized highway patrolman and his clipboard-carrying assistant walked up to each side of the SUV.

"This is just great," Bob hissed. "Don't say anything, anybody. I'll handle this." He rolled down the window with a friendly, "Howdy."

"I'd like to see your driver's license," the jumbo patrol man commanded. "Pull it out of the wallet, and don't make any fast moves." When Bob complied, the officer said, "Thank you. Now, put your hands on the steering wheel and keep them there."

At the same time, the skinny officer opened JT's door. "You," he ordered. "Step out of the car and show me your identification. Take it out of your wallet and hand it to me."

JT did so, then asked, "Why are you doing this? You didn't make the driver in front of us get out."

"Let's just say you're special," the officer chided. Then, without looking up he added, "Do not reach inside your pocket. I assure you that would be the wrong thing to do right now."

JT was read his Miranda Rights and handcuffed. Stupefied, I watched the smaller patrolman guide the top of JT's head through the car door, where he was settled into the backseat of the cruiser.

The bigger cop seemed to be in charge, as he spoke into a walkie-talkie. With all the static and unfamiliar terms, it was impossible to know what was happening. Out the front window I could see the side of Bob's head on the patrol car's hood. It started to rain again. His face was turned, but I saw large drops fall on his long hair which was spread out like a fan on a metal pillow; his hands were cuffed behind his back. The skinny cop spoke a few words to him before leading him to the backseat of the patrol car, as well.

The sheriff opened the front door of the SUV. There was a huge shift of weight as he sat down behind the steering wheel. He turned to the back seat and smiled at me. "I'm Sheriff Naughton. Well, you had a quite a morning, didn't you, young lady?"

I nodded, and then, probably because of his smile, I burst into tears. It was so hard being a spy, watching my hero get socked in the face and left bleeding in a parking lot. My heart was even heavy for JT, the singer/songwriter whose music still stirred me. There are so many heartaches that come with being talented. Years ago, I'd let go of any dream of fame, like a child releasing a balloon into the sky; but for him, this day meant another musical humiliation.

Smelling Hippy Bob's familiar soapy scent from my hiding place brought another uninvited flashback. With a spasm of regret, I realized after we had had sex, every encounter with my "summer fling" became worse. What would be next? Prison visits? *Me* peering out from behind bars? This world was revolving too fast and I couldn't stand it anymore.

"Hang on." The kindly cop took his sunglasses off and rummaged through his pockets. "I should have some tissues in the car. Be right back."

For the first time since the debacle began, I was alone. I let loose with a heaving howl that came from the base of my gut or maybe from another life, because it felt like a primordial wail of sorrow. My hands held my face, catching the flood of tears. By the time the sheriff returned I had sniffed and snorted my nose raw and managed to restore my breathing to ragged gasps. Although I could have used a beach towel, I was grateful for the couple of tissues he handed me through the window.

He opened the door and slid behind the wheel again. "We're just gonna move this off the road so vehicles can pass by safely. Okay, now, don't worry." He drove the SUV a few feet along the shoulder and we were now about five car lengths behind the patrol car. JT and Bob were reduced to patches of hair above a high-topped backseat window. A thick grate separated the front from the backseat. The thin patrolman was picking up cones as he continued to wave traffic along.

Don't *worry*, did the sheriff say? Weren't Jack and I supposed to be having room-service breakfast about now? I *had* to worry. I needed to come up with a quick story. Who knew what these cunning, serial charmers were telling the cops? That I was a *stalker*?

****

"What is this all about?" I asked, still belted into my seat.

Officer Naughton turned the key off, and put his arm across the back of the seat and turned to face me. "We got a call a few minutes ago about a stolen car and kidnapping. This car matched the description, and so did those two fellows. Of course, everyone is innocent until proven guilty." He let out a sigh that spoke of experience. He was about sixty years old and had a weathered face with kindly eyes. "The taller one with the brown hair and goatee said ya'll are friends and there's no kidnapping. Would you like to tell me what happened?"

"I lent the tall blond guy some money, 'cause they were going to Nashville to make his guitar album. When my friend and I met him at the Wingate—in the car—and listened to his songs again, well, I chickened out. But, I'd already given him the cash. He didn't want to give it back and we just started arguing and Bob drove off so there wouldn't be a scene in the parking lot."

Officer Naughton studied me without a word.

"Now he has my money," I said slowly, "and I want it back."

"I've seen this before, Miss. A girl with a few dollars saved gets involved with a pretty boy and he takes advantage."

I nodded too vigorously.

"So, this sounds like we can drop the kidnapping charge. Your friend reported the car stolen. I just radioed the station letting them know we got the car back, so they'll contact him at his hotel."

"Sir, since you've seen this before..." I started to cry. "Since you are so nice and you understand, could you possibly get my money back? The tall blond has my cash and I don't want to finance his album anymore."

"I patted down mister pretty-boy and I have to believe you since he was in possession of a large sum of cash. How much did you say you gave him?"

"Five thousand dollars, Sir," I said. "Do you know Sheriff Jimbo Clark?"

"Yep, why do you ask?"

"He judged my talent contest—what a great guy."

"I'll be right back. There're a few things I need to check out."

He stepped out and I unfastened my seatbelt. I considered doing the fifty-yard dash, myself. If JT didn't have that much cash on him, the cop would know my whole story was a lie. I realized my purse was still in the far backseat. I hung upside down over the back of the seat to retrieve it. My cell phone was inside, and in a flash of clarity I realized that I could get hold of Jack. I didn't know if he had a cell phone, but the officer said he had spoken with him. I called the Wingate and asked for room 333, his room. He picked up on the first ring. "Jack, it's me. Are you okay? Do you need to go to the emergency room? Is your nose broken?"

"My pride is a little more bruised than my nose." He managed a chuckle. "There's an ice machine down the hall and towels to ruin in the room. How about you? Where are you now, darling?"

"I'm on the side of whatever road it was that we came in on."

"So they got there quick, it sounds like?" Jack sputtered into the phone. "Oh, excuse me. I'm still getting used to breathing through my mouth."

"We were only driving about five minutes before the roadblock," I told him. "Actually, I'm watching the police car doing a U-turn and zooming off with JT and Bob in the backseat. Oh, my gosh. The main cop is coming back to question to me. Yikes, gotta go." With that I hung up and slipped the phone back in my purse.

It was impossible to read his expression with his sunglasses on. This time, Naughton climbed in next to me in the back seat. I unclipped the seatbelt to slide over.

He reached around and pushed the button to move the front seat forward, making room for his legs. I waited for him to settle in.

Finally, he let out a deep breath and said, "I 'spose I shouldn't get involved in this loan business between friends. That's between the two of you, but I got a little bent out of shape back there."

"What happened?"

"I needed to check out their story, like I said. So, I says to 'em, 'you were at the airport—where was you headed?' I'm waiting to see if he says Nashville. They both say Spain, out of JFK in New York. They said they didn't want any trouble and were heading out of the country for good. Some nonsense about a cousin living over there. I called the airline and they confirmed that two one-way tickets are paid for, in their names, leaving for Spain this afternoon. That's why they was getting so aggravated. They didn't want to come down to the station and miss the flight. I says to Blondie, 'so what are you doing with all this cash?' He tells me you need cash to travel, or some kind a bullshit like that."

I nodded. My lips were drawn so tightly I made a conscious effort to blow them out and it made the sound of a pony.

He continued. "I says to them, 'I got a pretty lady over there crying about lending you some money to make a record or some deal. You don't know anything about going to Nashville with her money? 'Cause one of you is lying. That's when the brunette speaks up and says, yeah that's true. It's her money.'"

Officer Naughton seemed to be enjoying the story because he slowly took out a cigar and clipped the end and then lit it. I suspected this was a story he'd be telling again. It had all the elements. Little lady crying, pretty boys going to Spain after they took her money to make a record in Nashville, and he intercepts the whole plot. "I hope you don't mind if I have a smoke."

"I actually love the smell of cigars." My voice was wobbly. "I used to smoke the lady Cigarillos."

"Like I said—" Naughton took a draw, "Blondie was wearing about seven thousand dollars on a money belt. We got a saying here in the South. 'If we can clean it up in an hour, it's heaven's paperwork.' We like to solve problems quick and simple, ma'am. You may have had a lover's quarrel—I don't know. But these wannabes got one-way tickets out of the country and I'd hate to have them miss their plane and stay in *my* jurisdiction." He squinted one eye. "You actually saved their ass, miss. If you hadn't told me your side of the story, I'd have to hold them at headquarters. You see, drug dealers and the like carry large sums of cash. When we have a justifiable cause to search a person—as in the reporting of a stolen vehicle—if the suspect is carrying a large sum of money, it's confiscated."

"What will happen to them now?"

Officer Naughton blew smoke out his open window. "We still have the stolen vehicle report."

I patted the seat. "This here is my boyfriend's car and we—"

"It's a rented car, ma'am," he clarified. "Mr. Swanson rented it. I need to question him."

The last thing I wanted was to involve Jack. The Associated Press would get hold of this story and there'd be the

National Enquirer at his door, among other inquiring minds. I wanted the fake cousins out of the zip code more than Officer Naughton.

"Please just listen." My words were coming faster than I could think. I was on auto-bull. "As you know, Blondie and me were listening to his songs inside the car. Like I said, after I gave him the money, I, uh, changed my mind. We were arguing about it while driving around. So it really wasn't a *stolen* vehicle. You already know I wasn't *really* kidnapped. We were just gone too long." I shrugged, threw my palms up and grinned, and with a folksy chuckle I added, "My new boyfriend, the one who rented this car—he kind of, heh, heh, overreacted."

He sighed and kept his head straight, looking through the window. "Someone once said, life is not black and white, it's gray and white."

"Is a rain like this the beginning of hurricane weather?" I asked, trying to switch the subject from criminal to banal weather. "Does this mean the hurricane has passed us by?"

He didn't seem to be listening. We both sat quietly listening to the drops hit the windshield and watching the stream of trucks and vans speeding past. At that moment I realized how much power he had. Did he want to make a name for himself and play the big hero catching punks in the act of grand theft auto and kidnapping? Or, was he willing to take it easy and let the thing slide off the clipboard?

"Would you like to hear the song?" I asked. Without waiting for an answer, I slid out of the backseat, went around to the passenger side, and got into the front seat. I turned the ignition key to the auxiliary position. The music kicked in loud. "You tell me what you think, sir." I wrinkled my nose. "Does this sound like a hit to you?"

JT's voice blasted through the car speakers one more time. *I try and imagine—t—r—y and imagine, my life without you... "*

Naughton swatted the air. "Enough—turn that trash off!"

I pushed the eject button and when the CD slipped out of the slot, I snatched it and sailed it behind me into the farthest backseat. It clunked against a window and fell to the floor. The car had returned to blessed silence. The only sound was Naughton's fingertips tapping on the clipboard. For the first time, I noticed the familiar light blue business-sized envelope under the clamp. He handed it to me and I counted the money in front of him, five stacks of paper-clipped hundred-dollar bills.

"It's all there, Sir. Five thousand dollars is *not* going to Nashville."

"I've got another two thousand and change in this evidence envelope right here." He held a smaller brown envelope in his hand. "Because the brown-headed one validated your story, I can return your money."

"I can't thank you enough," I said, through brand new tears.

"Sad thing is, honey—"

"W-h-a-t, NOW?" I bleated.

"I don't think your five-thousand was ever going to make it to Nashville. These river-dogs were off to Spain, at five o'clock today. Sweetheart, you were ripped-off. Especially for *that* crappy excuse of music I just heard."

I looked at the floor.

"As for the rest of his cash, he can reclaim it at the station. I'll see to it they make the plane. Now you hang on to your money and don't let no fool musician sweet talk you out of it. There's an old saying: *good riddance to bad rubbish.*"

I leaned back over the seat and shook his hand. "Another good old saying is the one about *heaven's paperwork.*"

He started up the car and we drove leisurely back to the airport Wingate.

****

I was so nostalgic and pleased with the blue envelope that I had forgotten to worry about the police report. We were pulling into the parking lot when the officer said over the radio that he needed to verify the story with the caller who reported his vehicle stolen. I was pretty sure at this point that he didn't realize who my "boyfriend" was, and that—I hoped—wasn't going to be an element of the story.

I plucked my cell phone from my purse and hit redial. "Room 333, please."

Jack answered on the first ring.

"It's me. Jack, you know how I was going to give JT the money *to record* in Nashville, and I was listening to the tape he made in the car while you *waited* in our room? And you couldn't go with me to listen because your *allergy* to strawberries made your nose bleed? Well, I'm sorry I didn't pick up my cell phone when you called a bunch of times, but I didn't hear it ring because JT was playing his demo so freakin' loud I couldn't hear it. Then we were arguing on top of that. You couldn't have known this but, at the last minute, I changed my mind about giving him the cash to take to Nashville. *Like an idiot, I had already handed it over.* So he was pissed-off and he wanted to drive around and talk me into it, and that's why we didn't come right back. I'm sorry I made you worry. So, I'm not mad that you called 911 and reported your car stolen and that I was kidnapped. But, everything is okay now. Officer Naughton will be up to talk to you in about five minutes. He lectured me about lending scumbags money. Oh, he got it back for me. Bye."

CHAPTER 45

Jack and I had room service all right. It wasn't the romantic one he alluded to when he checked in, however. Officer Naughton was with us. We sat back in our chairs after polishing off the fruit salad, three orders of eggs-Benedict, side order of country bacon, a platter of sweet rolls and two pots of coffee.

"Boy, this day started out a hum-dinger," Naughton said, wiping away the sweet roll crumbs that had gathered in his mustache. "And, enough of this officer stuff. My nickname's Notty."

"I won't ask how you spell that." Jack grinned. "I'm glad to hear you're a golfer, too. I'm going to see to it that we're partners tomorrow. Now, it's no problem getting down to the Harbour Town Course, right?"

"No problem," he said. He wadded up his cloth napkin and set it on the portable room service table.

"The weather cooperated, so it's back to tee time is nine-fifteen," Jack said. "They don't like to make it too early. All of us out-of-towners come in from different time zones. Gayle Wingo, the tournament manager, takes real good care of us."

The officer sat back and scratched his chin. "My daughter told me Davey Jones, one of The Monkeys, is supposed to be over there. She always goes out to the course the last day and stands along the fifteenth hole—I think it is—to get a picture when they come by in the cart. She's done it every year. She's got pictures with all the celebrities. Me? I'm not one to notice." He raised his glass of juice in Jack's direction. "Although I did like you in *Moon Over Miami*. Saw it a couple times. It comes on TV every once in a while."

"Thank you, Notty," Jack said. "We had a good time. Now I think of it as a job to watch and a vacation to make."

I spoke for the first time in a while. "Please have your daughter come as our guest to the big party tomorrow night. I'll make sure she gets a picture with Davey Jones and Jack. She can bring a date and you, naturally, can bring Mrs. Naughton. Is there a Mrs.?"

"I've got a gal I'm seeing. Thank you, ma'am. I'll be honest with you, I'm not the best golfer. Out here we call the game—excuse me, little lady." He looked at Jack, and placed his hand beside his mouth to hide the words from me. Softly, he said, "Out here we just call the game 'whack-fuck.' You stand there and swing—hear the whack, then say…well, you know."

When the laughter had run its course, Notty got serious. "Strawberries, huh?" He tapped his nose and shook his head with pity.

"Huh?" Jack said.

"Yeah, the strawberry allergy wack-fucked his nose," I explained.

******

Dear Diary,

Okay, page one. Jack left me this beautiful, gold embossed leather journal. He suspected by writing things down I'll have insights. Till now, the signs along the way were overlooked as I had my nose shoved into roses. But, hey I've still got half of July, August, and I just signed on for all of

September. In these eleven weeks, without the distractions of sexy men, finding talent, raising an estranged son, and uncovering sinister crimes, I can probably meet the deadline for Jack's Back.

Patrice and I still get together every Monday night. She met a great guy, an engineer who is gloriously normal, and it's helping to heal the cynical heart. She was so happy to get her money back, she took me to dinner at the Quarter Deck for lobster. Afterwards, we had "birthday cake ice cream" in the courtyard.

After dinner we started laughing about the bumper sticker on JT's Escalade: "Don't Blame Me! I never voted in my life." We used to think it was clever, but now, knowing the tidbits, we have new ideas on how to end the phrase. "Don't blame me I never worked in my life" started it, then we ran it into the ground. Spoke a word of truth...liked dogs anyway....liked hot women...By the end of the dinner we were stuffed and laughed out. Years from now we'll still be laughing about the whole thing. The good part is, I can see myself knowing her years from now.

Devin is writing me more often too and his sparse responses are moving into more syllables. This summer was edgy but good for us.

Finishing the book? I can do this. I have all I need in my little room. Any way, I can sleep at night; except for last night's hideous nightmare. I should probably write this down and figure out the symbolism later. It was The Island Idol Contest—but this time—I'm performing in it.

In my dream, for some reason I'm scheduled to be a standup comic. I am flop-sweating all night since I don't have an act, or forgot it. I'm stressing big-time and call downstairs before show time, and nonchalantly ask David Lindsay how long my act is supposed to be. He just barks, "one hour." I hang up with a cheery, "Great. Thanks."

As the clock ticks down my insanity grows. Think. THINK! Knock-knock jokes are always good. But, who knocks first? This format is too complicated. Hmm, writing comedy in your sleep is like cutting into a steak underwater. Just when you're ready for a bite, it floats away.

Maybe I could do some mime. You just don't see enough these days. How hard is it to lean into the wind? Then, with palms outstretched, I could feel the parameters of an invisible box. Wait, I can combine the two. I'll be inside the box with the wind blowing on me. No one has done that! There is a solid minute and a half right there.

When the dream finally grinds to an end, it is seven-forty-five and I'm dressed for the show. As the elevator zooms down to the lobby, I snap my fingers in relief. Oh yeah! I remember I'm a singer! I don't have to be funny. I know my music and don't need to cower in the back or slink along the side wall.

My name is called. With pride, I take my place at the piano bench. I swing the boom stand that holds the mic in front of me. The lighting is a soft flattering pink. The audience is almost reverent in its attentiveness. All eyes are upon me. I lift up the little shelf and look down on the keyboard. To my horror, instead of black and white piano keys, there are little square alphabet keys. Everyone is eagerly watching, even leaning forward in their seats. Yikes, the audience is made up of really cute guys and everyone in my life who is holding a grudge against me, dating back to stolen Crayolas, and sand stuck in the knobs of a borrowed Etch-a-Sketch.

Necks are craning, throats cleared. I dismally look back down and I'm only slightly relieved to see the letters are in alphabetical order. Will that make it easier?

I take a deep breath; exactly one teaspoon of air. I put my hands on the keys and press. With all my might, I hope the audience will like it.

THE END